The

LUC
UGLI

RISE OF TH
RAGGED CLO

Rise of the Ragged Clover

Paul Durham

Illustrations by Pétur Antonsson

HARPER
An Imprint of HarperCollins*Publishers*

The Luck Uglies: Rise of the Ragged Clover

 For information address HarperCollins Children's Books, a division of HarperCollins Publishers, 195 Broadway, New York, NY 10007.
www.harpercollinschildrens.com

Library of Congress Control Number: 2015951376
ISBN 978-0-06-227156-3

Typography by Carla Weise
16 17 18 19 20 RRDH/CG 10 9 8 7 6 5 4 3 2 1
❖
First Edition

For the Durham girls, always.
And for Shadow, our own Gloaming Beast,
who's previously been neglected in these dedications.

Contents

BEYOND THE SHALE
THE WEND
THE RILL
THE HOLLOW
SITE of THE DESCENT
BOG HOPPER'S SHACK
BOGS
VILLAGE DROWNING
SLATTERNLY FLATS
WESTERN WOODS
LONGCHANCE KEEP
GREAT EEL POND
UNNAMED PATH
TWIN CULVERTS
RIVER DROWNING
GRABSTONE
NORTHERN SHALE
TROWBRIDGE
THROCKING

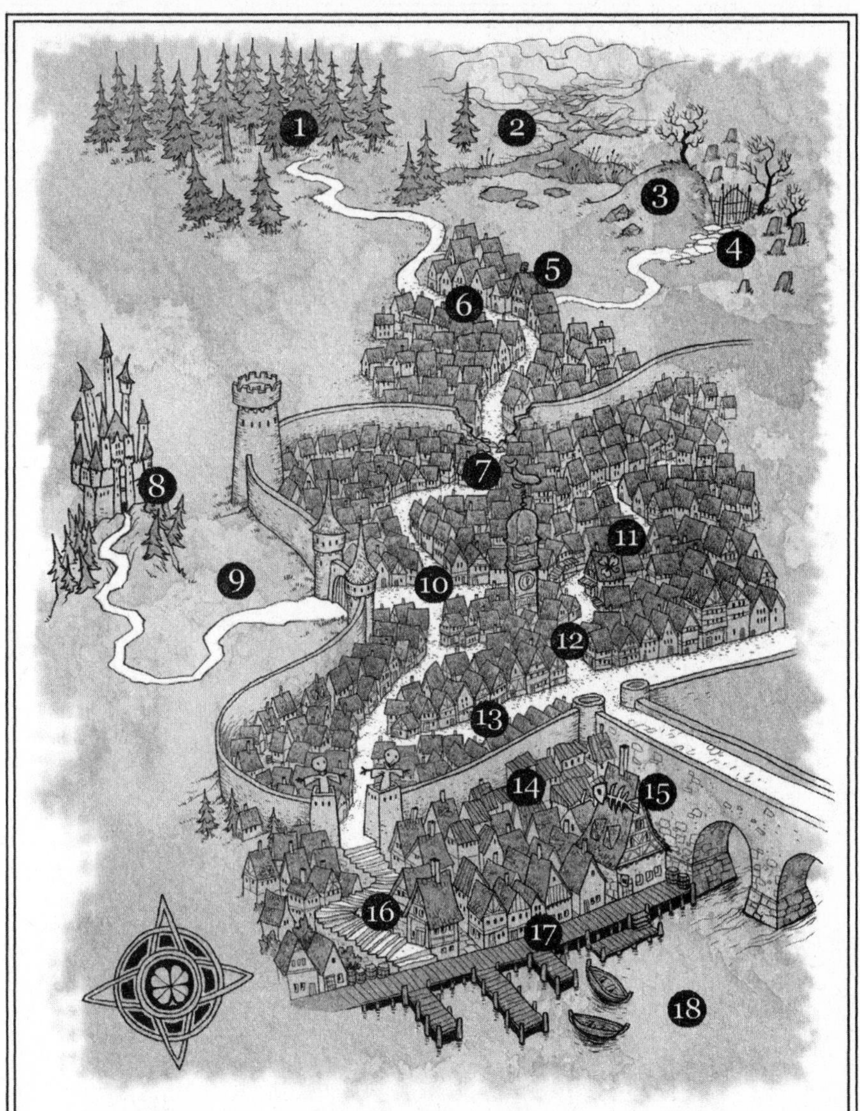

An O'Chanter's Guide to

VILLAGE DROWNING

1. BEYOND THE SHALE
2. THE BOGS
3. TROLLER'S HILL
4. MISER'S END
5. O'CHANTERS' COTTAGE
6. MUD PUDDLE LANE
7. NETHER NECK
8. LONGCHANCE KEEP
9. GRIM GREEN
10. OLD SALT CROSS
11. THE WILLOW'S WARES
12. MARKET STREET
13. DREAD CAPTAIN'S WAY
14. THE SHAMBLES
15. DEAD FISH INN
16. MUTINEER'S ALLEY
17. LITTLE WATER STREET
18. RIVER DROWNING

The Truth about Heroes . . .

A wise man once said that heroes can't be painted in black or white, they come to us in shades of gray. For the choices they make are hard ones, and the actions they take leave consequences that can't be undone. But wise men are prone to speak in riddles, and true words should be plain to understand. Hear these instead. There are no such things as heroes. After all, for every man we call a hero, is he not cursed as our enemies' greatest villain? So don your mask, young master. Don't be afraid to bend the laws of shadow and light. And leave it to history to brand you as it deems fit.

—Last words of Grimshaw the Black
(as quoted in Tam's Tome of
Drowning Mouth Fibs, Volume II*)*

H Is for Harmless

Rye O'Chanter crept through a dense maze of leafless branches sharp enough to skewer her. The towering pines in this stretch of wood were charred black like victims of a great fire, yet they hadn't been burned. It was as if the dark soul of the forest had poisoned the ground itself and bled into their roots, staining the trees forever.

Rye's nose twitched at the smell of a cook fire wafting from the small clearing ahead. She was confident that she'd visited this spot once before and found it empty, but she'd need to check more closely to be certain. The forest Beyond the Shale hid countless invisible secrets, its rolling hills and dense stands of pine and hemlock disguising hollows you might pass right by without a second glance. She understood now how the Luck Uglies, and others like them, might disappear into the forest for months, years, or even forever.

Rye listened carefully as she dug a rotting toadstool from the ground and rubbed it over her sealskin coat. The leather was already caked with the remains of smashed birds' eggs, mud from a beaver dam, and dung from some unknown animal. The stains hadn't gotten there by accident. If her friends Folly and Quinn could see her now, they would think Rye had gone daft, but the mixture of forest smells served to mask her own scent. Beyond the Shale was teeming with keen but unseen noses, too many of which might come calling if they caught wind of a human.

Satisfied that the small camp was unoccupied—at least for the moment—Rye stepped forward to inspect it. A tent made from animal hide housed a fur bedroll. Several small pots were arranged around the remains of a fire and the blade of a hand axe lay embedded in a fallen log. Rye's excitement grew. These were the types of supplies that could be packed and transported in a hurry—just the type of camp her quarry was likely to make.

She circled the clearing, pausing when she found the familiar trunk of a thick pine. There was her symbol in the bark: a circle with a capital letter R inside. It beamed white from dried sap that had filled the hollowed letter like a scab. She'd carved dozens of these in recent months. It meant Rye had searched this spot before and found it empty. But now there was another marking next to her own. The bark was still raw, as if recently cut.

A letter H.

She didn't blink, for fear she might reopen her eyes and find they were playing tricks on her. She was hunting for her father—the man she called Harmless.

Rye tried to temper her excitement as she glanced up at the sliver of sky peeking through the limbs high above, the muted sun hanging low behind the trees. The long days of summer were now gone, and roaming after dusk was far too dangerous. She bit her lip. Could she afford to wait to see if it was Harmless who returned to this camp? No, but she *could* leave a message of her own and come back at first light.

Rye removed the knife called Fair Warning from the sheath in her oversized boot and began to carve the stubborn bark.

"The sap in these trees is no good for sugaring," a coarse voice called out behind her.

Rye spun at the sound. A man appeared from the trees on the opposite side of the clearing, his footfalls nearly silent. A hunter's bow was slung over his shoulder and he dragged the carcass of a red stag behind him. His gaunt cheeks and wary eyes reflected the face of someone who'd spent many days alone in the forest. Unfortunately, it was a face she didn't recognize.

Rye's first instinct was to flee, but it occurred to her that this huntsman might have useful information. Here, in the lightly traveled reaches north of the Shale, information was more valuable than gold grommets. She sheathed Fair Warning, backed away a safe distance, then stopped, confident she could outrun the stranger if need be.

"Do you speak, child?" the huntsman asked when she offered no reply. "Are you a Feraling?" He eyed the grime that covered her coat.

Feralings were humans who lived in isolation Beyond the Shale. Reclusive and untamed, they'd adapted to the way of the wood in order to survive. In all of Rye's recent travels, she'd met only one.

"I'm no Feraling," she said. "And I'm not looking for sap."

The huntsman raised an eyebrow. "You do speak . . .

and with a Drowning accent, if I'm not mistaken." He sucked a tooth behind a rough beard.

"That's right," Rye said. "And if you know Village Drowning, then you're no Feraling either."

The huntsman abandoned the stag, pulled the hand axe from the log, and plodded to the tree she'd carved. He jabbed the bark with the axe head as he stooped and examined it.

"Letters *R* and . . . *H*. What do they stand for?" he asked, casting a suspicious glance at her.

When he looked back, Rye had removed her cudgel from the sling over her shoulder.

"*R* is for Rye," she replied. "And *H* is for Harmless. That's who I'm looking for. But make no mistake, he's not harmless at all." She tightened her grip. "And neither am I."

The huntsman chuckled. "Put your twig away," he scoffed.

Her *twig* was a High Isle cudgel, a dangerous weapon made from the hardest blackthorn in all the Shale. If the huntsman was as well traveled as he was road worn, he would have known it. Rye didn't put it down.

"Have you come across anyone in these woods lately?" she asked, gesturing her cudgel toward the trees. "A man maybe? Traveling alone?"

"Travelers are rare in the forest, as are young girls.

And yet, strangely enough, both have wandered into my camp in recent days." The huntsman studied her carefully before speaking again. "There *was* a man. Appeared like a ghost—startled me while I fixed my supper. He was cordial enough but didn't linger."

That sounded like Harmless, Rye thought.

"Did you notice anything else about him?" she asked. "Was he wearing an unusual necklace? Like this?" With her thumb, Rye hooked the runestone choker she wore around her neck so that the huntsman could see it.

She saw a flash of recognition in his eyes, then they shifted, as if calculating something. "It's possible, although I don't have a keen eye for jewelry," he said coolly. But his expression had already betrayed his real answer.

"When did he leave?" Rye demanded. "Do you remember which way he went?"

"I do," he replied, his face expressionless. "He was heading south along the Wend. But the rest of the details have already been bought and paid for."

Rye narrowed her eyes, unsure of what he meant.

"Several other travelers arrived the following day. They too had an interest in this man you call Harmless."

"Who were they?" Rye asked sharply.

The huntsman shrugged. "They wore no crest or colors. They weren't overly friendly—but at least they paid well for my answers to their questions. Well enough that I'll be able to spend my winter in the warm bed of a roadhouse instead of shivering in a tent. Can you offer the same?"

Rye's ears burned. "I have no coins."

"But if you are looking for this Harmless, he must be of value to you." He rubbed two grimy fingers through his beard. "Perhaps, you, in turn, are of value to him?" he asked, his voice darkening. "Or maybe . . . to those others who seek him?"

Rye took a step away.

"Now, now," the huntsman said. "Why not have a seat and join me without a fuss? I spend my days tracking fleet-footed creatures through this forest. If you run, I'll surely catch you. And then you'll have to spend the night in a sack with the rest of the game. I've got one right over there that's just about your size."

But Rye wasn't listening. She turned and ran, darting into the trees. She was no novice when it came to being chased and, if need be, she could bite much harder than some frightened hare. But just as she reached full stride, her legs kicked up and her body lurched skyward. The forest floor spun below and the blood rushed to her head. Rye craned her neck and peered up at the nearly invisible line strung over a limb. A snare had caught her around one boot and she now dangled upside down, several feet above the ground.

The huntsman shook his head as if to say *I told you so* and retrieved a thick burlap sack from his supplies.

Rye still grasped her cudgel and shook it threateningly in his direction. She doubted her effort was particularly menacing as she spun slowly and helplessly in a tiny circle at the end of the snare. She desperately wiggled her foot in her oversize boot, which only made her rotate even faster.

When the huntsman came back into view he was at the edge of the clearing, his axe raised in one hand, the burlap sack ready in the other.

A looming figure loped from the shadows opposite them, covering the space in two long-legged bounds. Rye sucked in her breath with such alarm that the huntsman paused to look behind him. A huge clawed hand sent him sprawling.

Rye thrashed her whole body, sending herself spinning furiously. She saw the blur of the massive beast. It regarded the huntsman's motionless body with bulging eyes set on top of its misshapen head. From its elongated jaws hung a plaited, rust-orange beard tied at the end with a child's bootlace. It snuffed at the air with a long, pig-like nose and, to Rye's great relief, briefly turned its attention toward the stag. Rye's own nose filled with the stench of the bogs.

She was no stranger to beasts of this kind. It was a Bog Noblin.

With one final tug, her foot slipped free from her boot with a cascade of damp straw stuffing. For once it had come in handy to wear her father's old boots that were three sizes too large. She met the ground head-first, the impact knocking the wind from her lungs.

The Bog Noblin looked up from its prize. First one bulging eye turned to meet her gaze, then the other. Hunched over the stag, its gray skin hung in folds from its broad, bony shoulders and ribs. Its floppy ears were pierced with an assortment of metal hooks, and around its neck dangled a crude necklace strung with the black-ened remains of human feet. The Bog Noblin sniffed the air in her direction and stood to its full height.

Rye pushed herself up from the dirt. She only hesi-tated long enough to draw Fair Warning and cut her boot down from the snare.

Tucking it under her arm, she rushed deeper into the forest without looking back, her runestone choker cut-ting through the shadows with a pale blue glow.

2 The Hollow

Rye scurried under, over, and around razor-sharp branches. She squeezed through the narrowest gaps she could find in the thicket, forging a path impossible for anyone larger than a young girl to follow. She didn't stop to catch her breath until she'd reached the edge of a narrow stream. The afternoon's dying light disappeared behind her.

Rye put her hands on her knees, examining her flushed reflection in the clear water. Where her brown hair wasn't stuck to the sweat on her forehead, it fell to her shoulders now, longer than she'd ever grown it before. Normally, by summer's end, Rye's face glowed like a creamy pecan after long days helping her mother in the garden. But life Beyond the Shale was one of perennial shade, and her cheeks still maintained last winter's pallor. At the moment, she was just relieved to see that her choker was no longer glowing either. Its runestones only stirred when Bog Noblins were near.

She stood up straight, water flickering silently at her feet. The stream was called the Rill. It flowed like a silver thread around a mossy glade and looped back into itself, hollowing the glade out from the rest of the dense forest. The Hollow was dominated by an enormous old oak tree, its thick roots engorged like veins bulging from the ground. A spiral staircase of knotted wood planks snaked around the oak's massive trunk, leading to a series of landings and ramshackle buildings embraced in its boughs. Rope bridges slumped like clotheslines between the main house and several smaller, overgrown cottages nestled in the tree's outstretched limbs.

A stocky, horned figure barely taller than Rye hurried forward, a handmade platform of intertwined rowan branches tucked under his arm.

"Miss Riley," the barrel-shaped man called breathlessly. "Where in the Shale have you been? It's practically nightfall!" He laid the makeshift bridge across the stream at her feet.

"It's all right, Mr. Nettle," she said. "I made it back, didn't I?"

Mr. Nettle lifted the bridge as soon as Rye crossed, his ferret-like eyes glancing at the shadows on the other side.

"Without an eyelash to spare," he replied, sniffing the air.

Mr. Nettle's curled horns were, in fact, part of the fur-lined mountain goat's skull that he wore on his head like a hat. His cheeks were buried beneath a curly beard the color of dried pine needles, and the hair on the backs of his hands and knuckles seemed as thick as the scruff on his neck. He wore a rather formal vest and coat that looked to have been quite regal at one time, but his trousers were made of raw, crimped wool that gave him the vague look of a woolly ram from the waist down. Despite his wild appearance, Mr. Nettle wasn't part animal or beast. He was a Feraling—a native forest dweller—the only one Rye had encountered in all of her months Beyond the Shale.

"I found a message from Harmless—at least, I *think* it was from him," Rye explained breathlessly. "There was a huntsman who said he saw him too, or someone who sounded like Harmless anyway."

"Perhaps that's who I smell," Mr. Nettle said, his

wary eyes still on the looming forest.

"I doubt it," Rye said. Her eyes followed Mr. Nettle's gaze across the Rill. "There's also a Bog Noblin out there, and he stinks worse than most anything on two legs or four."

Mr. Nettle turned to her in alarm. "A Noblin this far from the bogs?" he asked. "Just one?"

"That's all I saw."

"Traveling alone . . ." He furrowed his brow. "Even stranger. You're quite certain that's what it was?"

Rye nodded. "Trust me. I've seen more than my fair share."

Mr. Nettle pulled a curly lock of beard between his teeth with his tongue and began to chew. "Well, if he's foolish enough to linger, he may never make it back to whatever dank moor he crawled from. Worse beasts than Bog Noblins prowl these woods . . ."

"Is my mother back?" Rye interrupted, glancing up at the tree house high above them.

"Yes, she returned not long—"

Rye didn't wait for Mr. Nettle to finish. She raced past him, stomping up the spiral steps so fast she nearly made herself dizzy.

Abby O'Chanter raised her thin, dark eyebrows as she listened to Rye's story, looking up from her scavenged cook pot as she scraped the night's meager meal into wooden bowls. She placed one of them on the round stump of a sawed-off bough that served as their table, in front of Rye's little sister, Lottie. The youngest O'Chanter had donned Mr. Nettle's skullcap and now looked like she had grown horns from her ears.

"The letter *H* was fresh, couldn't have been more than a few days old," Rye emphasized after completing the tale. "And the way the huntsman described the traveler—it *had* to be Harmless."

Rye watched her mother carefully and waited for her reaction. Surely Abby would be as excited as she was. After nearly five months in the forest, the most they had heard of Harmless were vague rumors from wayward travelers. But now he had left them a message. Based on what the huntsman had said, he was not only alive, but nearby—not more than a day or two away.

"And the other men in search of your father?" Abby asked. "Did the huntsman have more to say about them? We haven't come across anyone in weeks."

"Just that they weren't very friendly," Rye said, recalling his words. "They don't sound like the type of travelers we'd care to run across."

Abby fell silent. Mr. Nettle watched quietly from his stump next to the sawed-off bough, the only sound the crunch of Lottie's small jaws. She chewed. And chewed some more. Supper consisted of tough meat and bland, boiled roots. Food of any sort was difficult to come by Beyond the Shale, where small game was elusive and the edible plants bitter.

"Tomorrow we can all set out together to search for Harmless," Rye added, grabbing her mother's elbow enthusiastically. "With luck, we'll find him before anyone else does."

She noticed a brightening in her mother's face, but one that was offset by some unknown weight, too. Rye could see the bones of Abby's jaw rising and falling as she plucked a root from the pot and chewed it between her teeth.

"Your discovery *is* promising," her mother said softly. "But we can't go tomorrow."

"But this is the first sign of Harmless we've seen! If we miss him now we might never have another chance."

Abby seemed to weigh her words carefully before speaking, and her tone was regretful when she finally did.

"I don't disagree, Riley. But we are running out of time. We've heard no news from Drowning in months. Any explorers will be winding up their travels and returning south with the coming of the cold."

Rye glanced at the gaps in the wooden floorboards. She could see all the way down to the mossy earth below them. The walls of the tree house were built around the boughs of the oak, vines crawling through the seams of its timbers. A draft fluttered the cobwebs in its corners. Their latest shelter was not a place well suited to handle the chill of autumn, never mind the deep freeze that would inevitably follow. It would only take one storm to leave them snowbound for the season.

"We too must return to Drowning before the first flakes of winter," Abby continued, her voice drifting off for a moment. "With . . . or without . . . your father."

Rye clenched her fists in frustration. They couldn't give up now! Abby raised her hand in response to Rye's inevitable protest.

"That's why I'm going to leave tonight to search for him," she said.

Rye swallowed back her objection. It was now replaced by another, quieter one. "But the forest—at night . . ."

Mr. Nettle shifted uncomfortably on his stump.

"I'll wait to leave until *after* our neighbors have made their evening rounds," Abby said, casting a glance toward the looming trees outside the shutterless windows. She flashed a reassuring smile. "Don't worry, Riley, it's not the first time I've ventured out alone after dark."

"We should go together," Rye muttered. "It would be safer."

"I'll return before dusk tomorrow," Abby said. "And I'll stay on the Wend. If your father *is* heading south that's the path he'll take. But if he's lingered nearby he may find his way to this Hollow. It's better that you remain here to meet him."

Rye frowned, unconvinced.

"Lottie, you'll be in charge while I'm gone," Abby said with a playful wink. "Keep an eye on these two until I return."

Lottie gave Rye and Mr. Nettle a watchful glare. "I'll try," she said solemnly. "Them's a lot of work."

"Indeed," Abby agreed with a smirk.

"Rye, is that you who be stinky?" Lottie chimed, already relishing her new role. "Leave your boots outside when you step in bear plop."

"Mind your own beeswax," Rye said.

"Me no beeswacker," Lottie objected. She leaned down and crinkled her nose toward Rye's feet, as if smelling something foul under her heels. Rye shifted away so that Lottie's horns wouldn't poke her in the arm.

Rye didn't protest against her mother any further.

"Now eat," Abby said, placing a bowl on the table for her. She gestured for Rye to sit. "None of us can afford to skip any more meals."

But Rye's stomach was already a twisted stew of

excitement and anxiety. She looked to Lottie and Mr. Nettle, who huddled over their own well-cleaned bowls. Lottie's dirt-streaked cheeks were less full than they once had been, and her soon-to-be four-year-old body had begun to stretch like an eager seedling.

"Lottie, you and Mr. Nettle can finish mine."

Lottie and Mr. Nettle brightened, but they gasped in surprise as the bowl was snatched from the table.

A furry creature the size of a raccoon scurried high up the stretch of the tree trunk growing through the wall. The thief was fawn colored, with a long, ringed tail and saucer-like eyes that blinked down at them nervously.

"How do they keep getting past the Rill?" Abby said in frustration.

"The brindlebacks are crafty little pests," Mr. Nettle groused with a tug at his beard. "A branch high up in the forest canopy must have grown over the Rill and intertwined the oak's own limbs. I'll have a look tomorrow and cull it back."

"Bingle-blacks!" Lottie huffed, and clenched her fists.

"Maybe he won't eat it," Rye said, looking up hopefully. "They don't like roots, do they?"

The brindleback held the bowl with his long black fingers, sniffed its contents with a wet, pointy snout, then cocked his head. Rye opened her hands in case the little bandit dropped it. Instead, it attacked it savagely with tiny teeth. Lottie and Mr. Nettle groaned in disappointment.

When it was finished, the brindleback dropped the bowl down onto the floor with a clatter and disappeared into a hole in the wall.

Abby sighed and stared at the hole. "Well, that's it for supper, I'm afraid. Let's get you girls to sleep while the forest still allows it."

The howls and cries came earlier and earlier each night—this time not long after the O'Chanter girls had huddled together in their blankets. Near and far, unseen voices of the woods seemed to call to one another as they surrounded the Hollow. Some spoke in wolfish growls, others in throaty warbles that sounded more like the clucking tongue of a hag than the beak of a raven or vulture. And yet the most unnerving sound wasn't a voice at all, but the plod and slither of something heavy dragging itself through the dried leaves and dead pine needles that carpeted the forest floor. With its arrival the rest of the nightmarish choir went silent, and the restless creeper circled the Rill over and over without crossing, dull teeth clacking as it went.

Abby sang softly in Lottie's ear until, eventually, the

slithering lurker abandoned its vigil, and its unnerving sound ebbed and faded into the distance. With the Hollow once again consumed by the silence of the massive trees, Lottie finally drifted off. Rye only feigned sleep, performing her best fake snore.

She listened as her mother gathered some supplies in the darkness, and when Abby headed for the tree house steps, Rye whispered loud enough for her to hear.

"You'll be back tomorrow, Mama?"

Abby paused. "Of course, my love," she said, and Rye heard her kiss her fingertips. Abby's hand fluttered in the air as if releasing a butterfly. Rye pretended to catch it.

Abby's silhouette disappeared, and Rye pulled a blanket tight under her chin in an effort to sleep. She pinched her eyes tight and tossed. Then turned. And tossed some more. But sleep proved elusive.

Before long, the glow of Rye's lantern wound its way down the oak tree's spiral steps. It passed over the mossy turf of the Hollow, then tumbled to the ground with a metallic clank.

"Pigshanks," Rye whispered, regaining her footing after stumbling over a root. She peeked back at the tree house to see if she'd woken anyone.

The windows remained dark. The only sound now was Mr. Nettle's snoring wafting from the porch in the limbs above. The Feraling still insisted on sleeping outdoors.

Rye set the lantern down at the edge of the Rill.

She crouched along the interior bank of the peculiar little stream, careful not to wet her feet. The lantern light flickered off the water against her face.

Rye didn't know why animals and other creatures of the forest could never cross the Rill. Mr. Nettle had told her it was one of those mysteries that was just accepted and understood, like the knowledge that trees would shed their leaves and feign death during winter, only to be reborn again come spring. The O'Chanters, Mr. Nettle, and other humans might splash through without consequence, but without the aid of bridge or branch, the narrow stream seemed as daunting as an ocean to the forest beasts. Whatever the reason, the Rill had made the Hollow a safe haven for the O'Chanters—and whoever had originally built the tree house long ago.

Rye took a deep breath. And waited. But not for her mother—Abby was probably already on her way down the Wend.

Finally, after many minutes, she heard a sound. Not like the restless predatory voices—but the faintest rustle of leaves and pine needles in the distance. She squinted and peered forward into the gloom. Then she saw them—two glowing yellow eyes watching her from the shadow of a twisted trunk.

Rye didn't move. The Hollow might provide sanctuary, but she still knew better than to cross the Rill after dark.

Instead, she toed the edge of the embankment, extending her hand as far across the stream as she could reach. She nearly lost her balance and had to brace herself just as the black beast emerged from the darkness.

The burly shadow padded forward and settled on the other side of the water. It opened its mouth, lantern light flickering off of its sharp white teeth. It licked its whiskers. Rye smiled.

"Shady," she whispered, and was just able to graze his thick mane with her fingertips. He pushed his head into her hand and shared a thankful rumble that sounded like a purr.

Rye had assumed she would never see her beloved family pet again—not that you could really call Nightshade Fur Bottom O'Chanter a pet anymore. Rye had grown up believing Shady to be nothing more than an abnormally large house cat. However, he was, in fact, a Gloaming Beast, a mysterious breed of creatures with a predisposition to hunt Bog Noblins. True to his nature, Shady had disappeared into the forest last spring in pursuit of his favorite prey. But not long after the O'Chanters had returned south and found the Hollow, she was shocked to discover that *he* had found *them*.

Shady kept his distance, and never crossed the Rill, but he had stopped by the edge of the Hollow each of the last few evenings. This was as close as he'd ever let Rye get, and the first time he'd let her pet him since their days together back in Drowning. His fur was velvety in her fingers, and she remembered the many nights he'd spent keeping her lap warm—and protecting her.

"I've missed you," she whispered.

His bushy tail batted the night air.

Rye's other hand fingered something in her pocket. She slowly brought it out, and Shady pulled away abruptly, dropping himself onto his side several paces away. He gave her what looked to be a disappointed glare.

"Sorry," she said, and examined the worn leather band strung with runestones in her hand. It was the collar Shady had worn all those years he'd lived with the O'Chanters. She gave him a sheepish shrug. "Wouldn't it hurt your feelings if I didn't at least try?"

There was a rustle from among the trees. Shady turned his chin to the forest with interest, but no alarm. His rough tongue licked a paw so thick it looked like it could belong to a bear cub.

"Who else is out there, Shady?" Rye whispered. "*What* else is out there?"

Shady just blinked his yellow eyes in reply.

Rye sighed. "Oh, how I wish you could talk."

He stretched and casually strolled back to where another pair of eyes now waited. Rye knew it must be Gristle, the Gloaming Beast who had set out into the forest with Shady many months before. She seemed to want nothing to do with Rye or the Hollow.

Both Shady's and Gristle's eyes flickered, just an instant before an animalistic, beast-baby wail pierced the still air like an unseasonal wind. Rye jumped to her feet. The eerie sound came from close by, and she knew very well what had made it. It was the cry of a Bog Noblin. Quite possibly the one she'd encountered with the huntsman. She stepped back from the edge of the Rill.

Shady narrowed his eyes, glanced over his shoulder at Rye, and darted into the trees.

"Be careful out there," Rye called. "And keep an eye on Mama."

But Shady and Gristle had already disappeared into the darkness.

Four Horsemen

The next day, the hours seemed to crawl. Rye sat in the moss at the edge of the Rill, her arms wrapped around her knees. She'd paced the Hollow's perimeter much of the morning, watching and listening for any sign of Harmless. But if he was still out there, the breeze brought no whisper of him. There was no sign of Abby either.

The only sign of life on the forest side of the Rill was Mr. Nettle. He'd set the rowan-branch bridge across the stream and stood on the opposite embankment, his hands on his hips and his round belly jutting over his belt. Mr. Nettle stared up at the limbs high above, trying to work out how the brindlebacks were getting over the Rill. He chewed his beard and scratched the curly hair that stuck up from his head. Lottie was using his horned skullcap like a makeshift net, trawling the gently flowing water, her small cage at her side.

"I think I see it," Mr. Nettle muttered, squinting. "That's quite a branch that's worked its way into the oak. No wonder those furry nuisances are making it across."

He walked over the bridge, lifting it up after he'd crossed. He peered down and frowned as Lottie drained water through the hollow eye sockets of his skullcap.

There was little that the youngest O'Chanter could offer in her family's search for Harmless, so instead she usually busied herself by searching the underbrush and streams for something that might replace her long-lost pet lizard, Newtie. Mr. Nettle had helped twist branches and slender twigs into a remarkable replica of Newtie's former wire birdcage. One day she had cheerfully filled it with some fireflies, two orange-bellied salamanders, and a knotty-looking toad of poor temperament collected from the forest. But by the time she'd made it back to the Hollow, the salamanders had devoured the fireflies before disappearing themselves, and all she was left with was a rather bloated, immobile toad that had apparently eaten itself into an early demise. She'd had even less success since then, and now the cage remained empty.

Mr. Nettle dropped himself down onto the ground next to Rye.

"I've dwelled in these woods my whole life," he said, following her gaze to the forest. "And I can tell you that staring at the trees won't hurry along whomever you are waiting for." He cocked his head back toward her. "It'll just blur your vision."

Rye looked over and smiled sadly.

Mr. Nettle crossed his eyes and stuck out his tongue. Rye giggled.

"Oh," he said, pressing his fingers to his eyelids. "I think I've made myself dizzy."

"I'll be glad when Mama's back, and I can do more searching and less waiting," she said impatiently.

"The forest moves at its own pace," Mr. Nettle said. "Live here long enough and you learn to take what it offers and ask nothing more. Those who try otherwise don't live here long at all."

Rye, Abby, and Lottie had met Mr. Nettle during their earliest days Beyond the Shale. They'd discovered a glade similar to the Hollow situated farther north along the Wend. The tiny shelter there was run-down and looked to be abandoned, but they'd found Mr. Nettle living in its remains. He didn't say much at first but was eager to join them when they were leaving. They were lucky to have found him when they did. If not for Mr. Nettle's intimate knowledge of the forest, Rye doubted they would have lasted this long Beyond the Shale.

"What is Harmless like?" he asked, when Rye once again turned her impatient eyes to the shadows of the pines.

Rye pursed her lips in thought. Truth be told, she'd only really known Harmless for less than a year herself. It seemed like every time she began to get a clear picture of him, she uncovered some additional detail that blurred her vision like a half-remembered dream. That, or he up and disappeared altogether.

"He's difficult to describe," Rye began. "He listens more than he speaks, but he's always answered every question I've asked of him. He can be funny and playful." She raised an eyebrow at Mr. Nettle. "Too much so if you ask my mother. But he's been called an outlaw—and worse."

Rye recalled some of the names Harmless had been tagged with: Gray the Grim, Gray the Ghastly, and, by the Bog Noblins, Nightmare and Painsmith. From what she had heard, those names had been well earned.

"And yet," Rye continued, "whenever he's near I feel safe. And the only reason he is out there"—she nodded toward the trees with her chin—"the only reason he exiled himself once again, to be hunted by Bog Noblins and men even more dangerous . . . was to protect me."

Mr. Nettle crossed his arms and furrowed his brow. "It sounds like what you have there . . . is a father." He gave her a tight smile. "Their ways are riddles to all of us, whether we're twelve or fifty-two." He pushed himself to his feet and brushed off his crimped wool trousers with his palms.

Rye buried her chin in her hands and narrowed her eyes at the forest once again.

That evening, after finishing the remains of a sparse supper Abby had left behind for them, Rye and Lottie climbed into their blankets.

"Mama should have returned by now," Rye whispered to Mr. Nettle.

"I'll keep an ear out," he replied quietly. "Nothing to be alarmed over. You and your sister try to get some rest."

Mr. Nettle bid them good night and retired to his nest of loose bedding on the tree house porch. But Rye *was* alarmed. Her mother wouldn't leave them waiting without good reason.

"Buggle snug?" Lottie asked, tucking Mona Monster, her hobgoblin rag doll, tight under her arm. Mona's polka-dot fabric was more gray than pink these days.

"Of course, Lottie," Rye said. "We can do snuggle bug."

Rye wrapped her own arm around Lottie and pulled her close, Lottie burying her head in Rye's shoulder. Lottie had allowed Rye to tame her unkempt hair into a long red braid after a colony of ants had taken a liking to some sap stuck in her locks. It still smelled like pine pitch and cook smoke, but Rye didn't mind. She just held her little sister tight until they both settled into a rhythmic breathing and eventually fell asleep wishing Abby was there with them.

Rye woke disoriented by the first voice of the night's choir. Lottie's eyes were still shut, her mouth open and drooling on Rye's chest. The voice came again. But this was no growl or slither of an unknown beast. She recognized it as the sound of a far more ordinary animal—the whinny of a rather unhappy horse.

Pulling her arm free, Rye rushed out onto the tree house porch. From the shadows of the oak tree's boughs she looked down upon the Hollow. To her disappointment, it was neither Abby nor Harmless. Instead, on the opposite side of the Rill, four hooded men struggled with a horse laden with packs. In the light of their lanterns, she saw the frightened animal buck and rear back as one man tried, unsuccessfully, to yank it by the reins across the shallow stream.

"Worthless mule," he cursed, splashing through the shallow water and onto the banks of the Hollow to improve his leverage. The others pushed at the horse's rump without success, and nearly got kicked for their trouble.

"Who are they?" Rye whispered to Mr. Nettle, who had joined her at the railing.

"I don't know. Surely they've come down the Wend. But I don't like their manner one bit."

The man in the Hollow lowered his hood and raised his lantern, peering up at the branches.

"Who's up there?" he called. "I can hear you warbling. Come down this instant. We seek shelter for the night."

Rye and Mr. Nettle stepped away from the railing, deeper into the shadows. They exchanged uneasy glances. Lottie stumbled out to join them, rubbing sleep from her eyes. Mona Monster was still tucked under her arm.

"*Come down*, I say," the voice bellowed, "before I burn you out of your tree."

The man's ashen face reflected in the lantern light, his dark eyes squinting as he struggled to see them.

Rye heard Mr. Nettle suck in his breath.

"What is it?" Rye asked.

"I don't know," he said. "But these men smell of danger . . . and death."

Rye dared to return to the railing, trying to get a better look at the four visitors.

"Wait here," Mr. Nettle ordered urgently. "And be absolutely quiet. You too, Miss Lottie."

Lottie turned an imaginary key at her lips.

"Innkeeper!" the hoodless man demanded, his black lips curling. "I'm readying the torches!"

"Coming," Mr. Nettle called. "One moment!" He gestured again for Rye and Lottie to stay put as he hurried off to the winding stairs.

Rye leaned over the railing. The man in the Hollow had smudged black face paint running from his lower lip, over his chin, and down his throat, where it split and curled at the end, like a long tongue. He gestured to his companions, two of whom left the horse and slogged through the Rill. In the light of their own lanterns Rye saw that, under their hoods, their faces were also pale and ashen, eyes and lips streaked black. She gasped.

"Mr. Nettle," she called in a desperate whisper. "They're Luck Uglies!"

Or to be more precise, they were Fork-Tongue Charmers.

But Mr. Nettle didn't hear her. He had already climbed down to meet them.

"What are you, some sort of troll?" the Fork-Tongue Charmer asked, as Mr. Nettle padded out onto the Hollow. He thrust his lantern in Mr. Nettle's face, and Mr. Nettle shielded his eyes with his hand and adjusted the horns on his skullcap.

"No . . . ," the man went on, a look of recognition in his dark eyes. "I've seen your kind before. I didn't know there were any Feralings left. I thought you'd all been boiled by superstitious woodsmen and eaten for good luck."

"Fortunately, I've proven to be unappetizing so far," Mr. Nettle said with mock cheer and a shrug. "Here, allow me to assist you with your steed. I think she'll be more agreeable with the help of this."

Mr. Nettle gathered the rowan-wood platform and laid it over the Rill. The other Charmers watched him with grim faces under their dark hoods, towering over the smaller man as he gently took the reins and coaxed the reluctant horse over the makeshift bridge and onto the Hollow.

"My name's Nettle," he said, affecting a steady voice. "And what should I call you and your companions?" he asked the hoodless man.

"I am Lassiter," the Fork-Tongue Charmer said,

lifting his arm so that his lantern light might catch the boughs of the oak above. He eyed the old buildings suspiciously. Rye was still watching from the porch, and stepped in front of Lottie, easing her back into the shadows.

"These are my brothers, doom, despair, and destruction," he added, flicking his chin over his shoulder. "They ride with me wherever I go."

The other Charmers laughed at his quip, although Lassiter's attention remained focused on the guesthouse built in the tree. He squinted upward through the shadows.

"Whose establishment is this? Are you the only one here, Feraling?" Lassiter asked with a crooked glance.

Mr. Nettle hesitated. "Yes . . . just me at the moment." He stroked the nervous mare's muzzle with his hand. "The master of the inn and his hunting party should be returning shortly."

"Master of the inn?" Lassiter said, his black lips curling into a smirk. "And what is this innkeeper's name?"

"Ab—that is . . . Able," Mr. Nettle said, catching himself midsentence. "You may have heard him called Able the Imposing. Or Able the Awe-Inspiring," he added quickly. "He's a legend. A giant among men."

Rye cringed as she listened. *Too much, Mr. Nettle.* He was not a practiced fibber.

"I've never heard any such names," Lassiter said, glowering at Mr. Nettle. "I'll look forward to meeting this master of tree houses upon his return. This is the shabbiest flophouse I've ever seen, but we've traveled far and long. Fix us a room and a hot meal while we wait."

"Oh, I'm terribly sorry, but there's not much I can do to help. We're all out of food."

"A guesthouse without food?"

Mr. Nettle bobbed the horns on his head with a nod.

"Are you out of rooms, too?" Lassiter looked up at the smaller cottages nestled in the boughs of the oak.

Mr. Nettle chewed his beard for a moment. "Yes, yes, full up." He gave Lassiter and the other glaring Charmers an apologetic smile.

"And yet you just told me you were all alone," Lassiter said flatly.

"Right," Mr. Nettle said slowly. He pursed his lips. "I did. What I meant was . . . well . . ."

"Pigshanks," Rye whispered to herself.

Lottie must have recognized the severity of Rye's expression. She didn't say a word about Rye's colorful language, just crossed her index fingers and rubbed them together in Rye's direction. *Tsk tsk.*

Rye put her own finger to her lips, reminding Lottie to keep hushed, and led her quietly inside, where she began helping her with her boots and cloak. The voices below were muffled, but Rye could make them out through the gaps in the treehouse floorboards.

"Perhaps you meant to say that the guests are all out with the hunting party?" Lassiter snarked.

"Yes, exactly," Mr. Nettle said enthusiastically. Rye could hear the misguided relief in his voice. Life in the forest had made Mr. Nettle resourceful, but he had no ear for sarcasm.

"Do you know who we are, goat boy?" Lassiter demanded, his voice rising.

Rye threw her arms through the sleeves of her coat, and was still pulling on her boots as she ran back to the porch railing.

"Certainly," Mr. Nettle said, blinking his eyes. "You're Mr. Lassiter, and that's Mr. Doom, and Mr. Gloom and . . ."—he tapped a finger on his chin before waving at the fourth man—"Mr. Desperation, was it?"

Lassiter unsheathed a blade from the scabbard at his hip. He clutched a handful of Mr. Nettle's vest.

"We're Fork-Tongue Charmers—and no greater nightmare than us roams this forest. We have searched this forsaken wood far too long in pursuit of our quarry, and now, at long last, he's been found and we are on our way home."

Rye bristled. Their quarry? *Surely he meant Harmless.*

"But at the moment we are tired and starving. If you truly have no food, we'll just have to test the old superstitions." Lassiter pressed the tip of his blade against Mr. Nettle's chin. "After all, everyone can use a little extra luck."

Mr. Nettle pinched his eyes tight.

"Let him go right now!" Rye yelled from the darkness above them. She wrapped her white knuckles around her cudgel in anger.

Mr. Nettle opened his eyes and, along with the Fork-Tongue Charmers, looked up.

"So there *is* someone else here." Lassiter nodded his head at one of his companions. "Gibbet, go get whoever's in there and bring them down."

Rye's heart climbed into her throat.

The Charmer named Gibbet moved in the direction of the oak but paused at a sound from the surrounding woods. The night choir had come to life—the first voice, a gravelly growl, took up its song on the other side of the Rill.

Lassiter loosened his grip on Mr. Nettle's vest. "The denizens of this forest are relentless," he said in exasperation. With his blade, he gestured for the other two Charmers to watch the trees opposite the Rill. They unsheathed their own weapons and moved to the edge of the little stream, angling their lanterns so their light might penetrate the shadows.

The chorus grew louder, their throaty warbles and wicked ramblings calling to one another, excitement in their mysterious tone.

"Gibbet, to the tree," Lassiter ordered again. "And you two, cut down any creature foolish enough to trifle with us." He gave Mr. Nettle a hard shove toward the two Charmers by the Rill. "Feed the Feraling to them if need be."

One of the Charmers took him by the shoulder.

"No!" Rye yelled. She pressed herself over the rails, her eyes flaring at them. "Stop it!"

As suddenly as it began, the night chorus fell silent. Mr. Nettle and the Fork-Tongue Charmers froze in surprise, none of them more shocked than Rye herself. Then she heard it—a thumping plod followed by slithering through the dried leaves outside the Hollow.

Mr. Nettle caught her eye, then glanced at the rowan-branch platform still lying across the Rill.

"Oh my. Shriek Reavers," he observed quietly, but when his eyes briefly met hers again they were wide with fear. "Climb, Miss Riley!" he bellowed. "Climb!"

4

Shriek Reavers

Three long shapes, low to the ground, scurried over the rowan platform with remarkable speed. Sharp fingers clawed the soil as they dragged their legless, serpentine bodies behind them, black tails undulating like eels through water. The first Shriek Reaver reared up, and Rye saw that its head was elongated like a stag's, its skinless skull charred the color of soot. Two jagged, multi-pronged antlers jutted menacingly from its head.

The Hollow echoed with the sound of clacking bone. Dozens of oversize teeth chattered not from cold, but purposefully—with hunger.

Like a cornered badger, Mr. Nettle lurched forward and buried his own teeth into the nearest Fork-Tongue Charmer's shoulder. The Charmer growled in pain, but before he could move to strike Mr. Nettle, a Shriek Reaver's whip-like tendril slashed the Charmer's arm and sent his lantern flying.

"Climb, Miss Riley! Go!" Mr. Nettle called out again, and she saw him dart across the Hollow, a hand on his head to keep his skullcap from flying.

Rye tore back into the tree house and grabbed Lottie by the hand. Lottie's eyes were wide as Rye dragged her through the main room, to the opposite landing at the top of the spiral staircase. She looked at the enormous oak ascending above them as far as her eye could see.

"Lottie," she whispered, crouching down to face her and placing her hands on Lottie's shoulders. "You love to climb trees, right? But Mama won't always let you?"

Lottie nodded suspiciously.

"Well, now's your chance. We get to climb the tallest tree of them all. I promise not to tell."

Lottie gave her an uncertain smile.

"Really. Go ahead. I'll follow you."

Lottie's eyes drifted down the staircase to the base of the oak. The Hollow was filled with the pained shouts of the Fork-Tongue Charmers as they called to one another; the hacking sound of metal into what sounded like damp, rotting wood; and the relentless gut-churning clack of bony teeth.

Rye put a finger on her sister's chin and gently lifted it so she was looking into Rye's eyes once again. "No looking down, Lottie. And don't worry, I'll be right behind you."

Rye saw Lottie swallow hard. She knew Lottie must be as frightened as she was, but the little girl was doing a remarkable job of hiding it. Rye gave her a boost onto the tree house roof, from which the thick trunk of the oak towered upward like an endless chimney. Lottie clung to the moss-riddled shingles on her hands and knees, and Rye moved to join her.

"Mona?" Lottie asked, peeking down over the edge at Rye.

"What?" Rye asked, and her eyes darted to the inside of the tree house. The pink polka-dot hobgoblin lay on the floor where Lottie had dropped her.

Rye checked the spiral stairs. She saw a dark shape scuttle over the oak's roots and disappear out of sight, the sounds of the calamity below still loud in their ears. She thought better of it but dashed into the tree house anyway, snatching up Mona Monster. She returned, showing the doll to Lottie before stashing it safely in the folds of her own coat.

"Now get to the trunk," Rye said, shooing Lottie on.

Lottie disappeared from the edge and Rye took hold of the roof, digging her fingers into the shingles and pulling herself up. She steadied herself and climbed to her feet, balancing on the sloped pitch. She gasped in alarm as she looked down, where the Fork-Tongue Charmer named Gibbet met her gaze. He was just below her, on the tree house landing.

But behind him was something even more terrifying.

A Shriek Reaver was deftly climbing the spiral stairs on two long tendrils that looked more like knotted roots than arms. This close, Rye now saw its teeth: grotesquely oversize for its jaw, their edges chipped from their relentless clacking and grinding.

Rye opened her mouth to scream but found her throat dry. Gibbet must have read her look of alarm, and pivoted on his heels.

The slithering creature pressed itself up on its long, spidery arms as it reached the top of the platform, extending its torso so that it stood as tall as Gibbet. It cocked its hairless, antlered skull and warbled something deep in its mouth, like the stub of a tongue flicking against the back of its throat.

Before Gibbet could attack the monster with his sword, the hideous creature lashed forward, pinning Gibbet's arms to his side with its own. Its long body coiled through the Charmer's legs, around his chest, and finally gripped his neck. They fell backward together, tumbling in a heap down the stairs even as Gibbet gasped for breath and struggled to free himself.

Rye didn't wait to see the outcome. She scurried toward Lottie, hurrying her up and onto the oak's trunk. She was thankful that they'd both spent so many days scaling trees together in Drowning, and fortunately the oak's branches were twisted and knotty—perfect for climbing. Rye followed her own most important rule whenever being chased: *Don't look back.* Or in this case, down.

Rye felt bark under her fingernails and scratches on her face, but she was otherwise unscathed by the time they reached a fork in the trunk where they could sit side by side. She put an arm around Lottie to be sure her sister was steady. Rye risked a quick glance down. Her head swam—they were higher than even the tallest rooftops of Drowning.

Only the faint flickering of scattered lanterns lit the Hollow far below, but in the shadows of the tree house, she could see the three black shapes weaving in and out of doors and windows, turning over every corner and cranny in search of some sign of life. One slid through a window only to emerge moments later from the crumbling stone chimney.

Rye heard nothing more from the Fork-Tongue Charmers . . . nor Mr. Nettle. She didn't know if the horrible Shriek Reavers would search the oak itself, and wasn't inclined to wait and find out. That presented a problem. They could keep climbing, but eventually the only way left to go would be down.

"Bingle-black!" Lottie huffed in a coarse whisper.

Rye looked in the direction Lottie pointed. Two saucer-like eyes stared at her a healthy distance away from the tree trunk, as if hovering in midair. Rye looked more closely. It was a brindleback on a branch—several branches intertwined together—where the limbs of the oak had mingled with a neighboring ash tree that grew outside the Hollow.

The brindleback blinked, then turned and scampered away along the branches, his long, ringed tail trailing behind him. *That's the answer,* Rye thought. She was suddenly relieved that Mr. Nettle was so fond of procrastinating his chores.

"This way, Lottie," Rye whispered, and on hands and knees, they shimmied across the branches. Rye cried out as they bowed under their weight, but their bridge held true, and she watched the Hollow and Rill pass far below them as they reached the other side. Climbing down the neighboring tree was more difficult, and they both fell from a higher distance than they would have liked, Rye cushioning Lottie's fall.

She pulled Lottie tight in her arms and leaned back against the base of the ash tree. Only now, with her sister's small warm body pressed against her, did Rye feel her own heart pounding like a desperate fist inside her chest.

But Rye's sense of relief didn't last long. She carefully craned her neck and peered around the ash tree. The Hollow and the oak were not far away, and she could still hear the chattering teeth of the stag-skulled monsters as they destroyed what was left of the tree house. Once finished, they would surely head back this way.

Rye put her hands on Lottie's shoulder. "Lottie, you stay here. Don't move, understand?"

Lottie looked at her in disbelief. Rye reached into her coat and dug out Mona, pressing her into Lottie's trembling hands.

"I'll be right back. Be brave for Mona."

Lottie embraced Mona and nodded. Rye took a deep breath and hurried cautiously toward the Rill. She hoped the Shriek Reavers would still be too busy hunting through the tree house to notice her coming.

Her plan seemed to work as she neared the edge of the Rill, but then there was a sharp crack at her feet. She sucked in her breath and looked down. She'd stepped on a fallen branch. Her eyes jumped to the tree house. The Shriek Reavers seemed to hang there for a moment, cocking their eyeless sockets toward her. Then suddenly they sprang to life, weaving their way down and around the spiral staircase.

Rye considered turning and running but realized it would be hopeless. Her only chance was to beat them to the Rill. She barreled forward, leaves and pine needles crunching under her boots. The three beasts were on the ground of the Hollow, dragging themselves on their spidery arms at a remarkable speed. Rye headed straight for them and reached the rowan bridge first. With all her strength she pulled it up in her arms just as the monsters reached the waterline. They flailed their sharp antlers and snapped their teeth a mere arm's length from her face, the smell of rot and mold on their breath. She fell backward toward the forest, the platform coming to rest on her chest.

When she pushed it off, she saw the Reavers circling the Rill frantically. Their nubby tongues warbled in their throats. Angry and agitated, they slunk around searching for a way over the water. Like every other nonhuman inhabitant of Beyond the Shale, they were unable to traverse the tiny streamlet without the rowan bridge.

The Shriek Reavers clacked their teeth in furious protest. They were now prisoners of the Hollow.

Whether or not the Shriek Reavers would find their way up the oak to the overgrown limbs was another matter altogether, and Rye didn't intend to linger to find out. She hurried back to the ash tree where she'd left Lottie, and slumped down to huddle with her sister in the dark. They might be safe from the trapped monsters for the moment, but they now found themselves on the outside of the Hollow looking in, along with all the *other* creatures of Beyond the Shale. It seemed that their long-term prospects had not greatly improved.

A nearby rustling of dried leaves startled Rye. She didn't have time to react before a body threw itself upon them. She shoved away its stocky form and raised her cudgel, but stopped when she felt the curved horns of a goat against her outstretched palm.

"Mr. Nettle?" she gasped in relief.

"Children! I was just heading back into the Hollow to find you. I'm not exactly sure what I would have done once I got there, but then I caught the scent of . . . your feet." He pushed his horned cap back up over his eyes, glanced at Rye's boots, then at the dark, sinister shapes circling the interior banks of the Rill. "I'm grateful for my sensitive nose . . . *and* your pungent toes," he added.

"What were those things?" Rye whispered. "You call them Shriek Reavers?"

Mr. Nettle nodded grimly. "Ancient guardians of Beyond the Shale. They are extremely rare, and normally only stalk the northernmost reaches of the forest. I've never seen them this far south."

"Monsters," Lottie huffed, and furrowed her brow. "Not nice ones," she clarified, patting Mona apologetically.

"There's no easy way to label the Shriek Reavers, Miss Lottie. They are neither good nor evil, just . . . single-minded," Mr. Nettle explained, chewing his beard. "The forest does not welcome outsiders. Feralings believe that when the balance shifts—when too many human outsiders penetrate the confines of these trees—the Shriek Reavers awaken from their slumber and take up their hunt. They don't stop until the balance tips back in the forest's favor." Mr. Nettle seemed to shiver at a memory. "It was a Shriek Reaver that destroyed the other hollow where you found me."

For a moment, Rye found herself hoping that the

Fork-Tongue Charmers had indeed found Harmless. At least that meant a Shriek Reaver hadn't beaten them to it. As for her mother, Rye could only hope she was already well on her way down the Wend.

"What happened to the other men—the Fork-Tongue Charmers?" she asked. "Did they get away too?"

"One clearly did. I heard other footsteps as I ran." He glanced toward the Hollow. "At least one other surely didn't."

Rye had seen all too clearly how quickly the Shriek Reaver seemed to squeeze the breath out of the Fork-Tongue Charmer named Gibbet.

"The Shriek Reavers aren't the only dangers out here." Mr. Nettle squinted at the shadows around them. "We need to find shelter until morning. Come on."

Mr. Nettle led Rye and Lottie away from the Hollow, carefully searching the gloomy terrain until he found what he was looking for. A fallen tree stretched far into the darkness in front of them. Its enormous root system had been torn from the earth and fanned out like jagged tentacles. Mr. Nettle helped Rye and Lottie duck into a gap in the broken limbs. The tree's knotted roots jutted around them like protective spines, but its pulpy core was soft against Rye's back.

Tomorrow they would set out at first light in hopes

of meeting Abby along the Wend. So for now there was nothing Rye could do but try to rest. She pulled Lottie close against her, and was eventually able to drift to sleep, comfortable in the knowledge that Mr. Nettle slept with one watchful eye open.

The Wend

The Wend resembled a tunnel more than a footpath. A menacing canopy of finger-like branches curled over the trail, as if ready to reach down and pluck any traveler who displeased the forest. Creeping roots bulged across the overgrown ground, seeking to reclaim the narrow corridor that had been forged through the trees.

Rye, Lottie, and Mr. Nettle bounced along the unforgiving trail, the clop of hooves thumping the ground beneath them. They had woken to find the Fork-Tongue Charmers' skittish mare drinking from a puddle not far from the Hollow. After some soothing words from Mr. Nettle, the horse had permitted them to mount it, making for an easier trip now that they didn't have to wait for Lottie's short but eager legs to keep up.

Rye watched the sharp branches pass around them as she bobbed in the saddle. The path's jagged canopy thinned the farther south they rode, eventually giving way to an overcast afternoon sky. The Wend ran north and south, twisting like a looming snake hole in each direction, and travelers hoping to cover any real distance had no choice but to traverse it. The Hollow sat along its more southern stretch. Village Drowning, the closest settlement, was still a two-day journey. But Rye's village might as well have been a mythical city in a book of fairy tales. Neither the House of Longchance nor any other noble family in all the Shale held sway over the inhabitants of these ancient trees.

There was a familiar odor in the air, and she had the unnerving feeling that something had been following them quietly through the brush. She quickly glanced at her choker. Fortunately, the runestones around her neck remained dull.

"My nose isn't nearly as good as yours," she said to Mr. Nettle, looking back over her shoulder. "But I can't get the smell of the bogs out of it."

Mr. Nettle grunted affirmatively from behind her.

"We're in the southern reaches of the forest. The bogs aren't far now, and beyond them . . . villages." He seemed to shudder at the thought.

"You don't like villages?" Rye asked.

Mr. Nettle shook his head adamantly. "Never been to one, luckily. But I've heard all about them from travelers. Trapped in dwellings, deafened by noise, and crawling with . . . *people*." He scratched his neck furiously like a hound fighting fleas. "Just the thought of it makes me itch."

"It's not all bad," Rye said with a nostalgic shrug, and watched the muted light filter through the treetops overhead. They hadn't come across Abby, and Rye's mind wrestled with a dozen unpleasant possibilities as the afternoon wore on. The obscured sun hung low behind the clouds by the time they stopped to rest. They dismounted and shared some of the skimpy provisions they'd found in the horse's saddlebags. Rye sat on the ground at the edge of the trail and wrapped her arms around her knees. The mare scuffed the dirt anxiously and tugged at her reins.

"We should have crossed paths with your mother by now," Mr. Nettle said as he tried to settle the nervous animal. Then he forced a smile and changed his tone in a manner that Rye knew was for her and Lottie's benefit.

"But I'm sure there's a good reason. She must have

decided to camp along the Wend for another night. Miss Lottie, don't wander too far . . ."

Lottie had taken Mona for a walk to "stretch her claws" and now took great interest in a small rodent scurrying through the underbrush.

Mr. Nettle's eyes followed a sharp turn in the path up ahead. "We may want to find a place to shelter for the night sooner rather than later. Better not to push on and then find ourselves exposed after dark."

Rye gnawed at a strip of dried venison with her front teeth and nodded, grateful to have a companion so familiar with the forest.

The mare jolted and startled her. Mr. Nettle tried to soothe it, but the horse tore off down the Wend with a furious snort, kicking up dirt and pebbles as it bolted away. Rye jumped to her feet as Mr. Nettle called and rushed after it, but she stopped abruptly. A cry caught her attention.

Lottie's familiar voice. Yelling. Angry.

Rye's mouth fell open, still full of chewed meat. "This way!" she yelled to Mr. Nettle, spitting it out.

Rye hurried off the Wend and through a thicket.

"Mean! You a mean monster!" Lottie's voice screamed.

Rye's heart raced at the sound of Lottie's words. She plunged into a small clearing in the pines, and jolted to a stop. Lottie stood at one end, hands on her hips with Mona Monster tucked under her armpit.

Just opposite her stood a Bog Noblin—the very one Rye had seen two days before. Its gray skin shimmered damp and clammy, the air around it thick with the smell of the bogs. Rye looked quickly to Lottie's neck, then her own.

Their protective runestone chokers did not beam blue.

Rye tensed and pulled Lottie close to her side. But the Bog Noblin didn't move. Surrounding it were two other familiar beasts.

Shady crouched alertly between the Bog Noblin and the O'Chanters, the thick fur on his back standing straight, eyes agleam with mischief. Gristle had positioned herself behind the Bog Noblin, blocking its escape. If the Bog Noblin was indeed following them, at least the Gloaming Beasts had stayed close behind. They looked as if they might pounce at any moment.

"Mean Gob Boblin did sneaky peek on me," Lottie huffed. "I think him tried to take Mona." She wrapped her arms around her doll protectively.

Shady circled the small clearing menacingly, Gristle working her way around the opposite direction, until the Bog Noblin shifted, its eyes rotating independently so it could keep watch on each of its antagonists.

Mr. Nettle arrived behind Rye, tugging the terrified horse by its reins.

"Perhaps we should be going now," he suggested out of the side of his mouth. "The Gloaming Beasts seem to have this well in hand, and I don't think we really want to see the results of their dance with this ugly fellow."

But Rye found herself studying this Bog Noblin carefully. It was clearly the one she'd seen at the huntsman's campsite two days before, and yet the familiarity ran deeper than that. She noticed the old bootlace at the end of his plaited, rust-orange beard; the fishhooks adorning his ears and nostrils. She had already seen more Bog Noblins than she cared to remember, and one thing she'd learned was that, like people, each had their own unique traits—after you got past their more common, toothy features.

The Bog Noblin watched Rye with its bulging, drippy eyes. There was a hint of fear but also an awareness, as if he too was searching Rye's face for recognition. She knew now that she had looked into those eyes before.

Leatherleaf?

The Gloaming Beasts closed in.

The Bog Noblin extended a veiny arm, its clawed palm open as if ready to defend itself. Around its wrist, she spotted a large decayed tooth strung on a string like a bracelet.

Shady's tail twitched, his body tense and ready to strike.

The Bog Noblin raised its distended jaw to the sky and let out a terrible beast-baby wail. Rye cringed, recognizing it clearly now—the first cry of a Bog Noblin she had ever heard. It *was* Leatherleaf, the juvenile Bog Noblin who had wandered into Drowning nearly a year ago and turned her life upside down. He had grown since she'd last seen him, but she was now certain of his identity.

"Wait!" Rye yelled and, inexplicably, found herself rushing to stand between the Gloaming Beasts and Leatherleaf.

"Miss Riley!" Mr. Nettle called out in alarm.

Rye raised her hands, gesturing to Shady and Gristle as if to hold them back. Gristle returned an indignant glare, and skulked off into the trees. Shady's eyes narrowed, more pensive. She doubted she could keep him at bay for long.

Rye looked to Leatherleaf. One of his strange, bulging eyes rotated from Shady to her. It was joined by the other. He fixed his gaze on Rye, and she could tell that he was examining the choker around her neck. He seemed as surprised as Rye that her runestones no longer glowed in his presence.

Shady let out a low rumble from his throat.

"Please, Shady. Wait," Rye urged.

Her hand went to her throat. The runestones were cool to the touch and dim—no different from ordinary stones. Why hadn't they warned her of Leatherleaf's arrival?

"Why are you here?" she called to him.

He extended a large fist, his gray skin bulging with knots and blue veins. Rye tensed.

"What do you want?" she tried.

He gestured his outstretched arm in reply. She didn't expect that he understood her words, but perhaps the confusion in her tone had resonated.

Summoning her courage, Rye took a step forward. Leatherleaf watched her approach intently. He didn't move to meet her, nor did he retreat.

"Miss Riley!" Mr. Nettle gasped from behind her, and held Lottie back.

Rye trembled but forced herself closer, close enough that she could smell the stench of the bogs on Leatherleaf's breath. She extended an open palm under the enormous fist that dwarfed her own. The Bog Noblin unfurled his long, clawed fingers as if he would snatch her, but before Rye could flinch, something fell from his grasp into her hand.

Leatherleaf quickly retreated several paces to a deeper gap in the trees. Rye backpedaled into the clearing before looking at what he'd offered.

She opened her hand, cupping it with her other palm as several hard objects spilled between her fingers. Runestones. In her hands was a broken leather necklace, similar to hers, Abby's, and Lottie's, but larger. She knew exactly whose it was.

The necklace belonged to Harmless.

6 The Descent

Rye stared blankly at the remains of Harmless's necklace in her palm. One of the House Rules she had been raised with, all long since broken, related to their chokers. *Worn under sun and under moon, never remove the O'Chanters' rune.* Had Harmless taken his off? The alternative churned her stomach. She wondered if this was why their own chokers hadn't glowed in Leatherleaf's presence.

Rye cast her gaze at Leatherleaf in shock. Her ears always grew hot when she was angry, and now they burned as if singed by a torch.

"Where did you get this?" she yelled, thrusting her hands outward. She marched forward, blind to the danger. "Did you hurt him?"

Shady followed eagerly at the sound of Rye's furious voice. He readied himself at her side, furry ears pinned back and chin on his front paws, eager to charge.

Leatherleaf didn't flee, but his watery eyes fixed themselves on Shady uneasily.

Rye stuffed the loose runestones into her coat pocket and then gently put a hand on the bristled fur of Shady's back.

"Easy, Shady, don't move," she whispered to him. "For now."

Rye tried to settle herself. Had Leatherleaf sunk his claws into Harmless then tracked her down to show her the evidence out of spite? That made little sense. It was the Dreadwater clan of Bog Noblins who had pursued Harmless Beyond the Shale. Leatherleaf was from the Clugburrow, and an outcast even among his own kind. Although he had grown larger and more imposing than when she had first encountered him last year, she doubted that Leatherleaf had the temperament to risk challenging Harmless alone.

"Why did you give me these?" Rye called. She tightened her grip on her cudgel and stepped toward him.

Leatherleaf rose from his crouch and Rye's body tensed. But instead of moving toward her, he took several strides deeper into the forest, stopped, and crouched again.

"Perhaps this would be a good opportunity to leave?" Mr. Nettle suggested urgently.

Rye waved a hand behind her back and shushed him.

She approached the spot where Leatherleaf had just been, Shady padding softly beside her. When she paused, Leatherleaf loped farther away, crouched once more, and looked back at her.

"I think he wants me to follow him," Rye said looking back over her shoulder at Mr. Nettle and Lottie.

"He probably has a nice picnic blanket set up back there and is waiting for the main course," Mr. Nettle said.

Rye hurried back to the frightened horse and pulled a torch and some flint from its saddlebags. Mr. Nettle's eyes went wide.

"What are you doing, Miss Riley? Have you gone mad?"

"What if he knows something about Harmless?" she said. "Maybe he's trying to show me."

Mr. Nettle sputtered his lips in protest.

"If he meant to hurt us, he would have done it

already," Rye said. She sparked the flint and the torch flared, and she peered into the darkening woods. "Besides, I'll have Shady with me."

Shady narrowed his yellow eyes at Leatherleaf. Rye knew it was taking every bit of his willpower to refrain from bolting after the Bog Noblin.

"Take Lottie to the Wend," she added quickly, before Mr. Nettle could protest further. "I'll hurry back as soon as I see where Leatherleaf leads me. If you find Mama, tell her which way I went. I'll catch her fury for this—but if Harmless is out there, we can't take the chance of missing him again."

Rye's boots sank into the swampy ground beneath her. Here the wetlands had broken the grip of the forest, the terrain around her filled with rotted stumps and the trunks of splintered pines felled by the water of the bogs. As fearsome as he could be when motivated, Shady was fussy when it came to wet paws. He trailed behind like some princess's lap cat as he carefully navigated the higher ground.

Darkness fell quickly that evening. Either that or Rye had been following Leatherleaf through the moors for far longer than she'd realized. She finally came to a halt when he did, keeping a healthy distance between herself and the Bog Noblin. He had crouched knee-deep in the shallow muck. His eyes reflected red in her torchlight as they glanced toward a clearing in the distance. Rye followed his gaze. A ring of lights—dozens of them—penetrated the darkness up ahead. She squinted to make out their source.

Rye turned back toward Leatherleaf in search of an explanation, but the Bog Noblin was now gone, the sound of his feet churning the swamp somewhere in the distance.

It seemed Leatherleaf had taken her as far as he intended.

A flicker caught the corner of Rye's eye. A light broke away from the others and approached with haste. Rye hurried to duck behind a stump covered in moss and blackened toadstools. She quickly snuffed out her dim torch.

The circular glow of a tallow candle spread out over the ground. The man who carried it scanned the bogs with probing eyes from under his cowl. Rye saw that his face was ghoulish white—covered in the traditional corpse paint of a Fork-Tongue Charmer. He paused just two short strides from her hiding place. Rye held her breath and hoped the sour smell of his candle would mask the smoke of her own smoldering torch. Not finding what he was looking for, the

Fork-Tongue Charmer returned to the others, sloshing across the damp turf with his heavy boots.

Rye exhaled in relief then hurried after him as quietly as she could, this time disappearing behind the splintered trunk of a fallen tree. She pressed her back against it and waited, making sure no one had heard her, then peeked over the top of the split bark.

An assembly of hooded figures had congregated in a crescent line on a mound of earth rising from the bogs. Each held a thick, bare candle, flames barely flickering in the still air and yellow wax drippings covering their fingers. If the wax burned them, they didn't flinch. A man was led to the center of the mound, the jagged point of an impish beak penetrating the dark folds of his hood.

Rye watched as one of the other figures stepped forward to meet him. This man was masked as well, but instead of the fiendish, leathery guise of the Luck Uglies, his mask was lined with scales and bore no nose. A hollow mouth and grotesquely distended jaw stretched down to his chest, a cavern so dark it swallowed the hope from Rye's heart. She knew of only one Luck Ugly who wore a mask like that. He was the leader of the Fork-Tongue Charmers—and the most dangerous Luck Ugly of all.

Slinister Varlet.

With a nod of Slinister's distorted chin, the Fork-Tongue Charmers on either side of the man removed his cloak and cowl. He offered no resistance as they shackled his wrists at his waist. Rye felt a lump rise in her throat. She was suddenly very aware of the thick smell of rotted wood and stagnant water around her. A Fork-Tongue Charmer reached up, pulled the mask from the prisoner's face, and cast it to the ground.

Rye had already guessed who she might see under the mask. Still, her face fell and her head swam—first in relief, but then with dread. She placed both hands on the fallen trunk to keep from losing her balance.

Harmless's wolf-like eyes glared back at Slinister, his jaw knotted behind a beard that was thicker and grayer than when Rye had last seen him. The faded scars on his face were drawn tight with defiance rather than pain. Harmless listened unflinchingly as Slinister recited accusations, the Fork-Tongue Charmer's words deep and booming from the hollow of his mask, loud enough that Rye could hear them over the stillness of the bogs.

"Gray O'Chanter, you stand accused of failing to answer a Call of the Luck Uglies. A charge you have not denied. You have raised your blade and shed the blood of no less than six of our own brothers since your disappearance, with several more missing and unaccounted for. Another charge you do not deny."

Harmless listened impassively.

Rye fumed silently. Five months earlier, Slinister had handed Harmless over to the Bog Noblins for that very reason—so Harmless would miss the Call, casting doubt on his commitment to the Luck Uglies. And surely the Charmers who Slinister had sent out in search of him had not brought any peace offering. Of course Harmless had fought them.

Slinister cocked his masked head. "Do you offer no explanation?" he asked.

Harmless's reply came calmly, but with venom.

"I have nothing to say to this assembly of snakes. Except that you all shame the brotherhood tonight." Harmless's fiery eyes moved from one Fork-Tongue Charmer's darkened face to another as he spoke. "This gathering is a farce. Where are the rest of the Luck Uglies, Slinister? I see only the freshly powdered noses of your allies here."

"Word was sent regarding the nature of tonight's meeting," Slinister replied coolly. "Just because the others were unable to attend in a timely manner, that does not mean justice can be delayed."

"No justice will be served tonight," Harmless said slowly. "But rest assured, it *will* find each of you someday. Justice is a patient huntress . . . and a merciless one."

Slinister stared back from the red-rimmed eyes of his mask.

"Since you have nothing more to offer, we are left with no choice," he said, and for a moment Rye recognized the tone of mock sincerity Slinister used when he once wore the guise of a constable. "You have broken our code. Our oaths are sacred and absolute, and the punishment for such transgressions is well known by us all."

Slinister paused, and the assembled Fork-Tongue Charmers seemed to hang on his next words.

"Tonight, High Chieftain, we gather to see you on your Descent."

Rye's heart jumped. His *Descent*? She'd never heard that term before.

The two nearest Charmers moved closer to Harmless. He flashed his teeth and eyed them with such ferocity that they both hesitated, even though Harmless's wrists remained shackled.

"Stay your hands," he spat through his gritted jaw. "While you may dishonor yourselves tonight, I shall descend with the honor of a High Chieftain."

He stepped away from them, to the edge of the mossy mound where it sloped and disappeared into the brackish darkness of the bog.

Slinister followed behind him, pausing to remove his own mask. His sandy beard, once waxed into elaborate spikes, now hung straight, its end tied into a loose knot. Where his head was not shaved smooth an elaborate plaited braid was pulled back and fell past his neck and down his broad back. In the candlelight, his eyes were splinters of cracked jewels. The other Fork-Tongue Charmers tightened around them.

Harmless stared down to the black water at his feet.

"You show no remorse, Gray," Slinister said. "But we still afford you a brother's farewell."

Rye waited for Harmless's next move. What manner of escape did he have planned? Would he run? Or perhaps lull Slinister into a sense of comfort before striking unexpectedly? She readied herself, calculating what she might do to help him when he took action.

But instead, Harmless stepped forward. His body lurched downward as he sank up to his knees into the bog.

The Fork-Tongue Charmers surrounding him began to speak in unison, reciting words that sounded like a scripted chant.

"Once a Luck Ugly, always a Luck Ugly. Until the day you take your last breath. It's our deepest regret that breath has come so soon."

Rye's insides clawed at her. This couldn't be happening. She watched wide-eyed as Harmless took another step and the marsh rose past his waist. The Charmers' voices droned on as one.

"Sleep well, brother. May the bogs fill your lungs so you never rise. Tonight we will toast you fondly for what you once were, and try to forget what you have become."

A third step and Harmless's body fell awkwardly before settling, the mire consuming him up to his shoulders. Rye's head reeled as the chant continued.

"The blackness of the bog reveals the truth in every man. It is the rare brother who takes the final step unassisted. So we offer our hand this one last time."

A Fork-Tongue Charmer handed Slinister one end of a thick rope and Slinister stepped into the bog, his open palm raised, as if eager to push Harmless's head under himself.

"Back," Harmless growled through gritted teeth. "The last step is mine alone."

Slinister hesitated and curled his lip, as if disappointed. "As you choose," he said, and gripping the rope, climbed back to higher ground.

No, Harmless! Rye cried from behind the fallen tree, but not aloud. Her plea was silent and went unheard.

Harmless took the last step without assistance. The black mud of the bogs covered his nose, then his eyes as the ground gave way beneath him, and finally the top of his head disappeared altogether.

Every muscle in Rye's body strained to rush forward. But she fought back her urge, and instead began to count silently in her head.

One . . . two . . . three . . .

The Fork-Tongue Charmers uttered their final words.

"As the bog fills your eyes and ears, we too blow out our lights, sharing the ultimate darkness with you for but a moment, a reminder of what awaits us all should we forsake our bond."

They blew out their candles, and all was dark.

Two hundred eighty-nine, two hundred ninety.

Rye counted. One second for every three beats of her racing heart. Her clothes clung to her body from sweat as she waited, her back pressed against the pulpy bark of the split tree. Despite her panic, she forced herself to focus. The count was critical; she couldn't lose track.

Two hundred ninety-nine. Three hundred. Five minutes now.

It felt like forever. And yet was it long enough for all of the Fork-Tongue Charmers to have left? She peered over her shoulder. The moonless night offered nothing but shadows and silence.

Rye kept up her count. She had seen Harmless hold his breath for six minutes under frigid water. But to wait that long would leave her with no room for error. It was now or never. With a flick of flint, she re-sparked her torch and tore out from her hiding place.

Rye ran as fast as she could, but the wet bog seemed to grip her boots and fight her every step. It was as if she could barely lift her legs. When she did, unseen roots and creepers lurched out to trip her.

Finally she reached the place where she had last seen her father. Dropping her torch, she plunged herself into the bog, clawing and digging at the muck.

"Harmless!" she cried out, this time as loud as she could. "Harmless!"

But the bog guarded its prize jealously as it tightened around her. Soon Rye couldn't move her legs, and her arms grew heavy. She struggled to free herself but its murky waters held fast. Too many minutes had passed. Rye looked to the darkened sky above, her voice lost.

"Harmless," she rasped. But there were no answers. She had run out of time, for both Harmless and herself. She felt herself sinking, and could no longer move at all.

There was a loud splash behind her. Rye was pulled up violently, popping from the ooze like a cork as she was hurled backward. She landed hard on moist but unforgiving earth, losing her breath with the impact. Through the light of her torch on the ground she saw a large gray shape plunge into the bog. It buried its head and shoulders beneath the surface, rooting and grunting like a pig in a trough.

Rye blinked her eyes in disbelief. After a moment, Leatherleaf emerged from the water, pulling himself from the bog with one clawed hand.

The other claw dragged Harmless behind him, her father's lifeless body stained black with mire from head to foot.

7 The Departed

A chill breeze rattled the swamp maples and sent a storm of crimson leaves fluttering down past Rye's shoulders like hundreds of tiny kites against a gray sky. The leaves joined their fallen companions around Rye's boots, covering every inch of turf in the tiny graveyard. A dozen or so worn and broken headstones peeked out from the rustling red piles.

Villagers who knew of this place called it Miser's End Cemetery. But most had long since forgotten it altogether, and didn't call it anything at all.

Rye examined the thick bouquet of clover in her hand, the long stems tied with simple twine. She trudged through the leaves to the center of the graveyard, where three irregularly shaped stones jutted from the overgrown weeds, their faces covered with ivy that had turned burnt orange with the season. She crouched and pulled aside the leaves from the first. The single carved name was faded but legible, and was unaccompanied by date or detail.

GRIMSHAW

It was a name she'd only recently come to know. Grimshaw the Black. Her grandfather . . . and former High Chieftain of the Luck Uglies. The second headstone was just as unremarkable, the ivy less dense as she tore it away.

LOTHAIRE

That was the name of Harmless's younger brother. Lothaire the Loathsome was an uncle she'd once heard mentioned, but had never actually met. Rye swallowed hard and moved to the last of the three irregular stones.

Here she didn't need to clear any ivy. The markings on this headstone were still crisp, its face unadorned by weeds or growth.

GRAY

Rye breathed deeply and looked around at Miser's End. She had first met Harmless in this very same burial ground. They'd shared breakfast and stories sitting among these headstones. She'd played here with her friends even before that, and yet she'd never known her very own ancestors had come home to this small, unremarkable place.

There was a metallic creak behind her, and she glanced quickly over her shoulder. It was just the old iron gate swinging gently in the breeze as another round of crimson leaves danced past her boots. She cast her eyes to the path up Troller's Hill, where its solitary tree cast a skeletal shadow in the afternoon light. She thought she saw another shadow flicker on the hillside, but in an instant it was gone.

Rye turned back to the ground in front of her and resolved herself to the task at hand. She stared at the bouquet of clover one last time, pinched her eyes tight, then set it at the base of the headstone etched with her father's name.

Rye hurried out of the cemetery and up the path to Troller's Hill. She was just outside the northernmost fringe of Drowning, and as she climbed the gentle peak, she could see the roof of her cottage and Mud Puddle Lane not far away. She squinted, in hopes of catching a glimpse of Quinn, or the Pendergills, or even crotchety Old Lady Crabtree. But the dirt road seemed strangely deserted for midday. It would have been easy to hurry down and rap on Quinn's door, to greet her old friend for the briefest of moments, but her instructions had been quite clear. She was to stay out of Drowning and return without delay. Abby would be waiting.

So instead Rye stopped atop Troller's Hill, where Mr. Nettle waited, leaning against the base of the tree.

"Did you do what you needed to?" he asked solemnly.

Rye nodded.

"Good," he said with relief. "Let's be going, then."

Mr. Nettle's uneasy eyes were on Mud Puddle Lane, and the shadows of Village Drowning's rooftops looming beyond it. He chewed his beard.

"All of those buildings," he said with a mixture of awe and apprehension. "What are they?"

"Home," Rye said with a tight smile. "Maybe I'll get back there one of these days."

❖ ❖ ❖

Rye and Mr. Nettle arrived at a small sod house built right in the side of a hillock, on terrain that was neither bog nor forest. Thick marsh grass grew from its turf roof, camouflaging the dwelling into its surroundings. It sat near the southernmost end of the Wend, and was the place Abby had led a shocked and desperate Rye to after finding her huddled in the bogs, still clutching Harmless's body in her arms. The dilapidated hovel was an abandoned bog hopper's shack—an artifact from a time when laborers would harvest the bogs for red marshberries and ship them by the cartful to Drowning. That was before the swamps crawled with Bog Noblins again.

Mr. Nettle tended to their mare, and Rye opened the shack's rounded door and stepped inside.

Her mother stooped over a cook fire, which warmed the earthen walls like a rabbit's warren in winter. She glanced over her shoulder at the sound of the door, and offered Rye a smile. Lottie was too preoccupied to acknowledge her with more than a grunt. She was playing with a fuzzy caterpillar that she'd corralled within a tiny fence made from Rye's hair clips.

Rye turned to the figure in the corner. He rested in a chair with a blanket over his legs, a steaming cup of pungent liquid sitting untouched by his side. The circles under his gray eyes were dark bruises, but the eyes themselves were keen and twinkled at the sight of her.

"Don't just stand there. Come give your dearly departed a hug," Harmless said.

Rye hurried forward and threw her arms around him. He let out a little groan, but wrapped an enthusiastic arm around her in return.

Rye pulled away. "I'm sorry, too hard?"

Harmless waved away the notion. "Never," he said.

"How are you feeling today?" she asked. "You sound stronger," she added hopefully.

"Much better now that you're back," he said warmly.

Harmless carefully lifted his left arm and slowly clenched and unclenched his fist. From the short sleeve of his loose-fitting shirt, Rye could see that the muscles of this arm were noticeably smaller than his right one. It was still covered in a green mosaic of tattoos from shoulder to wrist, but where skin was visible it had taken on a grayish pallor. And his forearm was etched with an angry pink scar, raised and jagged, as if the victim of a sawblade. Rye knew that, in fact, it was the remnants of the near-fatal Bog Noblin bite he'd received last spring. The night he'd disappeared into Beyond the Shale, the Dreadwater clan close behind him.

"This old companion has seen better days," Harmless said, running a finger over the damaged limb. "There's still a tooth in there somewhere. Alas, extracting it is beyond my crude medical skills. I'll get to Trowbridge to visit Blae the Bleeder soon enough. It's been far too long and I'm afraid his business must be suffering from the extended absence of his best customer."

Harmless gave Rye a wink.

"Your mother has helped me get most of the bog rot out of my lungs," he added with a nod to the steaming cup on the table. "Although if I have to drink another cup of her foul herbs I think I may jump right back into the muck."

He shot Abby a playful look. She narrowed an eye in reply.

"If you don't stop complaining and take your medicine, I'll throw you back in myself," she said.

"Riley," Harmless said, becoming more serious. "How was your visit to Miser's End?"

"I stayed there for a long while, just like you said. And left the clovers where you told me."

Harmless nodded, satisfied.

"I don't think anyone saw me, though," Rye added, recalling the unusually quiet afternoon. "Troller's Hill—and all of Mud Puddle Lane—seemed . . . deserted."

"*He* will have seen you," Harmless said, and Rye knew he meant Slinister. "With his own eyes or someone else's. And that's all that matters. Did you play it up?"

"I looked very sad. I almost shed a tear."

"Excellent. If nothing else, you'll have a future in the theater."

"I said 'almost,'" Rye clarified.

"Close enough," Harmless said. He picked up the cup with his good hand and sipped it. He grimaced and coughed. Leaning over to a wooden bucket, he expelled something black and thick from his throat, then wiped his mouth on his shoulder.

"What now?" Rye asked.

"Now we stay here," Harmless said. "And rest. And catch up on better times." He rubbed his chin, and his weary eyes turned wolfish. "Then, in another day or two, when Slinister will have assumed the O'Chanters have left for good, you will return to Drowning." Harmless's jaw tightened. "And summon a Call."

"A Call?" Rye asked.

Harmless nodded. "And not just any Call. It will be a Call of all Luck Uglies, near and far. And with it, we shall bring a Reckoning to Slinister and the Fork-Tongue Charmers."

8 Broken Stones

Rye sat on the grass outside the old bog hopper's shack as the sun began to dip low in the sky. She heard the door creak over her shoulder, and Harmless hobbled outside to join her. He let out a low whistle as he carefully eased himself down onto the ground beside her.

"I may need to find a walking stick like yours until I get my legs back under me," he said with a tight-lipped grin, eyeing the cudgel across her back.

Rye returned a smile and gazed at the clouds

overhead, tinted purple in the late-afternoon light.

"I wasn't acting, you know," she said.

"Come again?" Harmless asked.

"At Miser's End," she said, turning to him. "I wasn't acting. I *was* sad. Seeing that headstone there—just waiting for you." Rye clenched her jaw in silence for a moment. "When Leatherleaf pulled you from the bogs, I was sure it was too late."

Harmless nodded grimly. "After all these years of close shaves and near misses, I thought it was finally my turn to hop the fence."

"But you lasted for so long under there. You never gave up."

"Yes, well, that's not entirely true," Harmless said with a sigh. "In fact, in the darkness, with the pressure of the bogs closing around me, you might say that I accepted my situation. I wasn't waiting for some miraculous rescue—the unlikely arrival of you and your red-bearded friend was entirely unexpected. The reason I held on was so I might savor my fondest memories for as long as possible." His gray eyes met her own, and he placed his palm on her cheek. "I clung to my visions of your mother . . . your sister . . . and of you. For even in the most hopeless depths, your faces make me smile. And whenever my time *is* finally up, I plan to go with a smile on my face." He flashed her a smirk. "Not that I'm planning on going anywhere soon."

But Rye didn't find his words to be particularly reassuring. "What was it like—being buried under there?" she asked. She pinched her eyes tight and shook her head. "Sometimes I shut my eyes and try to imagine how awful it must have been."

"Don't," Harmless said firmly, but kindly. "It's not something you'll ever have to discover."

Rye reopened her eyes. "Slinister called it the Descent," she said, remembering his ominous words. "Is that the punishment for violating the Luck Uglies' code?"

Harmless nodded. "It's a cruel fate, but an effective deterrent."

"Have you ever sent someone to the Descent?" Rye asked hesitantly, then wished she hadn't.

Harmless just cocked his head toward her sadly, then narrowed his eyes and stared out at the bogs in the distance. Rye supposed that was answer enough.

"Have you seen Leatherleaf in recent days?" Harmless asked, studying the shadows falling across the mire. "Of everyone who has ever done me a favor, he is the most unexpected of all."

Rye shook her head. "I think Shady chased him off. Maybe for good this time. I haven't seen either of them since Leatherleaf burrowed in after you."

Rye reached into her pocket and retrieved Harmless's broken necklace.

"He gave me this," she said, and handed Harmless the loose runestones and torn leather band. "I didn't know how he came by it, but I feared the worst. It seems our own chokers no longer glow either," she added, fingering the band around her neck.

Harmless examined the stones in his hand. For the first time, Rye noticed how closely the circular pattern tattooed on his palm matched the runes on the stones.

"This was torn from my throat when I lost my struggle with several Fork-Tongue Charmers," Harmless said. "Leatherleaf must have found it. I sensed that a Bog Noblin was following me in recent weeks. I had assumed it was another one of the Dreadwater, but was puzzled that it didn't attack."

Harmless furrowed his brow. "The destruction of my choker explains why yours no longer glows. But that matters little now." Rye was stunned to see him cock his arm and cast the handful of loose stones out into the brush. "Whatever power the runestones once had to protect has faded anyway."

Rye shook her head quizzically. Harmless spoke slowly while his eyes stared ahead, as if observing a scene far in the distance.

"Many years ago, when the Luck Uglies drove the Bog

Noblins from the Shale, I led that charge. I was merciless. I unleashed the Gloaming Beasts on them—Shady and others—and when they fled and hid, disappearing in the bogs, I kept hunting. I surprised them while they were helpless and hibernating for winter. I dug them from their burrows while they slept, dragging them out one by one."

Harmless paused. He opened one fist, then the other weakened one.

"They had a name for me. The Painsmith—the greatest monster their kind had ever known." Harmless stared down at the faded pattern of runes etched into his palms. "The ink that stains these hands was spilled from the Bog Noblins themselves."

Harmless's matter-of-fact tone could not hide a hint of remorse.

"I have many regrets," he added finally. "But I've long since learned that regret is an emotion with few uses."

Rye blinked with a sudden realization. She'd often puzzled over how the extinct Bog Noblins could have returned, but sometimes the right answer was also the simplest one.

"You didn't honor your bargain with the House of Longchance," she whispered aloud. "You never finished the job. That's why the Bog Noblins have come back."

Harmless looked up from his hands.

"At the very end, when their numbers had been decimated and I could have made the Bog Noblins no more than fossils in a history book, I hesitated."

Harmless held Rye's eyes.

"Why?" she asked.

Harmless shook his head, as if he was still searching for an answer. "Perhaps because I saw the fear in their eyes—for themselves, and for their young. It made me step back and question who the real monster was. Was I really any better than they were? It's a question I still ponder. But, yes, I spared them in the end. And to this day, it remains the only bargain I've ever broken."

They both sat in silence.

"I left the Bog Noblins defeated and scattered," Harmless continued, "with a promise that the Luck Uglies would show no mercy should they ever return to Drowning. These stones," he said, plucking one last loose runestone from the ground at his feet, "were made using a dark and wicked sorcery best not dabbled in."

Rye swallowed hard and looked at her choker in a new light. It no longer gave her comfort.

"So now you know the truth, Riley. Our runestones were carved out of fear. But that magic always fades. The Bog Noblins no longer fear the Luck Uglies. Slinister and the Fork-Tongue Charmers' actions have shown them that the Luck Uglies are divided, and are willing to turn on their own."

With a flick of his finger, the last runestone flew through the air. Rye watched with sinking spirits as it disappeared where he'd thrown the others.

"But it seems *you* have tapped into a magic even more powerful," Harmless said.

"What do you mean?" Rye asked.

"Kindness," Harmless explained, with a curious smile. "You showed compassion for Leatherleaf, and he has repaid it in his own way. If not for your choice, I daresay I wouldn't be here to tell you these things now."

Harmless placed a hand on her knee.

"Leatherleaf has confirmed what I suspected so many years ago. Like Luck Uglies, not all Bog Noblins are cut from the same cloth."

Rye considered Harmless and Slinister, two leaders desperately tugging opposite ends of the same fabric.

"Can the rift between the Luck Uglies and the Fork-Tongue Charmers be mended?" Rye asked.

Harmless looked to her sadly. "It can't. Slinister had hoped my recent disappearance would be enough to elevate him to High Chieftain. But he overestimated his influence. After so many years apart, many Luck Uglies were unwilling to accept my demise based on Slinister's word alone. That's what his farce of a Descent was about—a hasty trial and punishment designed to discredit me and pave his own way to the High Chieftain's Crest." Harmless's face hardened from sadness to something darker and more primal. "Now he prepares to assume the Crest, unaware that we are still left to resolve our differences in the only manner possible . . . and that the Luck Uglies will ultimately follow whoever is left standing."

Rye's chest tightened. "That's the Reckoning you were talking about?"

Harmless nodded. "It's an ancient method of reconciliation reserved for only the most serious of differences—those that might otherwise lead to an endless war within the Luck Uglies themselves. Once summoned, the fate of the Luck Uglies will hinge on its result."

"A method of reconciliation?" Rye repeated suspiciously.

"Think of it as a competition," he said with a shrug.

"Like a pie-eating contest?" she asked flatly.

Harmless's face softened. "If you'd like to look at it that way."

"You want *me* to summon it?" Rye asked.

"I'd go myself, but I'm in no shape to travel and the Reckoning can't be delayed. Slinister will take steps to be named High Chieftain as quickly as possible. We need to beat him to it." He sighed and looked down in disappointment at his body, as if an old friend had betrayed him. "Growing old can be a cruel fate."

"I'd say it's a better fate than the alternative," Rye observed. "You were almost drowned in a bog." She looked at her father, and his eyes glinted at her in expectation. "So how do I do it?" she asked.

"It's not a dangerous task," he said, clearly pleased with her response. "But it may be a bit tricky. You see, the Call for a Reckoning has not been made in my lifetime. And—I'm embarrassed to admit—I am uncertain as to how that Call is made."

"You don't know what the Call is?" Rye said in disbelief. "Then how will anyone else?"

"No, Riley, the Call itself is unmistakable, sent via the River Drowning and spread through every port and village that lines its banks. What I mean to say is that the *method* to make the call is secret. A secret hidden in *Tam's Tome*."

Rye sat up straight at the mention of the banned book.

Harmless raised an eyebrow. "Although Longchance destroyed all the copies he could find, I understand that there may be one more hidden right under our noses."

Rye just blinked in reply. Harmless blinked back. A tiny smile creased his lips. Once again, Rye would lose the who-could-stay-quiet-the-longest game.

"How did you know?" she asked incredulously. It

had been a year since Rye, Folly, and Quinn had unwittingly made off with a copy of *Tam's Tome of Drowning Mouth Fibs, Volume II*. It had since lain hidden in the clutter of Quinn's cottage.

He touched a finger to the tip of his nose. "Those skilled at keeping secrets tend to be best at sniffing them out."

With great effort, Harmless climbed to his feet, using Rye's shoulder for support. She stood and helped him.

"There's a chapter in *Tam's Tome* called 'The Reckoning,'" he said, gathering his breath as they made their way back to the door. "It will be written there."

Rye held his elbow tight as they took small steps. It felt unnatural—and more than a little unnerving—helping her powerful father in this way.

"Your last attempt to resolve your differences left you buried in the bogs," she said quietly. "How can this all end any differently?"

Harmless paused, reached his good hand across his chin, and flicked the nub that remained of his left ear. He'd lost the rest of it to an accident years before.

"Because my ears—what's left of them—are burning," he said. A dark smile penetrated the faded scars on his face. "And that means I've got one more good fight left in me."

Homecoming

Rye wasn't expecting a welcome party; she was just looking forward to the familiar hustle and bustle of Mud Puddle Lane. Instead, she was greeted by a barricade of sharpened timbers and stakes spiked with nails.

Mr. Nettle had seen her safely to the village limits before once again turning back for the bog hopper's shack. It seemed that even just the smell of Village Drowning and its sprawl was enough to give him hives. Harmless still wasn't strong enough to travel, so Abby had stayed behind to look after him and Lottie.

Rye methodically navigated her way through the unexpected barrier, using her cudgel to push aside strings of brambles that snagged her coat.

The winding mud road before her was soft from recent rain and empty of foot traffic. Even the wandering hens had abandoned the street. Ropes of black smoke twisted from the chimneys of the lane's low-lying cottages. Rye's neighbors' plots were protected by nasty thorn-rigged fences she had never seen before. Hand-painted signs warned trespassers of dire consequences, complete with ominous illustrations for anyone who couldn't read.

The far end of the road dead-ended at the village wall—or what remained of it. A small section had collapsed years before, leaving a snaggletoothed hole. Now it appeared that the gap had been recently filled—not with stones or mortar, but with refuse. Rye squinted at what looked like scraps of metal and timber, a broken wagon wheel, and other debris, all crammed haphazardly in an enormous pile like a plug in a rat hole.

Rye walked cautiously down the street she'd grown up on. Cottage windows, shuttered even by day, seemed to watch her like narrow, suspicious eyes. This place felt foreign to her now. Silent but for the plod of her boots through the mud, the stillness of the neighborhood left her uneasy.

Rye stopped in front of the largest cottage on Mud Puddle Lane. Unlike the others, its yard was bordered only by a simple, unfortified fence. There were no warning signs. Instead, a purple door carved with the shape of a dragonfly beckoned to her. The cottage was her home.

The thump of metallic boots on damp earth caught Rye's ear. She glanced down the road, toward the broken wall. A gangly man in full armor rounded the corner, his steel helmet bobbing atop plated shoulders like the bulbous pumpkin head of a Wirry Scare. A shield was stowed across his back and the scabbard of the oversize sword at his hip nearly scraped the ground as he walked. Rye couldn't see the crest on his shield, but she recognized it as soldier's armor. Soldiers on Mud Puddle Lane usually meant trouble.

Rye darted through the purple door and quietly pressed it shut behind her, hoping the soldier hadn't seen her. The unexpected changes on Mud Puddle Lane had left her feeling out of sorts. She missed her home, and hoped that waiting in the cottage for him to pass might bring her some comfort.

Instead, she was immediately struck by how lifeless and hollow the cottage had become. Rye looked around sullenly, as if seeing it for the first time. The ashes in the fireplace were cold and dusty. Her eyes drifted to her and Lottie's artwork on the wall—the paper had curled at the edges and yellowed with time. One of the pages listed the O'Chanters' five unbreakable House Rules: five absolutes that had framed the structure of her childhood. She hummed their rhymes softly out of habit while she pushed open the door to her bedroom, finding the bed she shared with Lottie rumpled and empty. But the tune caught in Rye's throat as a door slammed behind her.

She spun on her heels, and found the armored soldier in the cottage's doorway.

Rye gasped in surprise. The soldier hesitated for a moment, as if in shock. Rye struggled to free her cudgel but was too late as he rushed forward. He flung his metal arms around her.

"Let go! You're crushing me," she groaned.

"I can't believe you're back!" a muffled voice cried from underneath the helmet. "We thought we'd never see you again!"

"What?" Rye said, squirming free. "Quinn? Is that you under there?"

The visor of the helmet flicked open with a clank. The wide eyes of Quinn Quartermast blinked back at her, his friendly face stunned but beaming.

"Where have you been?" he asked in disbelief.

"In the forest," Rye said. "We found Harmless."

Quinn's jaw dropped.

"I'll tell you all about it," Rye added, then paused and looked him up and down. He was a head taller than when she'd last seen him. "What happened to you? You've sprouted like a weed."

Quinn blushed.

"And what are you doing in all that armor?" she asked.

"Things have changed since you left, Rye," he replied. He shrugged his shoulders with a squeak of metal plates. "And not for the better, I'm afraid."

The Quartermasts' cottage was only three doors down from the O'Chanters', and since Rye had last seen it, the place had become more armored than Quinn himself. It looked like a giant, scrap-metal toadstool growing alongside Mud Puddle Lane. His father, Angus the blacksmith, had done an expert job of encasing it in protective siding. The cottage was as dark as a fortress when they entered, the windows covered with plated sheeting. Quinn sparked several lanterns.

Stacks of books were piled precariously atop a small bed—those were Quinn's. The rest of the cottage was filled with the products of Angus Quartermast's trade. Iron shields were stacked like plates in a cupboard, heaps of chain mail lay strewn like fishing nets, and all manner of blades and bludgeons poked out from weapons racks. They navigated a narrow pathway through the disorderly mess.

"Give me a hand," Quinn said, wriggling out of his breastplate. He kicked off his armored shoe and stuck out his leg.

Rye grabbed his greave and gave a firm tug, pulling the piece free from his shin.

"So why exactly are you wearing this shell?" Rye asked, falling back onto a pallet of woolly gray blankets that smelled of peat and stale cabbage. "I'm not sure what you're going for, but I'm afraid you look more like a tall, skinny sea bug than a soldier. All you need are claws."

To Rye's alarm, the blankets underneath her got up and ambled away with Rye still on them. She leaped to her feet. It was Woof, Quinn's old wolfhound. The huge dog blinked at Rye slowly, scratched an ear with a long hind leg, and settled himself back down in a corner.

"My father makes me wear it while I'm out," Quinn said, dumping his gauntlets in a pile. "To be honest, I can't stand it. It's hot in there, and I feel like I'm wearing a tin bucket on my head. I can hardly move, never mind run."

Quinn had always been the fastest runner on Mud Puddle Lane.

"I'd rather take my chances unarmored and light on my feet," he added.

"Take your chances with *what*?" Rye asked.

Quinn adjusted his shirt and plopped himself down on a stool. He tugged on his regular leather boots and gave Rye a sad smile.

"Bog Noblins, Rye," he said.

"Noblins?" Rye said, furrowing her brow. "Where?"

"Here, in the village."

"In Drowning? Now?"

"Well, not at this very moment, but soon enough. They come after dark. The raids were sporadic throughout the summer, but now, with the shorter days, they've become more frequent." He shrugged. "Lately, it's been every night."

Rye shook her head. "That's why the street's deserted? And why the neighbors put up all the fences?"

Quinn nodded. "Supplies have run scarce. With no soldiers to protect the caravans, goods don't flow into the village anymore. Merchants from other towns won't take their chances on the more remote roads."

"There are no soldiers?" Rye asked.

"No one has seen any in months. For that matter, no one has heard from the Earl himself."

Rye bit her lip. The last she'd seen of Morningwig Longchance, he was being dragged off by Slinister

Varlet. She wondered if the Fork-Tongue Charmer had finally exacted his revenge upon him.

"What about the Shambles?" Rye asked. "Surely the Bog Noblins can't block the river and sea. Goods must still flow in by boat?"

Quinn shook his head. "Drowning's luck has gone from rotten to worse," he said. "Rumor has it a beast as nasty as the Bog Noblins has taken up residence in the river. Some sort of sea monster. It's already made off with a dozen fisherman and three whole merchant crews. The Shamblers are calling it the River Wyvern."

"A sea monster?" Rye asked, incredulous. "That's ridiculous."

"Something's got the Shamblers spooked, Rye. And you know those port folk—they don't spook easily."

Quinn popped off his helmet and scratched his matted hair.

"The Floods have been keeping their eyes out for it," he continued, "but ale and wine is their game. They're pretty useless on the water. The port is effectively closed."

Rye shook her head. After their months of isolation in the forest, neither Abby nor Harmless could have any idea how dire things had become in Drowning.

"With winter coming, our prospects look bleak," Quinn added. "Those who can afford it are making arrangements to get out of Drowning. The rest of us don't have that option."

"Where's your father?" Rye asked.

"He works practically around the clock, now. Forging as many blades and shields for the villagers as he can. He spends more nights at the shop than he does here. I run errands and deliver his handiwork once it's done. At least I get to come and go as I please these days."

Behind them, there was a louder rap on the cottage door.

"Quinn!" a girl's voice cried from the other side.

Quinn flashed Rye a smile. "She's going to jump out of her boots."

He flung open the door.

"Quinn!" the girl shouted. "Where have you been? We were supposed to meet twenty minutes—"

The voice of the hooded girl in the doorway came to a dead stop. She pulled the hood of her cloak from her head. Quinn beamed and proudly pointed a finger at Rye, as if he'd found a long-lost treasure.

A heavy basket fell from Folly Flood's arms, spilling bundles of dried fruit and several whole fish wrapped in waxed paper. Jars of jam rolled across the floor. Folly's blue eyes were as wide as marbles. They welled as her cheeks flushed red.

"Folly—" Rye said softly, but lost her breath as Folly

plunged forward and wrapped her arms around her. Her affectionate hug soon became too snug for comfort.

"Folly . . . ," Rye repeated, gasping this time.

Folly pushed Rye away, her eyes now burning. "How could you leave like that without telling us?" she demanded, fists clenched. "We thought you'd been eaten by a Bog Noblin, or worse!"

"I'm not sure what could be worse than that," Quinn noted.

"I'm sorry, Folly," Rye said. "We had to keep it secret—"

"No, no, no," Folly said, holding up her hand and showing Rye her palm. She turned to Quinn. "Tell Rye I'm too angry to speak with her right now."

"Folly's at a loss for words at the moment," Quinn said to Rye.

"Folly, I never meant to upset you. I'm sorry you were so worried—"

"Shush," Folly said, waving her hands at Rye as she hastily stuffed the spilled supplies back into the basket. "Not talking!"

Folly crammed the last of the jars into the basket, huffed, and scowled at Rye out of the corner of her eye. "You're okay?" she asked under her breath.

"Yes," Rye said. "We all are."

"Good," Folly said. "But I'm still not talking to you.

And I'm so angry I could beat you with a fish."

Folly removed a herring from the basket and did just that.

"Ow!" Rye cried. "Stop that!" But she was smiling as she said it, and saw that Folly was struggling to hide a smirk too.

10 The Night Courier

Rye caught Quinn and Folly up on the highlights of her months in the forest Beyond the Shale, culminating with Harmless's directive to summon the Call for a Reckoning.

"As it happens," Rye said, looking to Quinn, then Folly, "I'm going to need your help."

"How so?" Quinn asked.

"This isn't just any Call," Rye explained. "It's a Call to summon all of the Luck Uglies, both near and far.

And the directions for how to make it are written somewhere in *Tam's Tome*."

Quinn's eyes went wide. "There are special instructions?"

Rye nodded. "Harmless mentioned that it requires some sort of chemical concoction."

"Like a potion?" Folly asked, her interest piqued by her favorite subject.

Rye shrugged. "Sounds like it."

Quinn dropped to his hands and knees and dug out an assortment of hidden treasures from under his bed. A tin of green licorice, a small coin pouch, and a raggedy doll shaped like a rabbit went flying.

"Quinn, is that *your* stuffed bunny?" Rye asked.

"No," Quinn answered quickly. "I mean . . . that old thing? That's just Woof's chew toy."

He picked up the doll and tossed it to Woof in the corner. The dog opened one lazy eye before promptly returning to sleep, entirely disinterested.

Finally Quinn found what he was looking for. A dusty old book that both Rye and Folly knew well—*Tam's Tome of Drowning Mouth Fibs, Volume II.*

He handed the book to Rye, then hurried to the window and peered through the seams in the metal covering. He frowned at the waning sunlight and turned to her. "If you plan on spending the night at the Dead Fish

Inn, we better get on the road right now. We can find out about the Call as soon as we're safely there. Unless you want to stay here."

Rye looked around the small, cluttered cottage. The only spare space was in the fireplace. She glanced at Folly hopefully.

"We've got plenty of room," Folly said with a nonchalant shrug. "Lots of folks are leaving Drowning, but not so many are coming to visit."

Rye was relieved that Folly was quick to forgive her—and she wouldn't be forced to spend the night in the soot of the Quartermasts' chimney.

Quinn emptied the basket Folly had brought him and refilled it with various hand-forged utensils, nails, horseshoes, and a variety of small tools.

"Any weapons for the inn?" he asked.

Folly shook her head. "We've got plenty of those."

"Okay," Quinn said, handing the basket to her. He retrieved a large leather satchel. "Rye, can you give me a hand?"

She nodded and placed *Tam's Tome* carefully in her own pack. Quinn handed her the satchel, and she held it open while he filled it with small daggers and a helmet. When he was done, Quinn took the heavy satchel and slung it over his shoulder. "Let's go. We've got no time to waste."

Mud Puddle Lane remained deserted as the friends hurried over long shadows cast across the dirt road. When they reached the loosely filled hole in the village wall, Quinn showed them a narrow path that had been hollowed through the discarded junk and rubbish.

"Who filled the wall?" Rye asked, making herself flat as she pressed past broken table legs and some old shutters.

"The villagers," Quinn said, ducking under a bent and rusted weather vane. "Trying to slow down any Bog Noblins that might try to come this way. Of course, they didn't bother to think it might slow the rest of us on Mud Puddle Lane too."

Once past the wall, Rye, Folly, and Quinn continued through the residential neighborhood of Nether Neck on their way to the narrow streets of Old Salt Cross.

Tall, skeletal wraiths in tattered black robes watched them from every corner. The eyes and jagged mouths of their carved faces gaped, orange and fiendish. Wirry Scares—pumpkin heads set atop scarecrow-like frames. Despite their ominous stick-finger claws, Rye and her friends knew better than to fear them. They were old-fashioned totems, built to ward off creatures that went bump in the night. Apparently, the villagers were leaving no stone unturned in their defense against the Bog Noblins.

Quinn explained that, unfortunately, they'd been of little help. The Bog Noblins just ignored them, hardly giving them a second glance. It seemed the local squirrels were even less deterred; Rye spotted one burrowed tail-deep in a Wirry Scare's head as it searched for tasty seeds.

Quinn extended his palm and gestured for Rye and Folly to stop when they finally reached the darkened end of a disused alley. The three friends stared out at the deserted cobblestones stretched before them. The crossroads were eerily silent. The only sign of any inhabitants was the dim glow of candles behind the wooden planks and scrap metal sheets covering barricaded doors and windows. This corner was known as Apothecary Row. Most of Drowning's merchants were situated on Market Street, but Drowning's healers and medicine men—members of the Apothecaries' Guild—had set up their shops in the pricier neighborhood of Old Salt Cross.

"Why are we stopping?" Rye asked. "I thought we were short on time."

"Just wait here," Quinn said. "I'll be right back. If you see anyone . . . or *anything* . . . just whistle."

"I can't whistle," Rye said, puckering her lips and blowing out a silent puff of air in demonstration.

"I used to be able to whistle between the gap in my

teeth but it closed up on me. They're all straight now," Folly added glumly.

"Oh, never mind," Quinn said. "Just yell instead." He hurried out to the center of the crossroads. He crouched low to the ground, peering down one road, then the other. When all looked to be clear, he set his satchel of weapons down on the cobblestones.

"What's that about?" Rye asked Folly.

"They're for the Night Courier."

"The who?"

"The Night Courier," she repeated. "He should be starting his rounds shortly."

"Shhh," Quinn said with a finger to his lips, hurrying back to join them. "You don't want to scare him off." He stared across the road to the opposite alleyways.

"Nobody knows who the Night Courier is," Folly explained. "But every night, just before dusk, he delivers parcels of supplies for the more remote villagers who don't have easy access to them."

"He just shows up?" Rye asked.

"At different spots around the village," Quinn said. "Most of the villagers have banded together—cooperating to share provisions as best they can. But the streets can be treacherous. The Night Courier collects supplies from one part of town when the villagers can't, then delivers them where needed. It seems impossible that he's avoided the Bog Noblins this long, but whatever he's doing, it's worked."

"Of course, not all of the villagers have been so cooperative," Folly added with a frown.

Rye raised an eyebrow.

"The Apothecaries' Guild voted to shutter their doors," Quinn said. "Now they only sell medicine to the highest bidder."

"That's awful," Rye said, a twinge of anger heating up her ears.

"Fortunately, the Night Courier has put an end to that," Quinn said. "He's been raiding their storerooms, taking whatever medicine he can get, and delivering it where needed. We don't know how he's getting in there either, but those of us who are short on coins are grateful for the effort."

"That's what we're doing here?" Rye asked.

Quinn nodded. "The Pendergills need a poultice for the babies. They've been battling fevers for a week . . . and we're afraid they're losing the fight."

The Pendergills were Rye and Quinn's neighbors on Mud Puddle Lane.

"Look," Folly said in a hushed voice.

They turned their attention to the crossroads.

A slender figure had appeared from the shadows. He was garbed in a fitted brown leather coat and a wide-brimmed hat cocked low over his eyes, a blue feather tucked in the hatband. He moved silently like a wisp across the cobblestones, a deep blue scarf wrapped over his lower face, masking his features.

"That's him," Quinn whispered.

The Night Courier paused at the satchel Quinn had left in the street. He seemed to examine it for a moment, tilted his head toward the shadows, then lifted it and slung it over his shoulder. A small brown sack dropped from his gloved fingers, taking the satchel's place on the ground.

He turned on a heel, his slender legs hurrying quickly toward the alley from which he'd come.

A low rumble echoed through the crossroads, like a wind through a forest corridor.

"Quinn, tell me that was your stomach," Folly said.

"That was my stomach," Quinn replied.

"Really?" Folly asked hopefully.

"Afraid not."

The Night Courier heard it too. He skidded to a stop, and was lucky he had. From the alley emerged a hulking gray figure, its skin hanging from its massive frame. Rye saw its wild rust-orange hair and the tusk-like teeth protruding from its lips. She craned her neck to check her choker but, of course, it no longer glowed.

"Bog Noblins," Folly gasped.

Quinn shook his head in disbelief. "It's too early," he muttered. "It's not even dark."

On the road, the Night Courier didn't waste any time. He darted away as fast as he could in the opposite direction. But a second Bog Noblin, one even larger than the first, appeared from the mouth of the southernmost street. It dragged the body of an ox behind it as if the carcass were no heavier than a traveler's sack, shoulders stooped as it hunched over to peek through windows and doors like a Market Street shopper. The second Bog Noblin straightened at the sight of the Night Courier and dropped its prize to the ground, eager to catch something a bit more savory.

Both Bog Noblins converged on the Night Courier as he rushed to the facades of two crooked brick buildings that leaned askew with age. Rye caught her breath when it appeared that he'd run out of places to go—the windows and doors were boarded up tight. But the Night Courier slipped into the narrowest crevice between the buildings, like a rat under a door, and the Bog Noblins were left staring into its dark shadow with no hope of pursuing him any further.

"Come on," Quinn urged. "Let's get out of here while we can."

"Not without the medicine," Rye said, pointing to the small pouch the Night Courier had left at the center of the crossroads.

She hurried out to snatch it before Quinn or Folly could stop her. But as she stepped into the roadway, another rumble echoed up and down the streets of Old Salt Cross. Rye glanced around in confusion. This sound wasn't a beast's groan, but a quick-paced thunder of hooves.

Before Rye could react, three black horses and hooded riders burst from the western stretch of road. They didn't slow as they approached her, and she had to throw herself aside onto the cobblestones to avoid being trampled. Without stopping, the lead rider stabbed the medicine bag with his sword as his mount stormed past it, plucking it up and stashing it among his saddlebags.

Rye caught a glimpse of the rider's ashen white face and the curled smile of black-lined lips under his hood.

"Fork-Tongue Charmers!" she spat as Quinn and Folly rushed to her side and dragged her to her feet.

The Bog Noblins turned their attention away from the Night Courier's hiding place at the sound of the horses, but the Charmers didn't slow. The gallop of hooves faded as the riders disappeared around a bend. Instead, the Bog Noblins found only Rye, Folly, and

Quinn in the middle of the crossroads.

"Back to the alley!" Quinn cried, but no sooner did he say it than the frame of a third Bog Noblin filled that alleyway, blocking their escape.

"They're everywhere," Folly gasped.

"Look!" Rye called, and pointed. "Follow him."

There, between the three friends and the Bog Noblin in the alleyway, was the Night Courier. He had appeared as if out of thin air, and now crouched on the cobblestones. Rye thought she saw the flicker of his eyes in the narrow slit between the brim of his hat and the scarf around his face.

They all rushed toward him. The Bog Noblin in the alleyway must not have believed his luck, and lumbered out to wait for the dimwitted morsels making straight for his mouth. But as he did, the Night Courier disappeared before all of their eyes, and the Bog Noblin paused in disbelief.

The three friends skidded to a stop where the Night Courier had been, hovering over the mouth of a round black hole just wide enough for a child to fit through. A heavy metal sewer grate was pushed aside.

"Down there," Rye said.

"Are you sure?" Quinn asked, squinting into the ominous void.

Rye glanced up at the snarling Bog Noblin just a

stone's throw away, spittle flowing from his distended jaws.

"Positive," Rye said.

And the three children leaped down into the tunnels below.

11 Creepers

Rye, Folly, and Quinn scrambled away from the dim column of light filtering down through the open sewer grate. Rye heard the snuffling of the Bog Noblins' pig-like noses, the grunting of hungry maws and flicks of salivating tongues as the creatures peered down into the sewers. But like defeated hunting dogs that had lost a rabbit to its hole, they soon wandered off, having caught the scent of easier prey.

Rye blinked, trying to adjust her eyes to the darkness.

"Those riders—the Fork-Tongue Charmers. Do they always try to take the Night Courier's supplies?" she asked.

"Sometimes," Quinn replied from the shadows. "Like Folly said, not everyone in the village has learned to cooperate."

"I heard they've holed themselves up in Longchance Keep," Folly added. "But if they're guests of the Earl, I think they've overstayed their welcome. No one's seen Longchance since before you left."

Based on Slinister's rough treatment of Morningwig Longchance when Rye had last seen them together, she doubted that anyone would be seeing the Earl again.

"What is this place?" Quinn asked. "Is it the Spoke?"

"Part of it, I guess," Rye said.

In the past Rye had accessed the Spoke through the wine cellar of the Dead Fish Inn, from a tattoo parlor in the Shambles, and by way of her mother's hidden workshop on Mud Puddle Lane. She knew there were other entrances and exits concealed throughout the village. Abandoned wells, forgotten cemeteries, and neglected basements all provided secret entryways into the Spoke's catacombs. It was the perfect highway to traverse Village Drowning invisibly—just as it had been used by the Luck Uglies generations before.

Her vision had adjusted to their gloomy surroundings. It was dim, but not pitch-black. A weak light flickered a short distance away, giving shape to a bend in the subterranean tunnel.

"I'd bet my boots that this is how the Night Courier gets around the village right under the Bog Noblins' noses," Rye said, glancing around.

Rye waved for Folly and Quinn to follow as she crept forward, carefully navigating the loose earthen floors and stagnant puddles at their feet. Folly and Quinn trailed close behind. With his recent growth spurt, Quinn had to duck to avoid clipping his head on the roots jutting from the crumbling walls and ceiling. They reached the light source. It was a torch mounted in a casing on the wall.

"And I bet *your* britches that someone lit this for us to follow," Rye said to Quinn, reaching up and taking the torch.

"Why do you say that?" he asked.

"Because I think I know who the Night Courier is." Rye pointed to where the tunnel snaked away. "It looks like he lit another torch for us up ahead. Come on, let's see where they lead."

When Rye last traveled the Spoke, it had been abandoned. She vividly remembered its dank, musty smell. But now, instead of the odor of abandoned earth, she could smell the pungent aroma of decay. Where once these tunnels greeted her with silence, she now heard far-off bumps and scrapings. Was it the mere settling of earth or the disturbance of footfalls? As they proceeded cautiously, they found another freshly lit torch smoldering in its casing on a wall. They moved on toward the next.

Rye had just gotten into a rhythm, using her cudgel to push herself along, when she stopped in her tracks. Somewhere, deep in the recesses of the Spoke, they could hear a low rumbling.

Folly and Quinn froze beside her.

A gust of stale, damp air tickled Rye's cheeks. The torch flickered in her hand.

"What was that?" Quinn said.

"I don't know," Rye whispered.

"Did you feel that?" Folly asked.

Something fell onto Rye's shoulder. Then her head. She plucked at her hair with her fingertips. It was gritty to the touch. Soil.

"Ouch," Quinn said, rubbing dirt from his eyes.

"It could be a cave-in," Rye said. "Hurry, maybe the tunnels aren't stable here."

They all rushed forward. Rye felt the patter of earth and pebbles like hail. Their boots slapped the ground below them and shallow puddles splashed at their feet. Rye didn't try to keep track of direction as they ran, she just followed the distant glow from one torch to the next. Then, just as the falling earth seemed to subside, a loose stone sent her tumbling. She felt the heavy thud on her back as Folly's and Quinn's bodies stumbled and tripped over her. Rye's torch fell several feet away and fizzled out. It was dark except for a dim torchlight around another bend.

"Pigshanks," Rye cursed. She felt water running over her hands and past her skinned knees. "There must be a leak in the Spoke."

"It was a wet summer," Folly said. "One day we used up all the inn's mugs catching leaks in the roof."

Rye climbed to her feet. "Let's get to where we can see again."

They slogged farther along the tunnel, the splash of their footfalls growing louder as they went. The three friends placed their hands on one another's elbows so they wouldn't become separated. When they arrived at the next torch, Rye saw that the ankle-deep water flowed freely through the tunnel. She unslung the pack from her shoulder, its canvas dripping from her earlier tumble. She reached inside and removed *Tam's Tome*. Its pages were damp and spongy.

"That's not good," Rye said with a frown. She examined the ink smeared on her fingers. "We'll need to dry this out."

"How are we going to do that?" Folly asked. "These torches seem to be leading us deeper and deeper underground."

"I'm not sure," Rye said, squinting into the darkness of the tunnels around them. The Spoke could be disorienting, and she struggled to determine whether any of their surroundings looked familiar. "Stop that splashing, Quinn," she said. "I'm trying to concentrate."

"I'm *not* splashing," he said, blinking widely in reply. Indeed, he was standing in the water just as still as Rye and Folly.

The splash was coming from close behind them, back in the stretch of tunnel they'd just traveled. The thump of limbs punched into the ground, followed by the swish of something heavy and thick. It sounded like an enormous fish trapped in the shallows at low tide. It seemed to be wriggling its way toward them.

"What . . . is . . . that?" Folly asked slowly.

"I don't like the sound of it," Quinn said.

There was an echo of teeth, the scraping of claws.

"Me either," Rye said quietly.

Rye, Folly, and Quinn weren't strangers to troubling noises, but the sound was so foreign and unnerving that they were left staring dumbfounded toward the end of the tunnel.

The shadow that emerged was impossible to identify, but the tight bend was filled by the silhouette of its long body and jagged, clawed hands.

The friends didn't linger for a better look.

"Run!" Rye called, but as the word left her lips a gust of air extinguished the torch on the wall with a pop. They were plunged into complete darkness.

Rye felt a hand grab her coat. She reached down and clutched it. "It's me, Folly. Don't let go."

"Let go of what? Where are you, Rye?" Folly cried, her voice several yards away.

"Ow!" Quinn's yelled from a different direction. "Folly, that's my ear you're pulling."

"I'm not pulling anything!"

Rye cast her eyes downward, not that it helped—she couldn't see anything at all. If she wasn't holding Folly's or Quinn's hand, then whose was it? She tried to let go, but the unseen fingers held tight.

In her alarm, something slipped from Rye's grasp. She heard *Tam's Tome* hit the water at her feet. Her heart lurched as she fumbled for it in the dark.

"Quickly, come with us," a voice whispered in her ear. It was a girl's voice. Unfamiliar.

"Who are you?" Rye asked.

"Shhh," the voice hushed. "Please, miss. There's no time to waste."

"Rye, who are you talking to?" Folly called desperately.

"Please," the unseen girl implored from the dark. "Stay silent. The creeper's sight is poor, but it can hear and smell us. We must be off."

Rye plunged her free hand into the water, fishing desperately for *Tam's Tome.* The girl pulled at Rye urgently. She felt other small bodies at her back. Before Rye could resist, she was pushed forward blindly, deeper under the earth.

Rye and her friends allowed the invisible hands to lead them in silence for a long while. The splash of their boots subsided, and whatever had been following them seemed lost in the distance. Finally, as they made their way through a section of the Spoke that began to glow with luminescent lichen, Rye felt the girl release her hand.

"Careful," the girl said, moving off in front of her. "There's a stairway ahead."

No sooner had she said it than they reached a set of carved stone steps. But instead of leading up, they spiraled and twisted down, widening as they descended deeper into the Spoke. In the dim light of the underground flora, Rye saw three short figures start down the stairs. Rye, Folly, and Quinn caught one another's gazes and hesitated. A small girl with dark, curly locks paused and looked back at them. She was younger than they were, but older than Lottie.

"Well, come on," she said with a wave, then continued back down. From her voice, Rye knew it was the girl who had taken her by the hand.

They followed cautiously. Gradually the walls parted and the ceiling rose. They stopped at the bottom, where the last of the steps disappeared into black water.

They'd entered an enormous chamber. Rye marveled at the carved granite pillars rising high above them to support an arched stone ceiling. Hundreds of lit lanterns hung from ropes of varying lengths, bathing the chamber in soft light. It was like they'd entered a subterranean cathedral.

From the steps, a series of narrow wooden beams stretched over the water's dark surface, leading to a towering maze of salvaged wooden planks and platforms. They formed an island of ramshackle walkways and shanties.

The three younger children quickly traversed the beam with expert agility, disappearing into the hive of wooden huts. Before Rye and her friends could follow, another person crossed the narrow footbridge in the opposite direction. He stopped to meet them at the base of the steps. Up close now in his long brown coat and boots, Rye saw that he stood about Quinn's height.

The Night Courier placed his hands on his hips, the scarf still obscuring his face from under his wide-brimmed hat. He removed his cap and tucked it under his arm. His straight black hair fell past his chin. Without the shadow cast by its brim, Rye was now certain of his identity, even before he untied the scarf and offered her a familiar smile.

One of the boy's eyes was brown, the other blue.

Beneath the Night Courier's guise was Rye's friend Truitt.

12 A Gongfarmer's Boy

Rye hugged Truitt enthusiastically. His arms were still rangy but, like Quinn, he had grown since she'd last seen him. His shoulders felt broader. Rye quickly introduced him to Folly and Quinn.

"We've heard a lot about you," Folly said.

"And I you," Truitt said, with a bow of his head.

"We had no idea you were the Night Courier," Quinn added.

Truitt chuckled, his mismatched eyes flickering in the glow of the lanterns overhead. "Is that what the villagers are calling us? Well, it's a fitting name, I suppose."

"Us?" Rye asked, looking him up and down. The rather comely leather coat, thick boots, and handsome cap were a far cry from the modest attire he usually wore.

Truitt's lips curled into a narrow smile. "Come. I'll explain." He waved for them to follow as he deftly retraced his steps across the narrow wooden beam.

"The water has risen over the winter," Truitt said without looking down. His heels didn't miss a step, which was remarkable given that Truitt was blind.

"Be sure to stay on the planks," he warned. "The snarklefish prefer fallen bats or mice, but their eyesight is even worse than mine. They've been known to sample a toe."

Rye peered over the edge as they crossed the beam. Dark shapes cruised beneath them.

"What is this place?" she asked.

"The Cistern. It was built separately from the Spoke, although they're now connected by a passageway. This was once the source of fresh water for Longchance Keep and much of Drowning. It hasn't served that purpose for many years."

He reached back and helped Rye over a small gap in the planks, Folly and Quinn right behind her.

"Now it is just our home," he added.

They all stepped onto a small shantytown of makeshift docks and tiered platforms in the middle of the chamber.

Rye examined the manmade island. From the rows of cots and bedding, dozens of pairs of eyes had fallen on the new arrivals. Children—many her age but most younger—watched them from among their ragged blankets and scant belongings. The children's faces were dirty and their hair bedraggled, but their expressions were not timid. Several older boys were bending scrap metal into hooks and crude arrowheads. They watched the new arrivals with wary eyes. A few of the younger children offered smiles. Rye recognized the curly-haired girl who had led them through the Spoke whispering with two friends. She couldn't be more than six or seven. The girl nodded an acknowledgment to Rye and continued whispering.

"The link children," Rye said quietly.

"Yes," Truitt replied. "Orphans mostly, although some of us have simply been abandoned. Those of us who were old enough once took to the lamps by night, guiding travelers through the shadows. We used to pool our earnings to buy supplies we couldn't scavenge."

Truitt hesitated, and Rye saw the pale skin of his jaw tighten.

"Of course, no one travels the streets by night anymore. That leaves little demand for the link children's services."

"Where is your caretaker?" Rye asked, looking around. Truitt had once told her about an old man who looked after the link children. He'd rescued Truitt from the sewers when he was just an infant.

Truitt shook his head and lowered his voice. "He was gravely ill. Unfortunately, an unseasonably cold and wet summer finally proved to be too much for him bear."

"I'm so sorry, Truitt."

Truitt waved his hand. "Let's not speak about it here. It is still too painful for the little ones, and they hear everything."

Rye heard him ask one of the boys to check the way posts for signs of the tunnel creeper, then he led them up some uneven wooden steps to a small platform she took to be his own. She sat on a blanketed pallet with Folly. Quinn leaned against the uneven wooden railing.

"That's not so sturdy," Truitt said with a kind smile. "Feel free to grab a pallet."

Quinn raised an eyebrow at Rye. She could only shrug in reply. Truitt might not benefit from sight, but he had spent his life illustrating the world around him with his nose and ears. Quinn peeked at the snarklefish-filled waters below, and cautiously took a seat on the pallet next to Folly.

"Our caretaker was once the gongfarmer for Longchance Keep," Truitt said.

Folly and Quinn exchanged glances. Rye crinkled her nose. She knew gongfarmers emptied cesspools and privies, hauling the foul night soil outside the village limits and spreading it as fertilizer across the fields. They were required to work after dark and only permitted to dwell in certain undesirable sections of the village.

"Because of his work, he never found a bride, but he was the most generous and kindhearted soul this village has ever known," Truitt continued. "He built a family of his own by taking in orphans and foundlings. The Cistern is where he raised me with the rest of the link children."

The small girl with the curly dark locks climbed the steps to the platform, chewing a chunk of bread torn from a baguette tucked under her arm. She was joined by a slightly older girl with a similar head of hair but warier eyes.

"I'm Hope," the younger girl said, and pointed behind her with the baguette. "This is my sister, Poe. Are you hungry?"

She offered the baguette to Rye.

Although Rye was famished, the idea of dining on scavenged rations wasn't appealing, particularly with so many mouths that needed them more than she did.

Rye declined politely.

"Go ahead, eat," the girl named Poe said from over Hope's shoulder. "We can always get more."

Rye reluctantly accepted the bread, breaking it into thirds and sharing it with Folly and Quinn. She expected to crack her teeth on stale crust, but was surprised to find the bread as soft as if freshly baked.

Only then did Rye notice the bone-white key hung from a string around Truitt's neck. The Everything Key. Rye remembered that it afforded Truitt access to every locked door in Drowning, including the storerooms of Longchance Keep itself. He used it to take what he and the other link children needed. Based on what Folly and Quinn had told her, it seemed to Rye that Truitt was now using the key for the benefit of all of Drowning.

"You've been putting yourself at great risk for the village," Rye said. "Why keep your identity secret? Maybe other villagers could help."

"It's not yet time to reveal all the secrets that the Spoke holds," Truitt said with a wry smile, and hesitated. Rye sensed that he was holding something back.

"We all agreed it's best not to draw attention to ourselves," Truitt explained. "In dire times, there are those who will not hesitate to take even what little we have."

Rye glanced at Hope and Poe, as well as the numerous faces busying themselves on the platforms below them. She wondered how long it had been since any of them had been able to think of themselves as children.

"You've been looking after one another," Rye said in admiration.

"Not much choice in the matter," Poe said.

"I wish we were doing a better job of it," Truitt said, his voice saddening. "Notice the beds. Half of them lie empty now. The Spoke is no longer the sanctuary it once was. When we last met, Rye, I told you something was hunting the link children. Unfortunately, it hasn't stopped."

"I thought it was a Bog Noblin," Rye said, recalling Slinister's pet, a woefully undersize Bog Noblin named Spidercreep that had once chased her through the Spoke. Last she'd seen of it, Slinister had left it to fend for itself in the forest Beyond the Shale. "I assumed it wouldn't trouble you anymore."

Truitt shook his head. "This creeper is no Bog Noblin."

"It's like no man or beast I've ever heard of before," Hope added.

"Is that what was following us in the Spoke?" Folly asked.

"I think so," Poe said with an ominous nod.

"Hope and Poe were two of the children who found you and brought you here," Truitt explained. "Whatever the creeper is, it hasn't yet discovered the Cistern. If we cannot stop it, there will be no safe haven left for us in all of Drowning."

They were interrupted as another boy hurried up the planks and joined them. He was thicker than Truitt but several years younger, with a bronze face and unkempt woolly hair. The boy took Truitt's arm in his hands and began jabbing at it with his fingertips. Rye wasn't sure if she should stop him, but Truitt seemed to be concentrating carefully, as if listening.

"Darwin tells me someone is waiting to speak with me."

"He told you that?" Quinn said in disbelief.

The boy named Darwin narrowed his eyes and studied Rye, Folly, and Quinn with suspicion. He clapped his palm on Truitt's shoulder three times, then used a finger to trace an *X* on Truitt's forehead.

Truitt chuckled. "No, Darwin, they're not daft, just a bit disoriented. They're also friends."

Truitt turned back to them.

"Darwin cannot speak, and I, of course, cannot see. We make quite the pair," he said with a smile. Darwin smirked too. "But we've come up with a sign language of sorts. In any event, I need to meet someone not far from here, where a fork of the River Drowning flows underground. It's near the Shambles. If that's where you are headed, I can take you there myself."

Rye had finished her bread, but a pit in her stomach remained unfilled as she recalled her clumsy loss of *Tam's Tome*. Surely there was no hope of recovering it in the dark recesses of Spoke. She placed her hand on her empty pack and looked to Folly and Quinn without words.

"That would be helpful, Truitt," Rye said in defeat. She'd failed Harmless, and it seemed they had no choice but to return to the Dead Fish Inn and try to sort out what to do next.

Truitt navigated through the dark, his fingertips grazing the winding tunnels of the Spoke where unseen nooks and crannies served as his signposts along the way. Rye, Folly, and Quinn followed, with Darwin and Poe trailing close behind. When they glanced back at the link children, Darwin made a fork with his fore and middle fingers, pointed to his own eyes, then back at them to let them know he'd be watching. Rye's own fingers were still buried in her noticeably lighter pack, clutching the spot where *Tam's Tome* had been.

"What have I done?" she mumbled under her breath.

"Maybe we can find instructions somewhere else," Folly offered.

Rye put her head in her hand. "Why didn't I read it right away?"

She'd have to return to Harmless and explain what had happened. There was no telling how long it would be before they could summon the Reckoning. Too long.

"Maybe we can get another copy?" Quinn asked.

"No, no, no," Rye said shaking her head, pressing her palm against her eyes so hard she saw flashes of light. "This was the last copy in all of the village."

"Are you sure?" Quinn asked. "If the Angry Poet had this one, couldn't there still be others?"

"It's not like Drowning has a library, Quinn," Folly said. "We can't go door-to-door asking to borrow a banned book."

Rye said little more as they made their way through the indistinguishable surroundings, but before long she could make out a recognizable sound. The rush of water.

When the passageway opened, she found herself at the underground fork of the River Drowning. They were near a large, round chamber that seemed to glow in the eerie light of more luminescent lichen. The chamber looked to be the floor of a large cylinder, like the bottom of a well. A stream of water fell from high above, creating a murky waterfall that splashed into the river.

From its source, fingers of moonlight beamed down onto the water's surface. Unlike the rest of the Spoke, the well was made from stone and mortar.

Rye studied the river's dark water just in case *Tam's Tome* happened to go bobbing by in its current. Of course, she had no such luck. But something caught her ear and attention.

"What was that?" she asked.

Quinn squinted into the gloom. "It sounds like a voice. From the well."

"Rye, there's something more I need to tell you," Truitt said quickly. "About the Night Courier."

"Wait," Rye said in alarm. "I recognize it."

"This is getting more and more dangerous," the high-pitched voice whispered from the well. "We're all likely to get ourselves skewered. Or worse."

The voice paused, as if listening. Rye hurried toward its source before Truitt could stop her.

"Of course, *you'd* run and hide," the voice said dismissively. "You steal kitchen scraps for a living."

Rye came to an abrupt stop. A person in a wide-brimmed hat sat at the edge of the runoff. A blue plume was tucked in the hatband, and a long brown leather coat covered slender shoulders. A dim lantern sat on the ground, where an enormous rat crouched nibbling a crust of bread. It twitched its red eyes and, at the sight of Rye, scuttled into a crevice, its ugly tail disappearing behind it.

Rye turned to Truitt in disbelief, examining his identical attire.

The second Night Courier tilted her head and looked up at Rye, the blue scarf loosened to reveal an undisguised face. From under the hat's brim, a girl's mouth pinched into a frown and her mismatched blue and brown eyes glared at Rye intently.

It was Lady Malydia Longchance. The Earl's only daughter. Rye's enemy.

And Truitt's twin sister.

13 Lady in the Well

Rye and Malydia turned to Truitt, each of them aghast.

"What's *she* doing here?" Malydia said, her voice sharp.

"Who was she talking to?" Rye asked Truitt. She turned her glare back on Malydia before he could answer. "Were you talking to that rat?"

"Of course not," she said defensively. "Why, were you eavesdropping on us?"

Malydia stood and pulled off her hat. Her bloodless

lips were pursed, her black hair pulled atop her head into a tight bun. Rye gripped her cudgel as her ears burned scarlet. She looked around. For once, Malydia was unaccompanied by the Earl or his soldiers. Maybe Rye would give her a long overdue rap upside the head.

"So the princess of thieves has returned to Drowning," Malydia said, narrowing her eyes. "The rumormongers said you and your criminal father had fled the Shale. I expected you would never return."

"We didn't flee anything," Rye snapped back. "Lucky for you, should you need saving again."

Rye stepped toward her. Malydia was taller and two years older, but Rye didn't fear her.

"Stop," Truitt said. "Both of you."

Truitt took Rye by the arm, gently ushering her away.

"Yes, Truitt," Malydia said. "Take her from my sight."

"Wait here," Truitt barked at his sister in exasperation.

Rye scowled back over her shoulder as she went.

"Your sister talks to rats?" Rye asked in disbelief.

"She talks to herself when she's under stress. I think the rat just happened to be there. I know it's a little unnerving."

"Stark raving nutters is more like it."

"Malydia grew up alone in Longchance Keep with no companions except soldiers and servants. I suppose she hasn't always made the best choices in imaginary friends."

"I'd be happy if I never heard from her or her imaginary friends again."

"Malydia's not all bad," Truitt whispered.

"I know she's your sister, but how can you say that?"

"Malydia lives her life in fear," Truitt said with a sigh. He gestured up at the dark, dripping stone walls above them. "When I was just an infant, my father threw me into that very sewer."

Rye's heart dropped in her chest. She looked back at the grim surroundings. A baby—cast into this place. It was amazing Truitt even survived the fall.

"Malydia has lived with that man her entire life—he's the only parent she's ever known. If that was the one person you relied on to protect you, wouldn't you be fearful too?"

Rye just frowned and chewed her lip in reply.

"Malydia is here to help me and the other link children. And Drowning itself. She's my eyes in the Keep . . . and on the village streets. Together we ferry critical supplies to those who need them most."

"There's more than one Night Courier," Rye said. "That's why you're dressed alike?"

Truitt nodded. "Not just us. Darwin, Poe . . . and other link children too."

He ran his palms over his leather coat. "Malydia chose these outfits," he said with a shrug and a tired grin. "Hopefully she hasn't made us look too ridiculous."

"I've seen worse," Rye fibbed.

"The Keep has been overrun, the Earl imprisoned by the men called the Fork-Tongue Charmers."

"Longchance is still alive?" Rye asked in surprise.

"For now," Truitt said. "And hopefully he shall stay that way for a while longer."

Rye was even more surprised that Truitt had any concern for the Earl's well-being.

"Not that I have any affection for him," he clarified, as if sensing Rye's suspicion. "But Malydia and I have a plan, and it will go much more smoothly if the Earl remains alive to help us see it through."

"You and *Malydia*?" Rye said, the skepticism rising in her voice.

"Maybe if you hear it from Malydia herself it might give you some comfort."

Rye crinkled her face and grunted without enthusiasm.

"Please, Rye," Truitt said. "In desperate times, we all need as many friends as we can find. Just listen to what she has to say."

They had reached Folly and Quinn, who'd stayed

back with Darwin and Poe, watching Rye's confrontation with wide eyes. Rye tightened her jaw and looked to them silently for their suggestions. Folly shrugged. Quinn gave her a slight, reluctant nod.

Rye crossed her arms and turned back to Truitt. "I'll listen, but I'd rather snuggle up to a porcupine with bad breath."

Rye didn't know which was more chilly, the splatter of the falling water or the glare of Malydia's eyes as she spoke. Rye sat on a damp rock opposite the young noble. Truitt had wisely situated himself between them. Quinn and Folly sat nearby. They had never been so close to a Longchance before, and although they remained tight-lipped, they kept careful watch in the event Malydia had brought any unexpected surprises.

"That hideous constable has locked my father in the deepest dungeon of the Keep," Malydia said. She leaned forward with her elbows on her knees, long white fingers digging at her already well-picked nails.

"He's no constable," Rye said. "His name is Slinister."

"Yes," Malydia said darkly, her eyes turning venomous. "A Luck Ugly."

"A Fork-Tongue Charmer," Rye clarified.

"Call them what you like, but one filthy scoundrel is

no different from another."

"Malydia . . . ," Truitt interjected, with a shake of his head.

"There's a big difference," Rye said, her ears starting to tingle. "As you've proven, even twins can be as different as poison and porridge."

"Both of you, please stop," Truitt implored. "Bickering will get us nowhere."

Rye held her tongue. As much as she hated to admit it, Slinister *was* a Luck Ugly. And while Harmless might say that not all Luck Uglies were cut from the same cloth, did they not all hoist the same banner? To the outside world, a blow rendered by Slinister might as well have come from Harmless's own hand.

"The Fork-Tongue Charmers have taken up residence in the Keep," Malydia said. "They bide their time while Slinister schemes what to do next. Outside the Keep, only Truitt and I know our father's real whereabouts. And now . . . so do you."

"Slinister despises your father," Rye said. "Why would he keep him alive?"

Malydia scrunched up her face and offered a patronizing smile, as if explaining mathematics to an infant.

"Because seizing power and maintaining it are two very different things. Slinister knows that the other noble houses are even greater vultures than the Luck

Uglies. Once they realize that the House of Longchance has been toppled, do you think our neighbors will be satisfied to see it become some outlaw republic?" She narrowed her eyes. "Not when there's an opportunity to claim it for themselves."

Rye considered Slinister's motivations. "But Slinister detests all the noble houses," she said. "He doesn't wish to become one of them. He wants to rule the Luck Uglies, and crush the nobles one by one. I don't think he intends to linger and rule over Drowning."

Malydia nodded. "So for now, he keeps Earl Longchance alive, if not altogether well, preserving the illusion that the House of Longchance still controls Village Drowning. And should our noble neighbors grow suspicious, he can always trot the Earl out like a puppet. In that regard, my father's head is worth more to Slinister in a stockade than on a chopping block. At least . . . for the time being."

"But in the meantime the Fork-Tongue Charmers hoard Drowning's resources while the village crumbles," Truitt added. "The Bog Noblins' raids grow ever more frequent and bold. The villagers have fended for themselves so far, but they are little more than a loose militia. Rumor has it that the Bog Noblins are gathering in great numbers at the edge of the forest. We fear that it's only a matter of time before they overrun the village . . . and do not leave."

The situation sounded even bleaker than Rye had imagined. "So what can be done?" she asked.

Malydia raised a sickle-like eyebrow. "Restore the House of Longchance."

"You want to free your father and put him back in power?" Rye asked, aghast.

"No," she said, and cast her eyes to Truitt. "The time has come for the Earl's natural heir to reveal himself."

Rye's eyes widened as she turned to her friend.

"It seems to be the only option," Truitt said quietly.

"It's the best option," Malydia interjected. "You are already better suited to lead than our father ever was."

"She's right," Rye said. She couldn't believe that she found herself agreeing with Malydia on anything, but she'd always known Truitt to be compassionate and selfless.

Truitt remained silent.

Rye thought for a moment before saying more. "But nobody knows Truitt is the Earl's son," she said finally.

Malydia pursed her lips. "Perhaps you are cleverer than you look," she said. "That, of course, is the problem. It is why *we* need our father alive. We need him to acknowledge Truitt as his rightful heir."

"How will you get him to do that?"

"That will be *my* challenge, when the time comes," Malydia said. "In the meantime, we keep Truitt's identity secret. Whatever Slinister's plans for my father may be, there's nothing more inconvenient than an heir with unknown intentions."

"I'm a gongfarmer's boy," Truitt said quietly. "My intentions are to help the link children, and the rest of Drowning's outcasts who are unable to help themselves."

"And yet such pure intentions are unfathomable to men such as our father and Slinister," Malydia said bitterly. "And because of that you will always be a threat."

"What about you, Malydia?" Rye said. "Aren't you an heir with unknown intentions?"

Malydia gave her a tight, sarcastic smile, and opened her palms. "I am a Lady Longchance, but still a lady . . . nothing more. Ladies are not heirs by right. Any title would have to be bestowed upon me. And truth be told, an Earl of the House of Longchance is more likely to bestow his title upon a half-witted nephew or war-crazed son-in-law than a lady of the line." Malydia shook her head, and her lips curled into a jeer.

"To put it more simply, Rye, our other dilemma is Slinister and his men," Truitt said. "As long as those fork-tongued snakes maintain a stranglehold on Longchance

Keep, they are a threat to both the Earl and ourselves. If they remain in Drowning, our chances to succeed are slim."

Rye chewed her lip. She still distrusted Malydia, and preferred not to speak of Harmless or the Reckoning in front of her. Not that it mattered—Harmless's plan was of little use without *Tam's Tome.* Rye cupped her head in her hands and cursed herself silently.

Then a sudden memory struck her like a foot in the gut.

Rye made her decision without hesitation. She didn't trust Malydia, but as Truitt said, in dire times, you needed to take friends where you could find them. Rye pulled her head from her hands and eyed the Lady Longchance carefully.

"I can help you with your snake problem," Rye said.

Malydia's sickle-like eyebrow raised in curiosity.

"I may be able to get rid of the Fork-Tongue Charmers. But first, I need you to get me into Longchance Keep."

14 Serpents of Longchance Keep

The stone steps were carved steep and uneven, slick with cave moss and difficult to climb in the dim light of Malydia's lantern. Rye stumbled twice, but Truitt was behind her to put a reassuring hand on her back. By the time they reached the top, Rye was eager to leave the winding, claustrophobic wormhole that was even narrower than the Spoke's tunnels.

Rye ducked to squeeze through a small door, then wriggled on her belly to make it under some sort of low-hanging canopy. Only when she followed Malydia out past a frilly dust ruffle did Rye realize that they had exited the Spoke behind a palatial bed.

Rye had been here before. It was the Chamber of the Lost Lady in Longchance Keep.

Malydia climbed to her feet, brushing the dust and dirt from her brown leather coat.

"Look familiar?" she asked, cocking an eyebrow.

"Yes," Rye said coldly. "I have a very vivid memory."

She adjusted the choker around her neck. It was in this very spot that Malydia had torn it from her throat, right before Truitt helped Rye escape the Keep. Ordinarily, she would have no desire to come back. But Rye recalled that Longchance Keep was also home to the only library in all of Village Drowning. One that happened to house a copy of a very rare and illicit book. *Tam's Tome.*

"We need to keep our voices down," Truitt warned.

Returning here made Rye's skin crawl. Somewhere underground, Darwin and Poe were leading Folly and Quinn through the Spoke to the wine cellar of the Dead Fish Inn. They'd wanted to join Rye, but it was agreed that five children wandering through the Keep would be much too suspicious. Malydia had argued vehemently that it was too dangerous for Truitt to accompany them as well, but he'd insisted on coming. Rye wasn't sure if he distrusted Malydia's intentions for Rye, or simply feared what might happen if he left the two rivals alone. Either way, Rye was glad to have him along.

"I'll just be a minute," Malydia said. She stepped behind an ornate folding privacy screen decorated with embroidered leaves and partridges.

Rye could see Malydia's silhouette as she changed clothes behind the screen. She rolled her eyes at the young noble's vanity. But when Malydia emerged, Rye was surprised to find that she was wearing the ill-fitting frock and shoes of a servant.

"Better to keep a low profile," Malydia explained as she undid the pin in her hair. Her carefully coiffed bun came undone and the jet-black locks fell well past her shoulders. She mussed her hair with her fingers. "As long as I look like a serving girl, I might as well be invisible. The Fork-Tongue Charmers speak freely in the Keep, as if I'm not even here. For all they know I'm content cooking their meals and washing their linens. They'd never think that I—a girl—would dare to plot against them on my own."

Rye couldn't picture Malydia bussing her own dinner plate, never mind scrubbing someone else's undergarments. But the thought gave her a twinge of satisfaction.

"I'd suggest that you change your attire too," Malydia said, eyeing Rye's filthy coat and mud-caked boots. "But you already seem to fit the bill just fine."

"Someone's coming," Truitt said in alarm, and rushed from where he was listening at the door to join Rye and Malydia.

They all hurried behind the changing screen as the door burst open. Malydia held a finger to her narrow lips and pinched her face in concern. The voice that called out in a harsh whisper belonged to a woman.

"Lady Malydia," it said. "Is that you back there?"

Malydia's eyes flashed with relief. She stepped around the side of the privacy screen.

"Hildie, you nearly frightened us back into that hole in the wall."

Rye peeked out from behind the screen to find Malydia's nanny. The nanny's wide eyes blinked out from her work-weary face.

"The hour is getting on," Hildie said slowly. "I was worried when you hadn't returned." She looked at Truitt and Rye in wonder.

"No need to worry, Hildie," Malydia said, placing a hand on her shoulder as she passed by. "You remember my brother?"

"Of course," Hildie said with a curtsy. "G' evening, Master Truitt."

"And this," Malydia said, with an unenthusiastic flick

of her chin, "is Riley O'Chanter. We weren't expecting her."

"Yes, I remember," Hildie said, and offered Rye a warm smile. "It's lovely to see you again, Miss Riley."

"And you," Rye said. She hadn't seen Malydia's nanny since Longchance Keep was attacked by the Bog Noblins. Rye was glad to find her still in one piece.

"Hildie," Truitt said, "we need to get Rye to the library. How are the corridors?"

"It's late, so the serpents are just waking up."

"Fork-Tongue Charmers," Truitt said to Rye, by way of explanation.

"Night crawlers, the whole lot of them," Hildie said, shaking her head. She nodded toward the door of the bedchamber. "These stairs are quiet for now. But a big crowd of them have gathered in the Great Hall while the rest make mischief in the other towers."

"There's no other way to the library except past the Great Hall," Truitt said, tugging his lower lip in thought.

"It will only get worse as the night wears on," Malydia noted.

Truitt's face was resolved. "Then let's not waste any time. We find Rye's book and then lead her back out through the Spoke. If we are lucky, the Fork-Tongue

Charmers will be nose-deep in their mead and too foggy to notice."

The last time Rye had been in the Keep, it was ransacked by a Bog Noblin named Iron Wart. Although Longchance's servants had surely cleaned up since then, the castle hardly looked much better now. Chairs were overturned in the hallways and dirty platters and goblets lay piled in corners outside bedchambers.

Hildie shook her head in dismay, turning up her nose as she led the children silently down the stairs.

"Filthy brutes," she whispered. "It's impossible to keep up with them. Fortunately, as long as we keep the cook fires hot and their bellies full, they're not the most demanding masters."

All was quiet until they reached the base of the stairs. The main chambers of the Keep echoed with voices, loud and harsh. Somewhere close by, Rye heard heated yelling followed by coarse laughter.

Malydia peered around a corner. "Clear for now," she said, waving them forward.

They all crept down the main corridor. A plush feather mattress had been dragged from a bedchamber and lay propped at one end, an uneven red bull's-eye smeared on its face and punctured with arrows. The Earl's artwork hung in broken frames on the walls, and

Rye paused when she reached the largest—a grandiose self-portrait painted by Morningwig Longchance himself.

The painting had been defaced—the canvas of the Earl's eyes cut out and swapped for two rotting tomatoes impaled on arrows. Rye cringed at the portrait's mouth. A cow's tongue from a butcher's shop was nailed over the likeness of the Earl's smug smile, dangling obscenely and split down the middle like a Fork-Tongue Charmer's.

A clucking at Rye's feet startled her. Several hens scuttled past her ankles. She looked to Malydia in disbelief. Across the hall, a goat gnawed on a tapestry.

"They've rounded up all the village livestock for themselves," Malydia said. "Apparently they don't mind sharing a roof with them." She flashed Rye a mischievous smile. "Watch where you step."

Rye looked down, where her boot had just met a soft pile. She wrinkled her nose. "*Now* you tell me."

"Snakes up ahead," Hildie said quietly, and pressed a finger to her lips.

Malydia turned to her brother. "Truitt, you stay here," she whispered. "Find a shadow and disappear into it. Hildie, Rye, and I will work our way past the Great Hall."

"I'm coming," Truitt said. "You may need my help."

Malydia shook her head adamantly. "Too risky. They might overlook Hildie and a couple of serving girls, but you'll stick out like a sixth toe. Wait, and be ready to get Rye back to the Spoke quickly."

"I'll be fine, Truitt," Rye reassured, although she wasn't entirely comfortable heading on with Malydia alone.

"Then Rye will stay with me," Truitt said. "You know what *Tam's Tome* looks like, Malydia. Bring it back to us."

Malydia looked at Truitt harshly, then Rye. A demanding voice interrupted their standoff.

"Washerwoman!" a man called. "Our platters and mugs are empty. Fetch those serving girls and come refill them!"

Down the corridor, a Fork-Tongue Charmer with dark circles under his eyes had staggered from the doors of the Great Hall. He shook the mug in his fist.

"Step lively now. I won't ask twice!"

Hildie swallowed hard and turned back toward Rye and Malydia. "Come, girls," she said theatrically, as loud as her timid voice could muster. "No more dallying."

She turned her back to the Charmer, pulled off her apron, and handed it to Rye. "Put this on over your clothes," she whispered, eyeing her oversize boots and weather-beaten leather coat. "You look more like one of *them* than a serving girl."

Rye pulled the apron over her head and tied it around her back. As she did, Malydia pressed her hand to Truitt's chest and pushed him toward the wall. After a lifetime of well-practiced lurking, he easily blended into the shadows of a bend. Rye tried to give him a reassuring nod as his brown and blue eyes disappeared from sight.

Hildie hurried forward, Malydia trailing behind her subserviently. Her quick glance back at Rye told her to do the same.

Rye could see the orange flicker of flames from inside the Great Hall as they approached the enormous double doors.

"I thought I saw another of you?" the Charmer said, eyeing them. His glare was unforgiving.

Rye tried to make herself small.

"Yes, sir. I sent her off to stir the pots," Hildie said quickly, maneuvering herself between the Charmer and Rye as they passed.

"Not a bad idea," the Charmer said gruffly. "There's a chill in the air tonight. Something warm would fill the belly nicely."

Hildie offered a tight smile but kept her eyes on the floor as she ushered Rye and Malydia into the Great Hall.

"Quickly, girls. Gather up the plates and bring them

to the scullery," Hildie barked, then dropped her voice to a whisper and pressed her lips near Rye's ear. "And whatever you do, keep your head down."

Despite the nanny's warning, Rye couldn't help but gawk.

A towering blaze raged in the Great Hall, but not from the fireplace. Instead, a massive pile of furniture burned in the center of the chamber like an enormous campfire. The largest table Rye had ever seen, the one where she had once dined with Malydia, had been reduced to embers. Rye saw the glowing metal of Longchance's gilded chair among the burning wreckage, black plumes billowing up toward the cathedral ceiling and disappearing into the night sky.

Rye blinked to clear the smoke from her eyes, but the flames weren't playing tricks on her. Stars twinkled high overhead, through a gaping hole that had been punched in the Great Hall's roof. Over the fire, the ornate chandelier had been bent and twisted into a makeshift spit, the well-charred carcass of an enormous boar skewered garishly from mouth to tail. A Fork-Tongue Charmer stepped forward with a plush footstool and pitched it atop the kindling, kicking up a rain of embers that sent a comrade cursing as he brushed sparks from his beard.

Everywhere she looked, men with shifting eyes and hard faces lounged on the floor or in broken chairs.

Some fixated on their dice games, others on the playing cards and gambling chips. But most seemed perfectly enamored with the enormous goblets in their fists. The Hall buzzed with the crackle of fire and the music of edgy conversations.

Malydia coughed to get Rye's attention and flashed her a stern look. She had already collected several bowls in her hands.

Rye crouched and began to retrieve some plates from the mess scattered across the floor. Judging from the caked remains, they'd been there for days. She flicked her eyes around the transformed Hall as she stacked them.

"Slinister's brung in Thorn Quill," a nearby Charmer was saying. "Wants the Crest to be ready for the final touches on the next Black Moon."

"Not wasting any time, is he?" a different Charmer replied.

"He's been waiting his whole life, guess'n he don't want to wait a minute longer'n he has to."

Their words made Rye straighten as she tried to hear more.

"Take this one," a voice called. Rye flinched in alarm as a plate was dumped onto her pile.

Rye just nodded and muttered, "Yessir," under her breath.

She smoothed her long bangs in front of her eyes to cover her face. She should probably just collect as many plates near the door as she could carry and get out, but the snippet of conversation had her mind racing. Thorn Quill was here. He was the owner of the tattoo shop in the Shambles who she'd once seen working on Slinister. What crest was he putting the finishing touches on? It could only be the High Chieftain's Crest—the tattoo that only the High Chieftain of the Luck Uglies could wear.

Rye worked her way around the fire, adding more plates onto her stack as she went. She glanced over her shoulder. Malydia still hovered closer to the door, her mismatched eyes wide in disbelief and anger at Rye's indiscretion. Rye ignored her and continued forward. The heat of the fire had already made her brow moist.

"Gibbet said anything yet?" a Charmer was asking.

"Nothing," another answered. "Ain't moved. He just sits there pale as a ghost without blinking, that blank look on his face."

The man named Gibbet was propped in a chair, his shoulders slouched and hands dangling loosely between his legs. Rye recognized him immediately. He was the Fork-Tongue Charmer who had pursued her and Lottie onto the tree house roof back in the Hollow. The one she'd seen attacked by the Shriek

Reaver. His companions must have saved him. Or had they? His face seemed as lifeless as the boar on the skewer. His head lolled to one side, eyes staring at something far in the distance. His jaw was slack, his skin sickly and devoid of color. If he was breathing, his lungs filled so shallowly they barely rustled the thin shirt over his chest.

"You know what he looks like? A great big butternut squash," the first Charmer observed. "Same color."

"That's no way to talk about a brother," a familiar voice said harshly.

The words made Rye stop and catch her breath. It was the voice of Slinister Varlet.

Slinister sat atop an overturned cupboard, a hand on his knee, boots flat on the floor. He was shirtless, and Rye recognized the stringy gray hair and spidery ink-blackened arms of Thorn Quill as he tapped his sharp metal tools into the flesh of Slinister's broad chest. It must have been extraordinarily painful, but Slinister didn't flinch. He no longer wore a mask or garish hat atop his head, but he stroked the long and elaborate braid that fell from the crown of his scalp like a cat's tail. The rest of his head was shaved smooth, covered only by tattoos and an enormous crescent scar over his ear—one rendered courtesy of Harmless himself.

From his perch, Slinister looked like the perfect lord

of chaos to oversee this motley band of outlaws.

"I'm not saying there's anything wrong with a butternut squash," the offending Fork-Tongue Charmer mumbled. "They just don't do much. Except sit there and rot if you don't eat 'em."

Slinister's return glare was as cold and icy as the sea, and sent the loose-lipped Charmer retreating to the opposite side of the Great Hall.

Rye noticed another familiar face at Slinister's side. The boy named Hyde watched the state of affairs in silence, his narrow-set eyes framed by his hair. But there was one difference now. A green tattoo ran from his chin down the length of his throat—two ominous forks curled like an extended tongue, four-leaf clovers at the ends. If he wasn't a Fork-Tongue Charmer before, he certainly was now.

Rye heard the stomp of heavy boots approach behind her. She quickly stepped between a smaller table and some chairs that had not yet been sacrificed to the fire. A tall Fork-Tongue Charmer strode past her toward Slinister, a heavy cloak trailing behind him. He stopped and dipped his hands into a deep earthen bowl, splashing water on his face. The white ash and black soot mask ran down his face. He rubbed his palms over his eyes. The bridge of his nose had been pounded flat as if broken one too many times, leaving the fleshy end long and pointed like a hawk's beak.

"Lassiter," Slinister said in greeting. "What have your horsemen found for our dear friend Gibbet?"

The Charmer named Lassiter dried his hands on his cloak, reached into a pocket, and withdrew a small pouch. Rye had seen him before too. He was the leader of the band of men who came to the Hollow.

"This," he said. "Left by the Night Courier on Apothecary Row."

Rye's ears simmered with anger. Apparently he was also the leader of the horsemen who'd stolen the package meant for Mud Puddle Lane.

Lassiter handed the pouch to Slinister.

"Rest your hand," Slinister said to Thorn Quill, who paused from his work. Slinister loosened the pouch strings, held it to his nose, then dipped his pinkie inside. Rye cringed as Slinister extended his forked tongue and touched his finger to both of its split ends.

"Yarrow flower," he said with a frown as his eyes met Lassiter's. "We've tried it already. Good for fever, but not whatever *that* is." He nodded his head toward Gibbet. He retied the pouch and tossed it in Rye's direction. It landed on the floor in a large pile of similar medicines not far away.

"We'll save it for Hyde next time he gets the sniffles," Slinister said with a tight smile. If Hyde was amused by the quip, he didn't show it.

Gibbet and the Charmers might not need the yarrow, but Rye knew two babies on Mud Puddle Lane who did. It was probably foolhardy, but she only needed to make it a few short strides to reach the supply scattered haphazardly on the floor.

Thorn Quill laid his sharp tools down and shook out his knotted fingers. He lit a briar pipe and gestured it toward the hole in the roof. "My brother is a carpenter if you need someone to take care of that," he said between puffs.

"It's perfect as is," Slinister said, looking up. His sea-flecked eyes were as cold and sharp as the distant jewels in the night sky. "After so many years in exile, I've found that I miss sleeping under the stars."

"What do you do when it rains?"

Slinister gave him a dark smile. "We toast our luck that it isn't snow."

Rye stacked the plates as high as she could in her arms, the pile so high now that it covered her face. She hoped it would be an effective disguise. She wiped the perspiration from her brow with her upper arm, and took a careful step toward the medicine.

"Lassiter, what do the scouts have to say about the Dreadwater?" Slinister asked.

Lassiter took a goblet off the floor and filled it from

a heavy porcelain decanter. "They've counted another half dozen at the edge of the forest since last week. Three came into the village tonight even before nightfall. It's the earliest we've seen them yet."

Slinister tugged at the knot in his beard. "They're all coming," he grunted. "It's just a question of when."

Rye made it to the medicine supply. Slinister, Lassiter, and the rest were only a few strides from her, but the pile was even closer—right at her feet. Sweat trickled down her forehead and stung her eyes. How could they stand the heat from the fire? Her hands were damp. With one arm, she pressed the stack of plates against her body and bent her knees so she might reach the pouch of yarrow flower.

"Should we take the fight to the forest's edge?" Lassiter was asking.

Slinister's reply came slowly. "No. Not yet. Let us—"

Rye didn't hear the rest of Slinister's words. They were drowned out by a booming clatter. The Great Hall fell silent.

Rye looked to her hands. They were empty. No pouch . . . no plates. She'd lost her grip on the stack, and now they lay cracked and broken in jagged pieces all around her.

Rye's pulse pounded in her ears. She could feel the eyes of the Fork-Tongue Charmers bearing down on her. She turned quickly so her back was to Slinister and ducked her head. Should she run? How quickly would Slinister be upon her? She listened for his inevitable footsteps.

But the silence was broken by a roar of gruff laughter across the Great Hall. There was a loud crash—a plate breaking. Then another. The Fork-Tongue Charmers had begun smashing dishes, throwing them at one another and against the walls.

Rye risked a peek over her shoulder, her bangs still covering her features. Slinister's eyes studied her.

"For the sake of the Shale, girl!" a voice shrieked. It was Hildie, charging forward. "I'll have you lashed for this." The nanny stepped between Rye and Slinister, blocking his view.

"Back to the kitchen before you cause any more problems!" Hildie gave Rye a wallop on the shoulder for good measure, a bit harder than Rye would have liked.

Rye took her cue, hurrying back toward the entrance to the Great Hall, where she saw Malydia waiting. Rye ducked as dinnerware hurtled past her head, the Fork-Tongue Charmers engaged in a heated war of flying plates.

Malydia met her with fury in her eyes. "What were you thinking?" she spat.

Rye glanced over her shoulder as Malydia pulled her

from the hall. Behind her, Slinister's tall shape emerged from the shimmering haze of the bonfire. His eyes flickered in the light of the flames as they surveyed the commotion.

He wore trousers of black animal hide tucked into formidable boots, and although shirtless, his broad shoulders and thick arms shimmered like scales under sleeves of elaborate tattoos. His chest beamed red from a fresh wound over his heart, and at first Rye thought he might have been kicked by an enormous draft horse. But the painful imprint wasn't a horseshoe. Rather, it was the fresh outline of a familiar design she'd seen once before.

The High Chieftain's Crest—the same one her father still bore on his own body. Except that Slinister's mark remained incomplete. The crossed swords and four-leaf clover had not been finished.

"He knows I'm here," Rye said as they rushed down the hall.

Malydia didn't break her urgent stride. "Just keep moving. He didn't see you."

"He didn't have to. He can sense things. It's . . . hard to explain."

Malydia glanced back at her. "Rye, I was just starting to believe that your head wasn't clouded by the same superstitious cobwebs as the other villagers. Don't prove me wrong now."

Rye wasn't about to try to describe the gift of Sight, or Slinister's lineage on the Isle of Pest. They turned a corner, and arrived at a thick wooden door. Its face was carved with the crest of the House of Longchance—a coiled hagfish wrapped around a clenched fist.

Rye moved to open it, but Malydia put herself between Rye and the latch. Her face was severe.

"Before I bring you in, I want something in return."

"So that's why you wanted Truitt to stay behind," Rye said with a glare. "What more do you want? I'm trying to help you rid Drowning of the Fork-Tongue Charmers."

"Which may or may not work," Malydia said harshly, then paused. Rye recognized the sound of gruff voices down the hall.

"That's Slinister and the others," Rye said. "I told you they were coming for me."

Malydia raised an eyebrow and seemed to consider the situation. "Quickly," she said. "Inside."

They hurried into the Keep's library, shutting the door behind them. Rye had been here before, but was once again awed by the stacks of books on floor-to-ceiling shelves. The library was further divided into aisles and rows with freestanding stacks. The Fork-Tongue

Charmers must not be avid readers. Unlike the rest of the Keep, the large room remained largely untouched.

"This way," Malydia whispered. "It's a good thing we came now. By winter, all these books will be kindling."

They ran to the farthest aisle of the library, stopping under a tall stack. Above them, on the highest shelf, Rye spotted the elaborate leather binding lettered in gold. A pristine copy of *Tam's Tome of Drowning Mouth Fibs, Volume II.*

Rye moved to scale the shelf but Malydia beat her to it. The taller girl stretched and her long fingers just grasped the illicit book. Malydia pulled it down and clutched it with both hands. She examined it for a moment, then extended the copy of *Tam's Tome* toward Rye. But as Rye went to take it, Malydia held the book fast.

Rye heard the library door open with a thud. Malydia's eyes darted toward the sound, then back to her.

"I told you I wanted something in return," Malydia hissed.

The voices were in the library doorway. Footsteps scuffled.

Rye couldn't believe her ears. There was no time to waste.

"What?" Rye whispered. "What is it?"

Malydia's eyes drifted to Rye's neck. Rye put her hand

on her choker. Not again. Her choker might not possess the power it once did, but it was still her family's.

Malydia's gaze continued up, where it met Rye's own.

"I want you to remember," she said.

"Remember what?" Rye asked angrily.

"Remember that I gave you what you asked for. And regardless of what happens to me, or the Luck Uglies, promise that you'll do everything you can to help Truitt become the Earl of Village Drowning."

Rye was stunned by Malydia's request. She could hear the Fork-Tongue Charmers closing in, calling to one another as they worked their way through the stacks of books.

Rye nodded. "Of course. I'll remember . . . and I promise."

"Good," Malydia said, releasing her grip on the book. "Run that way." She pointed toward the corner of the library. "You'll find a sorting room with a service door that should be unlocked."

And with her words, Malydia threw her narrow frame against the tallest shelf of books. It wobbled, then pitched forward. The books, then the shelf itself, tumbled like a felled tree onto the floor. A Fork-Tongue Charmer cried out from under the heavy rain of bindings.

The Treasure Hole

Rye hesitated before fleeing, intent on dragging Malydia with her. But the young noble's eyes flared back in reply.

"Go! It's already done!" Malydia barked through gritted teeth. She clutched her shoulder. It hung low as if loose from its socket. "Don't let them seize us both!"

Rye turned and ran the way Malydia had instructed, darting into the sorting room just as the shout of men's voices and a girl's shriek filled the library behind her. She found the door to be unlocked, and hurried along a narrow service hallway until it emptied out farther down the main corridor. Rye peeked around the corner of the small hall and paused. The library was a good distance away, but she could make out Hyde standing in its doorway, his eyes fixed on the disturbance inside. This might be her only opportunity to escape unnoticed, and she'd have to be quick about it.

But just as she stepped out from the service hall into the corridor, Hyde glanced in her direction. The surprise in his eyes turned bitter, and there was no doubt that he recognized her this time.

"Pigshanks!" Rye cursed, and rushed in the opposite direction. She darted down the next side passageway she found.

Rye didn't have a strong sense of direction as she tore through the Keep's stone hallways. She used the echoes of the pursuing boot steps as her compass, and simply tried to keep them as far from her as possible. The walls were lined with vandalized paintings and tattered tapestries, and after she passed the same tapestry twice she realized she was circling back on herself.

Checking over her shoulder as she ran, Rye collided hard with a tall, bony shape—a boy. Rye caught her breath and prepared to fight free. But it wasn't Hyde.

"Truitt! What are you doing here?"

"I heard a commotion in the Great Hall. It sounded

like something was amiss."

"Yes, you could say things have taken a bad turn."

Truitt's hands went to the surface of *Tam's Tome* in her arms.

"You've got the book?"

"I do, but they've discovered Malydia."

Truitt's face tightened with concern. "Let's get you out of the Keep," he said after a moment. "I'll come back and find out where they've taken her."

They resumed their hurried pace, Truitt's fingertips guiding the way along the Keep's walls. When he stopped short, Rye nearly collided with him again. She stumbled and caught herself by grabbing hold of a large tapestry, knocking it askew.

"What is it?" she asked.

"Footsteps. Up ahead," he whispered.

"Let's turn around."

"We can't," Truitt said gravely. He tilted his head. "They're coming from that way too."

Rye heard them now. Footsteps *and* voices.

She spun around, examining the walls. There were no doors or passageways to offer another option. Her stomach tightened, and her eyes fell on the tapestry. She had a sense that she'd seen this one before too, although not tonight.

She looked more closely at the dark fibers woven

into an ominous image. A circle of masked men holding candles. Another in shackles at their center. Surrounding them all were leafless trees and dark waters of the bogs. This time she recognized the depiction for what it was—the Descent. She'd nearly knocked over this very same tapestry last year during Malydia's guided tour of Longchance Keep. And she recalled that there was something behind it.

Rye pushed aside the heavy fabric with her fingers, revealing a long, jagged crevice. The crack was even thicker than she'd remembered it—so thick, in fact, that a small person might be able to squeeze through.

"Truitt, there's a hollow in the wall."

"So try to climb through it."

"I don't think I can."

"We're short on options," Truitt said. "Let me give it a try."

Truitt studied the opening with his fingers. He lifted a leg and carefully shimmied it through, then contorted his body in an impossible manner and slipped in a shoulder and arm. He flashed Rye a smile.

"Plenty of room," he said before ducking his head, and the rest of his body disappeared like a rat wriggling through a gap in a stone wall.

Rye couldn't believe her eyes.

"Come on, Rye," his voice called in a loud whisper.

"There's space for you, too."

"How did you do that?"

"I've lived underground my entire life. This is hardly the smallest space I've ever had to fit inside. Now hurry."

"I don't know about this, Truitt. I once got my head stuck in the cupboard and had to wait all day for my mother to come home and free me."

"I'm bigger than you are and I made it. Hand me a torch and *Tam's Tome*, and start squeezing."

The din of echoing footsteps didn't allow for further hesitation. Rye snatched a torch from the wall and, holding the tapestry aside, carefully extended her arm through the crevice, giving the torch to Truitt. She passed *Tam's Tome* through next.

"I'm coming in," she said. Rye slipped one leg through the crack just as Truitt had. Then she ducked and tried to tuck her head under. The walls met her shoulders and she stopped.

"Pigshanks! It's the cupboard all over again," she lamented.

She felt Truitt grab her from behind and tug. With a scrape and a bump she fell through the snug opening and landed hard in the darkness on the other side. Scrambling to her hands and knees, she reached an arm back out, and smoothed the tapestry into place so that it covered the damaged wall.

Rye looked back over her shoulder at Truitt. "Snuff out the torch and we'll hide here until—Truitt!" she whispered as loud as she dared. The torchlight was now several yards away, as if he'd wandered down a twisting tunnel. "What are you doing?"

"This isn't just a hole," his voice came back. "It's some sort of passageway."

"A passage to where?" she called in a whisper.

"Follow me," he said, his voice a surprising distance away. She did, and met him in the torchlight.

"Are we back in the Spoke?" she asked.

"No. I've never been here before. And feel the walls. Stone and mortar. This passageway wasn't hollowed out—it's aboveground, part of the Keep itself."

Rye squinted to make out their surroundings.

"There's something up ahead," Truitt said moving forward.

"How do you know?" Rye asked, following him reluctantly.

"The air's thick with clues. I smell bronze. And silver. Canvas and paper. And . . ." His voice trailed off.

Rye smelled it too. The pungent odor of something rotten.

"Truitt, stop."

"Too late. We're already here."

Truitt handed *Tam's Tome* back to Rye and extended

the torch over his head. Rye looked up. Although she could see little, she could tell that the passageway had opened up. Rather than reflecting off a ceiling, the torchlight carried high above them.

"What do you see?" Truitt asked.

"Not much. Let me have the torch."

Truitt handed it to her, and she waved it around to get a better look.

"We're in a tall chamber. There are stacks and piles everywhere—some sort of storeroom." A glint of glass on a table caught her eye. "Wait, I'm going to light a lantern."

The ground crunched under her feet as she moved, as if she was stepping through gravel.

Rye opened the lantern and lit it. As it flared to life, the entire chamber twinkled around them. She sucked in her breath at the sight.

"What is it?" Truitt asked.

"Coins," Rye said in disbelief. "Jewels. Mountains of them."

All around the circular chamber, loose hills of gold grommets seemed to grow like mounds of earth. A carpeted floor of silver shims shifted under her boots. Coin purses, large and small, were stacked like sandbags. Towering shelves much taller than Rye overflowed with ornate platters and bejeweled picture frames.

"Longchance's Treasure Hole," Truitt said. He crouched and picked up a handful of loose coins, letting them fall between his fingers. "Slinister must not have found it; otherwise they'd have emptied it by now."

Rye found a casing to house the torch, picked up the lantern, and wandered about the chamber in disbelief at the wealth strewn around her.

"There are more coins here than all the shops on Market Street will see in a lifetime," she said. "And—oh!"

Rye leaped back when she came to a large wooden worktable. A chair was occupied by an emaciated body, thin onion-like skin pulled tight over its skull that lay slack-jawed on the table. Gray hair stuck up like dried thatch from its balding head, and ragged clothes hung from its skeletal shoulders. The jewel-encrusted scabbard of an ornamental sword dangled from its belt. She saw only one arm, and suddenly felt sick. Tied on its sole wrist was a familiar, faded blue hair ribbon—one that was once worn by her mother.

"What is it?" Truitt said.

Rye covered her nose with her arm. "There is—well, there *was*—a man here. Constable Boil. He's seen better days."

Truitt's face tightened. "I've heard of nobles who wall up guard dogs in their treasure holes. One was even said to keep a full-grown cave bear in his. They'd throw down just enough food and water to keep the guardians alive, but the solitude made them deranged and vicious—a final defense against any unwitting robber who stumbled upon the hole."

"It seems Longchance took it one step further," Rye said flatly.

"With the Earl locked away, nobody would have known he was here," Truitt said solemnly. "He must have starved."

Boil had been a vile man, but even he didn't deserve such a fate.

Rye gave the condemned Constable a wide berth as she explored the Treasure Hole. In addition to the mountains of coins and piles of precious stones and fine jewelry, the secret storeroom was filled with other, less conventional treasures. Goblets and platters, precious silks and sculptures. Rye examined some of the fine paintings stored on easels and protected under drop cloths. But her eyes were soon drawn to a less obvious one, a portrait housed in a silver frame much smaller than the cover of *Tam's Tome*. This painting lay on its side and was covered only by a layer of dust. But when she blew it off, it was clear that, unlike Longchance's own paintings that lined the walls of the Keep, this one had been the work of a master. The lifelike details were extraordinary given the small size of the canvas.

It was a portrait of a seated young woman with lush black hair pulled up in a graceful bun. She held an infant on each knee, the babies swaddled in fine black-and-blue gowns. Rye studied their faces. The artist had made their cherubic cheeks rosy and full and, in each case, their big wet eyes were mismatched—one brown, the other blue.

Rye's own eyes darted to Truitt, who was running his fingers over various items in the Treasure Hole. She looked back at the face of the woman in the portrait. Her high cheekbones and delicate nose were vaguely familiar. This was Lady Emma—Truitt and Malydia's mother.

"Truitt," Rye said, clutching the painting carefully. "There's something here you should have. It's a pocket portrait. Of you . . . and Malydia, and . . . your mother."

Truitt paused and approached Rye. She held out the frame and placed it in his hands carefully. Truitt felt the ornate edges, and ran his fingers over the canvas's small surface, as if trying to glean an image from the topography of oils.

"I've never known what it's like to see, so I can't say I've ever missed it," Truitt said. "But for the first time, I wish I had my eyesight."

Truitt furrowed his brow. "What does she look like?" he asked quietly.

Rye watched as his unfocused eyes ran over the surface of the painting.

"Beautiful," she said.

Truitt nodded. "Thank you for finding this, Rye. I shall keep it." He eased it inside one of the many large pockets lining his leather courier's coat.

Rye glanced again at the awe-inspiring wealth around her. "Truitt, if you become Earl, will all this be yours?"

"I suppose it will," he said. "Not that I have much use for a dark hole full of gold and silver."

"But think of all you could do with it," Rye said. "You could provide homes to the link children. Rebuild the bridges and walls, and make sure that every villager could have a feast on Silvermas."

"That's certainly more sensible than hoarding it in the walls of a castle," Truitt said. "But all of that remains a job for another day. Right now, we need to get *ourselves* out of the Keep."

Truitt was right, of course. While *Tam's Tome* might be able to tell her how to summon a Reckoning, nobody would be able to see any signal inside this decrepit vault. She studied the walls with her lantern. Rye didn't like the idea of heading back into the main corridor while Slinister and the Fork-Tongue Charmers were still searching for her, but she could find no other exit except for the way they'd come.

"Longchance sealed the passageways," Rye said, "but he must have gotten his treasure in and out of here somehow. What good's a Treasure Hole if you can't get to your treasure?"

"Maybe that's what the lift is for," Truitt said.

"What lift?" Rye asked, pivoting the lantern toward him.

"Have a look, and you tell me." In his hand, Truitt held a thick rope fixed to a pulley, its length stretching high up into the darkness above them.

For a long while, Rye just squinted up to where the rope disappeared in the shadows, trying to see how high it extended overhead. With her foot, she tested the small wooden platform rigged to the ropes. It wobbled under her weight but remained reasonably secure.

"Will it hold us?" Truitt asked.

"Not together, but maybe one at a time," Rye guessed.

They both turned at the sound of dull, distant voices from the far end of the hollowed passage. The Fork-Tongue Charmers were still searching the corridor.

"Do you think they'll find us?" Rye asked.

"Does it matter? We really can't wait to find out."

"Then we better get started," Rye said. "Who's first?"

Truitt thought for a moment. "You go. You're lighter,

but more importantly, you'll be better able to see what's at the top of this chamber. Take the lantern, and be sure we're not going from bad to worse."

Rye positioned herself on the wooden platform, shifting her weight to achieve an uneasy balance. She gripped the rope tightly in her palm.

"I'm ready," she said.

Truitt wrapped his hands around a length of rope closer to the pulley. "Me too. Pull with all your might."

Truitt pulled downward, hand over hand. Rye did the same, as best as she was able, until the platform slowly wobbled and began to rise under her feet. Rye felt the wood pitch beneath her and dropped into a crouch to keep from tumbling over the side. She could feel the strain in the ropes as she inched ever-so-slowly higher.

Rye pulled until her shoulders ached and the skin of her palms burned. She carefully peeked over the edge, where she could still see Truitt far below in the light of the torch they'd placed at his feet. She looked up, where the looming shadows of a circular ceiling neared.

"Almost there," she called down, nerves in her voice.

"You're not afraid of heights, are you?" Truitt called back.

"Not of heights," Rye clarified. "Of falling."

Rye kept tugging and heaving until she was out of breath. Finally, the platform came to a stop, nestling into a smaller alcove at the top of the Treasure Hole that housed the upper pulley. She stepped out onto a narrow but sturdier landing and took a moment to appreciate the solid footing. Just overhead was an even smaller portal. With her skinned palms, she pushed aside what felt like a flat wooden covering.

"That's it," Rye called down. "I'm here. There's some sort of hatch. It's small but we can fit through it."

"Send it back down," Truitt called.

They reversed directions on the rope, and with Truitt's help from below, the platform quickly descended to the floor of the Treasure Hole.

Rye caught her breath and waited for the rustle of ropes to indicate that Truitt had boarded the platform. When they remained still, she carefully peered down and could just make him out in the torchlight.

"You're not afraid of heights, are you?" Rye joked.

Truitt tilted his head up, then back at his surroundings in the Treasure Hole. He seemed to hesitate.

"Come on," she called again. "Climb on."

But she heard only the shuffle of coins in reply. Truitt was stooped over, gathering up as many coins as he could carry in his arms. Rye couldn't believe her eyes.

"Truitt! What are you doing?"

But he disappeared, hurrying away from the torchlight. Then she heard his voice again, muffled but calling loudly, somewhere farther in the distance.

"Help!" he cried out. "Here! In the wall! She's here in the Keep's Treasure Hole!"

Truitt was at the crack behind the tapestry, crying out for the Fork-Tongue Charmers.

16
A Tome Guards Its Secrets

Truitt's words shocked Rye worse than a hornet in the ear, and she had to grip the ledge to keep from tumbling off.

Just as she righted herself, the ropes lurched and the platform bobbed far below.

"Come on, Rye," Truitt's voice called out again. "Give me a hand."

He was on the platform, urgently working the lower pulley. Still stunned, Rye took hold of the rope and pulled. Truitt clambered off quickly when it reached the top, and she just stared at him blankly.

"We should get moving," he said. "It won't take them long to chisel through that wall."

"I thought . . . I thought you . . ." Her words trailed off.

"You thought I what?" he asked with a bewildered look.

Rye just shook her head. "Never mind."

Together they squeezed through the small portal above them.

Rye and Truitt hurried through what turned out to be Earl Longchance's master chamber. Judging by the mess, the Earl's private living quarters had long since been picked clean by the Fork-Tongue Charmers. But Rye now understood why the Keep's new occupants had yet to find the Treasure Hole.

The hole itself, and its lift and pulleys, were hidden beneath what appeared to be the tower's garderobe—the Earl's toilet facilities. The portal Rye and Truitt had crawled up and through was built to look just like a stone privy. It was an ingenious disguise, as no looter was likely to carefully investigate *that*.

"Why did you lead them to the Treasure Hole?" Rye asked, finally regaining her composure as they continued through an antechamber and cautiously descended a flight of stairs. Truitt had spent years secretly exploring the Keep under the cover of darkness, and they were back in an area he knew well.

"Because we needed to give them something they'd find even more interesting than you," he said. "A handful of gold grommets helped whet their appetite."

"I don't understand."

"Stop and listen," Truitt said.

They both paused. "What do you hear?" he asked.

"Nothing," Rye said.

"Exactly. I'll bet Slinister and the Fork-Tongue Charmers are attacking that wall as we speak, probably already squabbling about how they'll divvy up their riches. Otherwise, they'd be searching this tower right now."

Rye and Truitt continued downward. When the stairway ended at the main corridor not far from the Great Hall, they found the stretch of Keep quiet except for the crackle of fire from inside the Hall's doors.

"You cleared the way for us," Rye said quietly, and felt ashamed for ever thinking otherwise.

Truitt just shrugged. "It might buy Malydia some time, too. Let's get you to the Spoke, then I'll come back for her," he said.

"All right, but just one more thing," Rye said, hurrying toward the double doors. "Keep an ear out."

Rye rushed into the Great Hall, where the fire still

raged over a carpet of broken plates and goblets. But the towering chamber was empty of all Fork-Tongue Charmers, except for one. From his chair, Gibbet's blank face stared out at her as she made her way to the pile of medicinal pouches in the corner. If he took notice of her, he gave no indication. Someone had balanced a ripe apple on his motionless head. The fruit didn't even wobble as she passed by.

Rye filled her pockets with as much medicine as they would hold.

"It serves you right, you know," she said, pointing an accusatory finger at Gibbet. "Shame on you, chasing little girls up into trees."

Rye turned to make a hasty exit but paused, her conscience getting the better of her. She sighed and approached Gibbet carefully.

From an arm's length away, she snatched the apple from his head and placed it into his cold hand.

Better that the Fork-Tongue Charmers not get the idea to use it for target practice.

Rye was exhausted by the time she dragged herself up from the familiar wine cellar, her oversize boots heavy on the worn wooden steps. The hour was late but there was no need to be silent—she knew the Dead Fish Inn never slept. And yet, when she reached the main floor, she found the inn deserted. Its great iron portals were securely barred but unguarded. No barkeep manned the taps, and overhead the candles of the inn's looming sea monster skeleton chandelier burned low. All the tables were clear of patrons and platters. All except one, that is.

Two bodies rested their heads on the carved top of the table called the Mermaid's Nook. A boy's sleepy face pushed itself up from its spot among the mermaid's curves.

"Rye!" Quinn called, rising to his feet.

Folly's white-blond hair stirred and she blinked her blue marble eyes awake.

"We've been waiting up all night," she said groggily. "We were afraid you'd never get here."

"You found *Tam's Tome*," Quinn said in awe, spotting the leather-bound book wrapped tightly in her arms.

Rye placed it on the table with a thud and dropped herself into a chair, fatigue catching up with her.

"Like taking sweets from a baby," she said.

"Really?" Quinn asked.

"No," Rye said with a slump of her shoulders. "It was awful. But I got this, too." She placed the pouch of yarrow flower on the table. "For the Pendergills."

Folly pushed herself up and wrapped her arms

around Rye's shoulders. "No more waiting around for you," she whispered. "From now on we stick together."

Folly walked behind the bar and began to steep some tea.

Rye glanced over her shoulder at Folly, then turned back to Quinn. "Where is everyone?" she mouthed.

"Asleep," he said with a shrug. "Turns out there's not much to do around an inn when you have no guests."

Folly returned to the table with three steaming mugs, and Rye told them about Malydia and the Fork-Tongue Charmers, of the Treasure Hole, and of her narrow escape from Longchance Keep. Rye's friends had been through too many scrapes with her to doubt a word of her story.

"So what now?" Folly asked once she'd finished.

"Now we summon a Reckoning," Rye answered.

"How do we do that again?" Folly said.

"*Tam's Tome* will tell us."

"What part?" Quinn said, eyeing the thick volume.

Rye shifted the heavy book so that it lay between them on the table and cracked open the cover. "Harmless said there's a chapter called 'The Reckoning.' So I guess we start there."

The daunting, tight-knit scrawl of the tome's handwritten words stared up at them. There must have been a hundred lines per page, occasionally broken up by painstakingly lifelike illustrations.

Quinn sputtered his lips and scratched his hair. "I hope this tea is strong, Folly."

The three friends scoured the pages of *Tam's Tome* well into the early morning hours, until they could no longer see straight. They were on the verge of giving up for the night when they finally found the chapter titled "The Reckoning." A pit grew in Rye's stomach as they read about the contest. As Harmless had explained, the Reckoning was a harsh and ancient method of trial by combat—one used to resolve only the most serious differences among the Luck Uglies. In order to avoid a civil war that might destroy the brotherhood, the parties in dispute and their designated men-at-arms would compete under a set of agreed-upon rules. No other Luck Uglies were permitted to intervene. There could be only one winning team. Those who lost but otherwise survived the Reckoning were forced to leave the Luck Uglies in one final manner. Via the Descent.

It was the thought of yet another Descent that churned Rye's stomach.

But despite reading and re-reading the text, studying its words, and debating their possible meaning, they had yet to find any clue as to how to actually summon a Reckoning. As a distant cock began to crow outside, announcing the imminent arrival of dawn, Rye tried to shake a disheartening thought.

Even after her narrow escape from Longchance Keep, they were still no better off than when she'd first dropped *Tam's Tome* deep within the Spoke.

17
What's Worth Saving

Tiny black letters danced across the inside of Rye's eyelids, the tight-lipped prose of *Tam's Tome* haunting her even while she stole a few hours of much-needed sleep.

Muffled sobs echoed nearby. Her own? No, they belonged to another child. It was not a cry of great pain or despair. Rather, it reminded her of the fussy screech of a baby who had something warm and pungent in his britches.

Rye opened her eyes and pushed herself up from her blankets. Light streamed through the shutters of Folly's bedroom, glinting off the glass jars and beakers that lined the shelves around her. Folly's experiments had multiplied since Rye had last slept in this room. Small vessels of swirling liquids now bubbled atop oil burners. Stacks of notebooks covered a worktable, guarded by the unblinking eyes of the Alchemist's Bone—the tiny skull charm Harmless had once given Folly was now strung on a silver chain.

The sobs came from downstairs. Rye slipped on her coat, left Folly's room, and descended the stairs to the main floor of the inn. A dozen people stirred around the Dead Fish, most of them Folly's older brothers preoccupied with various menial tasks.

Quinn and Folly were in the Mermaid's Nook, Quinn's head buried in *Tam's Tome,* which still lay open on the table. A dull snore droned from his covered face. Folly sat across from him, bouncing a perplexed, pink-cheeked baby on her knee. Wisps of white-blond hair stuck straight up from his round head, and huge blue eyes as wide as Folly's swam with tears. He pursed his lips as Folly tried to encourage him to sample a bite from a spoon.

Rye couldn't contain a wide grin. "Is that . . . ?"

"Baby Fox," Folly said with a smile. "He's not very happy about his mashed beets and quail eggs at the moment."

Fox whimpered and pouted by way of confirmation.

"Hard to blame him," Rye said. "May I hold him?"

"Be my guest." Folly placed her little brother onto Rye's lap. "Here, Fox. Meet your Auntie Rye."

Rye cooed at the warm bundle in her arms. He eyed her curiously, but his crying tapered off. Quinn jolted awake at the silence.

"What happened?" he said, wiping drool from the pages of *Tam's Tome* with the back of his hand.

"Nothing," Folly said. "Go back to sleep."

Quinn groaned and dropped his head back onto the book.

"Quinn stayed up reading after we went to bed," Folly explained. "He's determined to find something in there even if he has to go cross-eyed trying." She handed Rye the spoon and slid over Fox's bowl. Fox's face flashed with betrayal.

"No, no, Fox," Rye said, "it's not bad. Look." She sampled the spoon with her lips and almost gasped at the revolting taste. She choked back her gag reflex. "Delicious," she croaked between gritted teeth.

Fox reached up and grasped the spoon with his round fingers. Folly gave Rye an impressed smile.

"Yes, good, Fox," Rye said nodding enthusiastically. "Yum."

Fox pushed the spoon against Rye's face.

"Oh, no, Fox. Not . . ." The beets and eggs caked Rye's face as he clumsily tried to find her mouth. "Yuck," she said.

Now Fox's toothless gums smiled widely.

Rye gave up trying to feed the littlest Flood, and was content to let him nestle in her lap.

"So Quinn slept here in the Mermaid's Nook?" she asked.

"I tried to wake him, but it was like trying to stir a stump."

Rye glanced around at the inn, careful not to disturb Fox's steady breathing. She had never heard the Dead Fish so quiet. Aside from the clink of dishes and the footsteps of Folly's family, the inn was still. Folly seemed to sense Rye's surprise.

"The port's as good as closed thanks to the River Wyvern," Folly said. "And those who brave the river are only sailing one way—out of Drowning."

Rye couldn't believe how much the village had changed. Bog Noblins in the streets, strange creatures in the Spoke, and now a monster in the river? It was starting to seem like Beyond the Shale was a safer place to call home.

"Have you ever seen this River Wyvern?" Rye asked.

Folly nodded adamantly, then hesitated. "Well, parts of it anyway. One morning at sunrise, I saw its head break the surface. It was a black and shimmery, then it ducked back under. It had a long tail trailing behind it."

"Like an eel, or a big sea snake?"

"I've never known an eel to drag a fisherman from his boat. Or scuttle up on four legs onto the dock and make off with a deckhand between its jaws."

"It did that?"

"That's what I heard. Whatever it is, it's been terrible for business. If my father and brothers ever get ahold of it, they'll turn it into a new chandelier."

A gentle hand touched Rye's shoulder. Rye looked up to find Folly's mother standing over her. Rye was about to stand to greet her, but Faye Flood pushed the gray streak in her white-blond hair behind an ear, and put a finger to her own lips. Then she pointed to Fox. Rye hadn't realized it, but the infant had nodded off on her shoulder, his pink lips open and his closed eyelids flickering slightly as he dreamed.

Rye smiled and handed Fox to his mother. Faye leaned over and pressed her lips to the top of Rye's head. Her eyes were warm and full of concern.

"Folly told me about Abby and Gray," she whispered.

"You've always got a home here until they can return." She carried Fox away to tuck him into his cradle.

Faye's words were kind, but brought Rye's troubles flooding back to her.

"I could use some air," Rye said. After a long night in the tunnels and passageways of the Spoke and Longchance Keep, she welcomed a trip outdoors.

Folly shook Quinn's arm. His head lurched up again.

"What happened?" he asked groggily.

"Nothing," Folly said. "We're going to walk some rust off. You could use it too."

"No," he said, rubbing his eyes. "I want to keep looking. The answer is in these pages. The print's so small it's making me see spots, though."

Rye reached to the loop sewn in her coat and retrieved her leather-and-brass spyglass. "Here, try this," she said with a smile. "I don't want to be blamed if your eyes fall out of your head."

"We'll bring you back some breakfast," Folly said, getting up from the table with Rye and approaching the inn's doors.

Folly's brothers Fitz and Flint leaned in the doorway. The burly conjoined twins crossed all four arms as they stared out onto Little Water Street, glowering from under their thick heads of white-blond hair. They looked down at Rye and Folly.

"Rye O'Chanter?" Fitz said. "Haven't seen you around here—"

"In ages," Flint added, finishing his sentence.

"Where've you been?" Fitz asked.

"Here and there," Rye said. She doubted the twins would have the patience for the long version—and probably wouldn't believe her if they did.

She peered past Fitz and Flint to the dirt road that had turned to mud under a steady drizzle and the clop of many boots. A line of damp villagers snaked along the edge of the river, eyeing the waters nervously and talking among themselves.

"What are they doing?" Rye asked.

"Getting out while they can," Fitz said.

"And while they can afford it," Flint added. "The fare goes up with each passing week."

"Last night was a bad night," Fitz explained. "Noblins broke into a row of houses in Nether Neck."

"Wasn't pretty," Flint said, shaking his head.

"I'm going to have a look," Rye said.

Folly moved to follow her.

"Uh-uh," Fitz said, placing a thick hand on his sister's arm. "You're staying away from the river."

Folly's eyes flared and she tugged her arm free.

"Don't worry. If I spy any sea monsters, I'll be sure to send them your way." Folly was one of the few villagers who would dare to ignore an order from the imposing twins.

Rye pulled her coat tight around her neck and they stepped out into the drizzle. She had never seen the river's banks so high. Water lapped right up over the docks onto Little Water Street itself. It splashed at the well-heeled feet of the villagers who waited in line, turning the dirt walkway as muddy as a spring field. The villagers shifted and tried to pluck their boots from the muck. Closer now, she saw that many of them carried heavy packs or pulled handcarts behind them.

Rye stepped down onto the street and walked parallel to the line, following it where it led to the end of a pier.

A hook-nosed fellow cleared his throat haughtily, rain dripping from the brim of his richly appointed hat. "Ahem. The line ends back there, young lady." He scowled and pointed a crooked finger far past the Dead Fish Inn.

"Don't get your bonnet in a bunch," Rye said without stopping. "Nobody's trying to take your place."

The villagers in line all bore the signs of affluence—not the types of folks who normally turned up in the Shambles. Their eyes glanced around at the shopkeepers and neighborhood residents apprehensively. The Shamblers themselves leaned in doorways and took shelter from the rain under small awnings, staring back at them with suspicious glares that did little to settle the outsiders' nerves.

At the front of the line, villagers crowded the pier and climbed into bobbing longboats. Each longboat was manned by thick-armed sailors, menacing harpoons over their shoulders. Rye squinted. In the distance, at the mouth of the river, a familiar-looking ship rocked on the waves. Its sails sagged and its hull looked to have seen better days. At the top of its mast, a green flag with the silhouettes of three soaring gulls rustled in the breeze. The banner of the freebooters.

"It can't be," she muttered to herself.

Rye had sailed on this ship before—or at least one that looked just like it. But the *Slumgullion* had been sunk.

"Patience!" a man barked. "No pushing. There's room enough for everyone. Gold grommets in your left hand, hold the rails with your right. As soon as I collect your fare, you're free to board."

A one-eyed freebooter made his way along the line. He smoothed his steel-gray ponytail with one palm and held out a well-filled sack with another. Coins clinked as the passengers dropped them in.

Rye looked to Folly in surprise. "Captain Dent?" she called out.

The Captain squinted at the sound of his name, and

his weathered face cracked a wide grin when he recognized Rye.

"Riley O'Chanter," he boomed cheerfully. "A pelican's ghost! I thought I'd seen the last of you! And good morning to you, too, Folly."

He hurried forward and threw an arm over Rye's shoulder. Her bones creaked as he squeezed her with a bit too much enthusiasm.

"Glad you're well, Captain," Rye said. "Is that . . ." She looked out toward the ship at the mouth of the river.

"Ah, your eyes aren't playing tricks on you, lass. My beloved *Slumgullion* still lies in her grave off the coast of Pest. That little beauty out there is the *Slumgullion Too*. Just as quick as her dearly departed sister, but a little thicker through the hull."

"What are you doing here?" Rye asked, looking around at the assembled villagers.

"Isn't it obvious?" Captain Dent replied. "The roads in and out of Drowning are impassable with those bog beasts running amok. That leaves the waterways, but the port is closed. Few seamen are willing to sail in or out with the threat of this water devil that's taken up residence in the river. It's quite a calamity."

"I'll say," Rye agreed.

"But the Captain is always willing to lend a hand when needed," he said, raising a fist. "I'll see to it that every villager who desires to leave—and possesses, shall we say, the wherewithal to do so"—he shook the sack of coins in his hand—"shall have a spot on the *Slumgullion Too.*"

The Captain winked and lowered his voice. "A wise old smuggler once said, 'With every great calamity comes an even greater opportunity.'"

Rye narrowed her eyes and gave Folly a knowing look. She had no doubt who that wise old smuggler was.

"Aren't *you* concerned about the River Wyvern?" Rye asked.

Dent reached over to where a thick harpoon rested against a pylon. Its barb was long and sharp enough to run through an ox. He took it in his hand and tapped it against the ground.

"That's what these are for," he said, then leaned forward conspiratorially. "Although the harpoons are mostly for their benefit," he whispered, nodding toward the villagers. "To give them the illusion of being safe. My crew has already put three of these into the monster and barely slowed it down."

"You've seen it?" Rye said.

Dent nodded gravely. "Aye. Once. A few weeks back. It was late afternoon around dusk and we were ferrying the last boatful back to the ship. It came up under us and capsized the longboat."

Both Rye's and Folly's eyes went wide with alarm.

"I remember they once had water dragons in the royal canals O'There. Generally lazy creatures, they'd loll about basking in the sun at the water's edge; would only get nasty if you disturbed them from their naps. Then water-dragon boots became fashionable among the noble ladies and you don't see many anymore." The Captain pursed his lips. "This River Wyvern is different, though. It's aggressive, with a mean streak. Smart. And fast. My guess? Nobody's finding it unless it wants to be found."

"How did your crew escape it?" Folly asked.

Dent gave her a tight smile. "My advice, if you must take to the water, don't do so alone. And while you need not be the fastest swimmer, you best not be the slowest. The good news is that most of these folks have never dipped a toe in anything deeper than a tepid bath."

Rye looked at the nervous faces stretched down Little Water Street, and hoped for their sake that the River Wyvern didn't find himself hungry today.

Dent put a hand back on Rye's shoulder. "There's always a spot for you and your family at the front of the line," he said quietly. "Consider your fare prepaid. I'd offer you the same, Folly, but I know you Floods are rooted tighter than barnacles."

"Thank you, Captain," Rye said. "But I think our

spot remains here in Drowning for the time being."

"I understand, lass," he said with a tight smile. "But if you reconsider, come find me. Don't be too long making up your mind, though. There's a storm brewing out there. It'll be barreling this way sooner or later, I can smell it. The next ferry out of Drowning just might be the last."

Captain Dent clapped Rye's shoulder and continued on down the line. He shook his sack of coins as he passed the villagers. "Orderly now! No pushing and shoving! And I suggest you snack lightly. Get seasick in my boat, it'll cost you extra."

Rye cast her eyes up at the gray sky. Above her, atop the great arched bridge that spanned the river, hundreds of pairs of coal-black eyes peered down on the spectacle. The sprawling flock of rooks gathered on the bridge's railing, preening their feathers and bobbing their heads excitedly, although their long gray beaks remained silent. Rye wondered who they were keeping watch for. The Fork-Tongue Charmers, or perhaps distant Luck Uglies? Then again, maybe they were just waiting to scavenge the remains of the River Wyvern's next meal. Perhaps she shouldn't have been so quick to decline the Captain's invitation.

Rye studied the deserted river. Except for Captain Dent's longboats, the slips were empty. No vessels, large or small, dotted the water. Except for one. At the center of the river, a flat-hulled barge that looked to be cobbled together with wood and rusting metal bobbed peacefully. A crimson sail was folded on its single mast. Several gulls circled overhead, like scavengers stalking a fishing boat.

"Folly, what is *that*?" Rye asked.

"That's the fortune-teller's junk," Folly said. "She's some sort of soothsayer. Arrived a few months ago. Villagers would row out to have her read their palms or study tea leaves—some nonsense. Folks don't go out there much anymore."

"Because of the River Wyvern?"

"There's that," Folly said. "But also, the fortune-teller has nothing but bad news to share."

Rye stared out at the strange barge, but didn't have time to ponder it further. They still had a pressing task at hand, and nothing she'd heard today gave her the impression that time was on their side.

"Come on, Folly, let's get back to *Tam's Tome*."

They worked their way back down Little Water Street toward the Dead Fish Inn. As they neared the iron doors, a voice called out from somewhere along the line of villagers.

"Lady Flood! Miss Riley!"

In the mass of villagers, the flush and beaming face

of their friend Baron Nutfield waved a flagon of wine from his spot in the line. Baron Nutfield was the ever-present barfly who had taken up residence in the Dead Fish Inn, or more often than not, in the alley behind it when he didn't pay his bar tab.

"Baron Nutfield?" Folly called in surprise. "You're leaving too?"

"Fear not, Lady Flood. I'll return with reinforcements!" he declared loudly. The other villagers around him turned up their noses and pretended not to hear his drunken ramblings. "Drowning is far more of a home to me than the sun-splashed meadows of my realm will ever be."

Often, after a long night in his cup, Baron Nutfield would prattle on about his noble lineage and vast land holdings to the south. That was usually right before the twins tossed him into the alley. Despite all his boasts, Baron Nutfield could barely scratch together two bronze bits. It was widely known that he told more lies than a fisherman.

"For what my land may offer in creature comforts, it lacks that which Drowning possesses in abundance—heart!" He thrust his fist in the air. "And that, my young friends, is something worth saving!"

Baron Nutfield's enthusiasm set him off balance, and he toppled backward into the mud. After struggling unsuccessfully to remove himself from the muddy hollow, he resigned himself to his spot and promptly shut his eyes.

"I'm going to miss the old nutter," Rye said as they turned back toward the Dead Fish Inn.

"Me too," Folly added. "Although he better get on that ship before my father realizes he never settled his bar tab."

"Rye! Folly!" Quinn's voice cried. His boots splattered mud as he leaped down the steps from the Dead Fish Inn.

"I found it!" he gasped with excitement, his face beaming. He glanced around, then lowered his voice. "I know how to summon the Reckoning."

Hogsheads

Rye, Folly, and Quinn hurried back inside, Folly sticking out her tongue in reply to the twins' reproachful faces as she rushed past. The three friends gathered around the table in the Mermaid's Nook.

"Rye had the right idea," Quinn said.

"What idea?" Rye asked.

"I used your spyglass to see the words more closely." He held up a small circle of glass between his thumb and forefinger. Rye frowned. The rest of her spyglass lay dismantled in pieces around the table.

"Sorry," Quinn said. "I needed the lens."

Rye waved him off. "Just show us."

Quinn reached into his pocket and carefully placed a small wooden stickman next to the open book—the Strategist's Sticks, a charm given to him by Harmless. He gave a sheepish shrug.

"It helps me concentrate," he said. Then he held the lens over the page titled "The Reckoning," placing it over the letter *T* in the heading. "Look."

Rye and Folly squinted.

"That's a big letter *T*," Folly observed.

"No, look *closer*. In the ink itself," Quinn coaxed.

Rye lowered her head until her eyelash nearly flicked the surface of the lens.

"There's a . . . word. *In* the letter *T*."

"That's right," Quinn said.

The word was so small it looked like a straight stroke of a quill to the naked eye, but now, under the makeshift magnifying glass, the letters *within* the letter became visible.

"*B . . . l . . . e . . . e . . . d*." Rye looked up from the lens, a sour look on her face. "Bleed?"

"Yes. Now the next." He slid the lens over the letter *h*.

There were two words in this letter. *The* ran vertically, and *hogsheads* arced around the bend in the letter *h*.

"The hogsheads," Rye read aloud.

Quinn nodded enthusiastically. "You've been practicing, Rye. Look, each letter contains more hidden words."

He moved the lens along each letter in the chapter title, reading aloud as he did. Putting them all together, they formed a sentence. An instruction.

Bleed the hogsheads under Ned Cooper's mill, 'til the river runs with their froth and spill.

"Brilliant way to hide a message in plain sight, isn't it?" Quinn said with a smile.

Rye winced. "I suppose," she said. "But that's awful. We have to find a hog's head and bleed it? I think I'm going to be sick."

"No," Folly said, jumping in with enthusiasm. "I think we'll find that everything we need is already there."

"Where?" Quinn asked.

"Ned Cooper was a barrel maker," Folly explained. "His old mill is on a pier at the end of Little Water Street. It's been closed for years, but under the pier, there's a mountain of old casks they never removed."

Rye looked at her blankly.

"Casks, barrels . . . *hogsheads*. They're all the same thing, Rye."

Rye and Quinn looked at each other, putting it together.

"See?" Folly said. "Sometimes it comes in handy to have a friend who's a barkeep's daughter."

Quinn insisted that Rye and Folly wait for him to check in with his father before venturing to the old coopery. It was late afternoon by the time he rejoined them. Folly tasked him and Rye with distracting her parents while she gathered supplies. It wasn't difficult—Quinn peppered Fletcher Flood with questions about the shelf life of his malts and Rye accidently lit a broom on fire while helping Faye sweep one of the fireplaces. So when Folly emerged from the storage room and announced that they'd be conducting some experiments, Faye agreed that it was a wonderful idea, and didn't even question the heavy sack in Folly's hand. The three friends hurried upstairs. With the increase in vacancies around the inn, Folly had commandeered a large guestroom as her workshop.

"Go on in," Folly said. "I'll be right there."

Rye realized that the concoctions she'd seen brewing in Folly's room were only a fraction of her friend's latest projects. She and Quinn looked wide-eyed at the makeshift laboratory, the floor covered with steaming vats and cauldrons connected by glass tubing.

Rye took particular interest in a swirling mist in a stoppered bottle. She picked it up and eyed it closely, a thin layer of clear liquid bubbling at the bottom.

"For the sake of the Shale, be careful with that," Folly said, entering the workshop with a pile of ropes slung over her shoulder. It was the rope ladder Rye and Folly kept stashed under her bed. "If you get it too close to that blue flask over there, the chemical reaction is liable to blow the roof right off the inn."

Rye carefully placed the bottle back where she'd found it and took a healthy step away.

"Are these mushrooms?" Quinn asked, jabbing his finger into a cluster of orange-red fungi growing in a flat tin.

"It's called deadly webcap," Folly said. "And if you eat it your brain will melt inside your skull."

Quinn frowned and wiped his hand on his trousers.

"Listen, you nosy nellies, there's no time to play right now. Quinn, hold this." She handed him the heavy sack and unfurled the rope ladder out the window toward the alley below. "If we hurry, we can still make it to Ned Cooper's and back before dark."

"What are these for?" Quinn asked, removing a heavy mallet and wooden tap from the sack.

"The hogsheads," Folly said, stringing her Alchemist's

Bone around her neck and climbing into the window frame. "Those barrels aren't about to drain themselves."

The rain had ceased and the late-afternoon sun now reflected crimson off the lingering clouds. Rye noticed that the *Slumgullion Too* no longer laid anchor at the mouth of the river. It must have set sail with the departing villagers, leaving Little Water Street nearly deserted of foot traffic. The waterway was similarly vacant except for the lonely, ramshackle barge floating silently on the dark current.

They were headed to the opposite end of the Shambles from the Dead Fish Inn, past Mutineer's Alley and the stone steps that led up to the village proper. Rye eyed Thorn Quill's darkened shop warily as they passed by, but it seemed that Thorn Quill must still be at the Keep.

The old coopery was a sprawling, nondescript warehouse of weathered gray wood, set on an aging pier above the river. It had been converted into a marine supply store, but was shuttered and closed at the moment, there being no mariners in the market for its goods.

Folly led Rye and Quinn down the steep embankment under the shadows of the pier. The river ran high, lapping at their feet. Barnacles climbed the wooden pylons around them, and the air was stale with wood rot. Stacked on their sides, from the river's edge all the way to the top of the embankment and the underside of the pier, stretched a mountain of oaken barrels. The bulging staves of the barrels were covered in mold, straining the metal rings that had turned green with corrosion.

"How long have these been here?" Rye asked, splashing through ankle-deep water to examine them more closely. The bottom row of casks lay half submerged in the brackish river.

"As long as I can remember," Folly said. "It would be quite a job to move them. When Ned Cooper closed shop, the new owners couldn't be bothered. Everyone's more or less forgotten about them."

"But they're full," Rye said. She tried to give one a shove. It wouldn't budge.

Folly placed her ear against a cask and rapped it with her knuckles. "There's definitely *something* in there."

"The river's awfully quiet," Quinn muttered, his eyes on the slow creep of River Drowning's black water.

"So how do we bleed a hogshead?" Rye asked.

"That's what the tools are for," Folly replied with a smile. "Quinn, stop daydreaming and hand me that sack."

Quinn frowned and brought it over. Folly removed a mallet and a wooden tap. She ran her hand over the circular end of one barrel until she found the round keystone near its rim. She licked her thumb and cleared off the caked grime. Rye saw a small X cut into the softer wood of the keystone. Folly lined up the tap and gave a hard swing of the mallet. It dented the hole, but didn't pierce it. Folly set her jaw and swung harder. This time her stroke drove the tap through the keystone, and liquid sputtered and spurted from the seams, trickling down the cask onto the ground.

"Is it blood?" Rye asked, peering at it.

"I don't know," Folly said. "It doesn't smell like rum. Or mead. Maybe we should taste it."

Rye and Folly both turned to Quinn.

"Why me?" Quinn asked in alarm.

"Because you'll eat anything," Folly said.

"No I won't."

"You *are* the only person I know who likes green licorice," Rye added.

"Fine," Quinn said, stepping forward. He dabbed a pinkie into the flowing trickle and touched it to his tongue. He contorted his face and spat it out quickly.

"Blood?" Folly asked excitedly.

"*No*," Quinn said. "But it's strong. Bittersweet. Whatever it is, it's been in that cask far too long."

"Well, it will take forever to drain like this," Folly said. "Give me a hand, Rye."

Rye joined Folly in gripping the tap. They gave it a wiggle and a firm tug, pulling it free. Now the contents of the cask flowed freely out of the new hole.

"Much better," Folly said. "Do you suppose one is enough?"

Rye looked at the mountain of barrels above them. "*Tam's Tome* didn't say. But I'd hate to have to come back and do this again."

"We better get started, then," Folly said. She handed Rye a mallet and tap of her own, then gave another set to Quinn. "Time to use some of those new blacksmith muscles," she said with a smile.

Folly and Quinn got to work, Folly tapping another lower barrel while Quinn climbed atop the casks to work on the ones higher in the stack. Rye examined the mallet in her palm and hesitated. She had never been particularly handy with tools. A shadow over her shoulder caught her attention. The broad wings of a large rook fluttered as it settled on top of a broken pylon not far out in the river. It bobbed its head and watched her with its coal-black eyes.

"Stop looking at me," she muttered in its direction. "You're making me self-conscious."

Rye crouched in the water, careful not to wet the seat of her leggings, and lined up the tap against the keystone of a lower barrel. She stuck her tongue between her teeth in concentration as she readied the mallet. She swung and it bounced off the edge of the tap, sending it scraping down the side of the barrel but causing no real damage.

"Give it a good swat," Folly encouraged. "You're not going to hurt it."

"It's my thumbs I'm worried about," Rye said, lining the tap back up against the keystone.

She gritted her teeth, cocked her arm, and heaved with all her might, as if swinging her cudgel. This time she missed the tap entirely, the head of the mallet cracking right through the circular end of the barrel. The liquid splashed and sprayed out like a fountain.

"That's one way to do it," Quinn said with a chuckle above them. He caught his laugh in his throat as the entire mountain of hogsheads shifted.

Rye watched as her cask imploded in on itself with a crack of wood, the weight of the stack crushing it. Several tumbling barrels crashed and broke themselves, and Quinn leaped from his perch before they could take him with them. The three friends rushed out from under the pier to avoid being flattened. They watched as the rest of the stack came to an uneasy balance, a third of them now broken and scattered in the shallows, dumping their mysterious contents into the river. Several floated off in the current. The rest of the stack remained precariously piled up the embankment.

"This won't take any time at all with your help, Rye," Folly said.

"Look at that," Quinn said pointing to the top of the pier. The solitary rook had been joined by a large flock of companions, much like the one Rye had seen atop the bridge earlier. The black birds took up posts on the pier, hopping about and bobbing their beaks eagerly.

"What do you suppose they're so interested in?" Quinn asked.

"I don't know," Rye said. "But let's finish the job and get out of here before we find out."

They returned under the pier and carefully examined the shifted mountain of casks.

"Maybe if we break the ones right there," Folly said, her hands on her hips, "the rest will roll right in."

But Rye wasn't looking at the oaken barrels. The friends were no longer alone under the pier. Two unblinking, predatory eyes had cracked the surface of the shallows, followed by the head of an enormous reptile.

19 The River Wyvern

The River Wyvern floated toward them as slowly and quietly as a fallen leaf, yet its length was even greater than that of Captain Dent's largest longboat. Rye could see the knotty ridges of its back where they protruded from the water like stepping-stones. Trailing an impossible distance behind, the barbs of a sharp crest on its tail wove silently through the water like a sail. The effect was hypnotic, and Rye, Folly, and Quinn stood in awe, paralyzed with fear.

The spell was broken when the River Wyvern

lurched from the water violently, and the three friends scattered backward, scrambling over several fallen casks.

The beast's forelegs splashed onto the embankment, and a long whip-like tongue snapped out, just missing Rye's arm and sticking to a broken barrel. It recoiled its tongue and chomped the wood between jaws large enough to consume her whole. As the Wyvern dragged itself from the water on four scaly legs, Rye saw it was nearly as tall as a horse, its black, dripping body shimmering almost blue in the fading sunlight that snuck through the cracks of the pier. It cocked its head one way, so that one eye faced them, then the other.

"What's he doing?" Folly asked.

"I think he's . . . measuring us—" Rye began, then gasped and leaped higher up the mountain of barrels as the River Wyvern ambled forward, flicking his tongue. Folly and Quinn did the same without a moment to spare.

The River Wyvern landed on a lower row of barrels. Several collapsed under the reptile's weight and Rye could hear its sharp claws grinding against the casks' metal bindings as it struggled to balance on the uneven surface.

"Keep climbing," Quinn called, and they all clambered higher still.

But the River Wyvern had stabilized itself, and began climbing too. Rye, Folly, and Quinn dropped themselves on their backs at the top of the stack, staring down helplessly at the approaching beast. Rye pressed her feet against the side of a barrel and pushed with her legs.

"Give me a hand . . . or a foot," she croaked, straining her thighs.

Folly and Quinn did the same, rocking the barrel with all their strength. It started to wobble, then it moved and finally rolled under its own weight down the side of the stack until it bounced off the River Wyvern's nose with a thud. The River Wyvern pinched its eyes tight and shook its head as the barrel landed on the embankment with a crack and split open, spilling its contents into the river.

"It didn't like that," Rye cried. "Do it again."

They pushed down another barrel. Then a third. The River Wyvern snapped at the tumbling projectiles with its teeth. Now others began to plummet down on their own, the delicate balance of the stack shifting. The River Wyvern lashed at the rolling casks with its long tail, the tall serrated crest cutting through the air like a sawblade.

Rye climbed to her feet and balanced atop the wooden curves underneath her. "It's working," she called, then lost her breath and fell hard on her backside as the cask rolled out from under her. Quinn grabbed her by the hand and pulled her up, but they all tottered as their footing shifted and rolled beneath them. The mountain of hogsheads was in motion, steadily rolling down toward the agitated River Wyvern.

Rye, Folly, and Quinn struggled from one rolling cask to the next, but no sooner did they gain ground than it disappeared beneath them. The River Wyvern crushed barrels in its jaws and swatted them with its tail. Rye lost her footing again and flung her arms around the rim of a cask just as it toppled down toward the waiting mouth of teeth below her. All around her, the entire stack gave way, and she could only pinch her eyes tight as everything, and everyone, slid and tumbled down the embankment and into the River Drowning.

Rye opened her eyes and found herself floating atop the cask, her arms still clutched around it. She had drifted out from under the pier, the shallow waters that lapped the embankment now littered with broken wooden husks. In the shadow of the pier she could see a monstrous, frenzied thrashing. The River Wyvern splashed and assaulted the barrels that had not already been destroyed, taking out its wrath on its wooden attackers.

With a final angry slap of its tail, it plunged back into the river and eased out into deeper water as silently as it first had come.

As darkness settled over the river, Rye heard a rhythmic ping of metal in the distance. She didn't waste time trying to locate its source, and instead slipped from her perch and hopped through the shallows to dry ground. Folly and Quinn sat damp and haggard on the embankment.

"Are you all right?" Rye asked.

"Splinters," Quinn said with a groan as he examined his elbows. "Lots and lots of splinters."

Folly nodded, her wet hair dripping over eyes.

Rye rushed forward in alarm. "Are you sure?"

"Yes, why?" Folly asked.

"Your hair. It's nearly as red as Lottie's."

Folly's white-blond hair was stained the color of rust. Rye examined her scalp closely but was relieved to find it free of holes or punctures.

Folly pulled a strand down over her nose and crossed her eyes for a better view. "Huh. Must be from the barrels."

"Well, that's one way to drain the hogsheads," Quinn said, looking out over the wreckage around them. A few remaining unbroken casks floated away with the current. "Do you think we need to open more?"

"That's enough for one day," Rye said. "Let's head back before the River Wyvern realizes his belly is still empty."

The rhythmic ping of metal caught her attention again. Closer now. They all turned toward the water. Through the shadows of dusk, a light drifted along the surface, making its way to the shore.

"It's not the Wyvern, is it?" Folly asked in alarm.

"No," Rye said in disbelief. "I think it's . . . a boat."

A small flat skiff eased toward them, a single lantern blazing at its helm. Its passenger set down his oar and stood up in the boat.

Rye had never seen the man before. He had hulking shoulders so thick his neck seemed to disappear into them, and hands as large as baskets. But his eyes were as watery and sullen as an old hound's and the hair on his head looked like an ill-fitted bird's nest. His accent was foreign, yet familiar.

"Which one of you is Rye?" he asked.

Rye and Folly looked at each other, then at Quinn.

"I am," Rye volunteered hesitantly.

"Sum'n wishes to so see you, lass. Get in."

"Someone like who?"

The large man blinked slowly, then turned and pointed to the lights of the barge twinkling on the river. "A very old friend," he said.

Rye was quiet for a moment, a suspicion taking hold. Hopeful but still wary, she narrowed an eye. "I'm not going anywhere without my friends."

The man sighed and stooped over to place a triangular dinner bell and brass striker on the floor of the skiff.

"Fine. I'll make room. But be quick about it. No telling when that river monster is coming back." He extended an enormous palm to help her aboard. "And it's best not to keep the fortune-teller waiting."

20 The Fortune-Teller

The boatman didn't say much as he rowed Rye, Folly, and Quinn out to the fortune-teller's flat-bottomed river barge. Folly's and Quinn's eyes shifted nervously over the water, wary of a reappearance of the River Wyvern, but the river's secrets were shrouded by the dying light.

Rye's curiosity was piqued by her unexpected summoning, and she studied the ramshackle boat as the skiff eased next to it. Its hull was a mosaic patchwork of mismatched wood and scrap-metal sheeting. Paper lanterns lit its long deck, and a dilapidated cabin sprang up from its center, candlelight glowing behind its shrouded portholes. Smoke puffed from a tin spout on its roof, fluttering up past the junk's single mast and crimson sail.

The boatman tied the skiff to the side of the junk and stepped onto the deck, then reached down to assist the children. Rye extended her hand in return, but he simply clutched her under the arms and hoisted her as if she were no heavier than a bucket of grain. He similarly plucked Folly and Quinn from the skiff and deposited them on the deck next to her.

"You two have a seat with me," the boatman told Folly and Quinn, pointing to a wooden bench that ran along the rails. "As for you, you'll find the fortune-teller inside." He thrust a thumb toward tattered silk curtains that hung like cobwebs over the doorway to the cabin.

Folly and Quinn cast concerned glances toward Rye.

"It's okay," Rye reassured. She had a suspicion as to who awaited her. It left her anxious, but not fearful. "I won't be long."

Rye glanced up at the seabirds perched on the rigging before parting the curtains and stepping inside. The interior cabin was a cluttered burrow, the ceiling strung with hanging lights, herbs and kettles, and smelling of dried fish. The floor was covered with worn tapestries and a hodgepodge collection of modest furnishings. A stooped figure huddled over a large cast-iron pot, her silver hair sparkling in the lantern light. She pinched a strange assortment of spices into her simmering cauldron before brushing off her hands and turning to greet her visitor. The face that welcomed Rye was a maze of wrinkles melted by the ages. But when the old woman raised the folds of skin where her eyebrows had once been, sea-glass-flecked eyes twinkled at Rye.

"Hello, Annis," Rye said quietly.

"Fine evening, duckling. Finer now that you are here." Annis's voice was an ancient but pleasant lilt, a remnant of a time and place far away.

"Let me look at you," Annis said, shuffling over to her. With her bent back and hunched shoulders, they met eye to eye. "Your hair's longer than when I last saw you," she said, touching a strand of it with a crooked finger. "And you've lost weight," she added, poking Rye in the ribs in a manner that tickled more than hurt.

Annis stepped back to her kettle and plunged a bowl inside. "Try this," she said, handing it to her.

Rye eyed the steaming potion cautiously. On the Isle of Pest, this withered old woman was called Black Annis—the most fearsome of legendary hags, not to mention Slinister Varlet's mother. But she had also become Rye's unlikely friend.

"What is it?" Rye asked.

Annis dipped a second bowl. "Dinner, dearie. To put some meat back on your bones." Annis sipped it with her thin lips, then flashed Rye a grin that revealed her toothless gums. "What else would it be?"

Rye pressed the bowl to her lips carefully. The rich, creamy broth was a medley of mild fish and flavorful spices.

"It's delicious," Rye said in surprise, and took another long sip.

"I'll send bowls out for your friends, too," Annis said with a pleased nod, and waved a hand to a small table where they both pulled up stools. "Sit."

Annis still wore a simple frock, but now a delicate string of sea glass circled her neck and a matching bracelet dangled from her twig of a wrist.

"I like your jewelry," Rye said.

"These old things?" she said, waving away the compliment, although she was clearly pleased that Rye had noticed. "I was expecting you, so I thought I might gussy up a bit. I don't get much company these days, except for Horace out there and my old feathered companions. Sadly, none of them are much for conversation."

"My friend Folly tells me you've been working as a fortune-teller," Rye said skeptically.

Annis chuckled. "I hate that term. *Fortune-teller* just

screams 'huckster,' wouldn't you say? As you know, I don't stare at crystals or read lines in people's palms. I study eyes . . . and faces." Annis's own eyes narrowed, as if probing Rye's face for clues. "I find omens in everyday events. There's no magic to it if your Sight is keen . . . and you have the patience to look."

Annis held Rye's gaze without saying more. Rye was always terrible at the who-could-stay-quiet-the-longest game. Fortunately, Annis looked away after giving Rye a tight smile, as if she'd already found what she was looking for.

"Whatever you call it, that line of business has dried up like an August mudhole," Annis said. "It's a meager living under the best of circumstances, made even more modest if you don't tell people what they want to hear." She shrugged. "I've always been a bit too forthcoming. Ran into a similar problem on Pest in my youth. Luckily, I don't require much." She spread her frail palms and gestured at their surroundings, her skin the texture of dried leaves.

"Why are you living on this boat?" Rye asked, feeling the rock of its hull underneath them. "Why did you leave Grabstone?"

"I could tell you it was too quiet without the thump of your feet," Annis said with a chuckle. "But the truth is, it's almost time for me to return home, and these old fins won't take me there." Annis wiggled her elbows playfully. "Besides, the gulls tell me there's damp weather on the way. Sometimes, when it gets really wet, a boat's the best place to be."

"Aren't you afraid of the River Wyvern?"

"Of course not, lamb." Annis snorted. "Why would I fret over the wildlife?"

"Oh, I don't know," Rye said dubiously. "In case he gets *hungry*."

"Well, he's *always* hungry, dear," Annis said, as if Rye had just declared that ice was cold. "That's why I have Horace feed him. Sure, it could still choose to eat us, but that would make its breakfast much harder to come by tomorrow . . . and the day after." Annis gave a dismissive wave. "Reptiles aren't the brightest creatures, but they're not stupid either."

When she put it that way, it did make some sense.

"Horace is your helper?" she asked.

Annis nodded. "You wouldn't know it by looking at him, but he too has the makings of an Intuitive. I've taken him under my wing, so to speak. I help show him how to see, and in exchange he fetches supplies and mans the boat."

Annis sipped her bowl and licked her lips with a tongue that was more purple than pink. A keen eye flickered in Rye's direction.

"So tell me, gosling," Annis said, in a tone that signaled it was finally time to get to why she'd brought Rye here. "How is *your* Sight? Share with me what you've seen and I'll do the same."

"Little in my dreams, if that's what you mean. I don't sleep well, and when I do my dreams are dark and murky. But I've found Harmless." Rye hesitated. "And Slinister, too."

Annis just nodded in reply, as if Rye needn't say more.

"You've seen Slinister? I mean . . . Slynn?" Rye asked.

"Not with my eyes," Annis said, sharing a somber smile. "I know that he's holed up in that dreadful Keep not far from here. I called on him myself but he refused to see me, his henchmen denying me entrance at the gates. That was many months ago. So I wait."

"That's why you've stayed here in Drowning?" Rye asked. "In hopes he might change his mind?"

"That boy won't change his mind," Annis said. "I'm just waiting for events to run their course."

"But do you already know his fate?" Rye asked, leaning forward across the small table. "Do you already know Harmless's? It seems the two are tied together."

"What is fate but the result of a series of choices?" Annis asked in return. "Each choice you make takes you one step closer to your fortune."

Annis leaned forward so that her face was close to Rye's.

"Sight . . . perception . . . it's all just an ability to guess what choices a person will make along the way. If you watch closely enough, you begin to recognize the patterns. Certain types of men and women are likely to make similar decisions, and those decisions are more likely to lead to a given outcome. But, remember," she said, raising a finger. "Everyone has a choice."

Rye tried to divine the meaning in Annis's sea-flecked eyes but they remained as unfathomable as the ocean. She wondered whether Annis was referring to Slinister, Harmless, or herself.

"You told me that things will get worse before they get better," Rye said.

Annis gave her the slightest nod.

"Worse than this? I hardly recognize Drowning anymore. Bog Noblins have gathered to overrun the village, Harmless and Slinister seem determined to destroy each other, and in the meantime the villagers have no one to help them with their struggle."

Annis just returned Rye's earnest look with a sad smile. Her silence was answer enough.

"Back in the Bellwether, you told me I could change the ending," Rye exclaimed, slapping her palms on the table. "You said I just needed to be willing to pay the toll. What's the toll, Annis? Please help me understand."

Annis sat back and clasped her fingers. She cast her gaze to the bowl of soup in front of her, blinking eyes that seemed suddenly weary. "Sight is a cruel gift indeed," she muttered to herself, then looked up.

"A storm is coming. Someone dear to you will be swallowed by it. That's the toll. Who that will be, I cannot say, because there are still choices yet to be made."

Rye felt the color drain from her face.

"Finish your soup, minnow," Annis said kindly. "A warm belly will help you sleep soundly, and ensure that your dreams remain sweet. Even if just for a short while . . ."

Rye left the cabin, the web-like silk shroud falling over her heavy shoulders. Folly and Quinn were at the rails of the junk with Horace. Quinn held an enormous dead fish by the tail and Folly clutched a metal striker excitedly.

She watched her friends' cheerful faces. She would get around to telling them about Annis, but not now. Her fatigue left her nearly speechless, like she was dragging an impossible weight. She couldn't bring herself to think about the toll.

"Rye!" Quinn called. "You won't believe this. We're feeding the River Wyvern."

Horace gestured to Folly. She reached up to the hanging dinner bell and rapped the metal triangle with her striker.

"Go on," Horace said to Quinn. "Give it a good toss."

Quinn hoisted the fish with both hands and hurled it over the side, the force of his throw spinning him in a circle, and he found himself deposited backside-first on the deck. Folly let loose a belly laugh that Quinn, and even Horace, couldn't help joining.

After two more offerings to the River Wyvern, Horace rowed them back to shore without incident. The three friends made their way to the Dead Fish Inn and slipped inside undetected. Folly set Quinn up in a vacant guestroom and soon joined Rye at the window of her bedchamber. The black water continued to flow leisurely under the bridge and toward the sea. The surface wasn't broken by fish, gull, or mythical River Wyvern. Only the dim lanterns of Annis's junk bobbed on the surface.

"Can you see anything out there?" Folly asked hopefully. "Any sign or signal?"

Rye shook her head.

"Well, that was underwhelming," Folly said, and bit her lip. "I hope we got it right."

"I read the same thing you did, Folly. I don't think we missed anything. I mean, *Tam's Tome* didn't say what would happen *after* we emptied the hogsheads."

Still, it *was* perplexing. When she'd lit the Luck Cauldrons, they had flared blue, their smoky plumes racing into the sky like ghostly tendrils. Rye would have thought that a Call for the Reckoning, one meant for all Luck Uglies near and far, would be much more impressive.

"Let's give it an hour," Rye said, "then check again."

Folly slumped from the window and collapsed on her bed. Rye followed her lead and deposited herself in her blankets on the floor with every intention of waiting out the hour. But after their grueling day, both friends soon drifted off, the bedchamber silent but for their snores.

Rye dreamed of her friends—of those days that seemed so carefree, when they'd played in Drowning's alleys and graveyards. She had visions of catching salamanders with Lottie at the edge of the bogs—before they crawled with Bog Noblins. She could feel Abby's warm embrace and taste her bumbleberry pie. And, more recently, she remembered leaping across rooftops, hand in hand with Harmless, before she had ever heard of Slinister Varlet or Fork-Tongue Charmers.

When Rye awoke, the room streamed with the light of a new day, and for a moment, it seemed that everything she'd seen and heard the night before was part of her dreams. She heard the muffled squawk of Baby Fox down the hall, crying for his breakfast or a linen change.

"Rye, Folly!" a breathless voice called from the door. "Come out here. You need to see this."

It was Quinn. Rye rubbed her eyes and Folly stumbled out of her bed. They joined Quinn on a small terrace overlooking Little Water Street. Rye blinked hard to be sure the sun's reflection wasn't playing tricks on her.

"Do you think we accidentally poisoned the River Wyvern?" Folly asked.

Rye shook her head in disbelief. "I think we'd have to poison a hundred of them to do that."

Stretching before them, upstream and downstream as far as the eye could see, and continuing under the bridge and into the ocean itself, the River Drowning flowed red as blood.

Echoes of a Distant Call

Rye and Quinn sat on the edge of the great arched bridge, Rye's oversize boots dangling over the unseemly red waters far below them. They weren't alone. Despite their fears of the River Wyvern, curiosity compelled many villagers to come see the river for themselves, and speculation ran rampant as to what the ominous changes might mean.

"I never seen anyt'ing like it," a stone carver said. "The river was its normal color just last night. A nice brackish swill."

"It's an omen," a straw-haired peddler warned. "A warning. Them Bog Noblins are coming and it won't be long now."

Rye and Quinn exchanged glances before quickly turning their eyes downward, trying to disappear.

Another villager speculated that it was a curse, while still others suggested it was evidence of some unknown tragedy far upstream.

"I've seen it like this once before," a weaver woman croaked over the banter. She looked nearly as old as Annis. "Long ago, when I was a wee girl, River Drowning bled for a whole week."

The stone carver and peddler turned to her in surprise.

"Was it an omen?" the peddler asked. "Did the Bog Noblins follow?"

The weaver shook her head of gray hair. "Not Bog Noblins. Worse."

The other villagers' eyes went wide.

"Worse indeed," she muttered with a click of her teeth. She pulled her shawl snug over her shoulders and hurried off with urgency, the peddler and stone carver chasing after her with questions.

A smaller villager in a green wool head wrap pushed past them and dropped herself next to Rye and Quinn.

"Where did you dig up that old thing?" Rye asked,

noticing the scarf-like material covering her ears and neck. Only Folly's blue eyes and lips peeked out.

Folly frowned and tugged a fold aside with her finger, giving them a glimpse of her hair. Although no longer the crimson of the night before, it had turned the color of wild roses.

"I tried soaking it in vinegar. Don't think it's much better."

"I'll say," Quinn said, crinkling his nose at the smell. "Did you get a look at the river water?"

Folly reached into her cloak and retrieved a small stoppered vial filled with red liquid that matched the River Drowning. She held it in her lap between her fingers where only Rye and Quinn could see.

"It's not blood—but we knew that already. I compared it to some of the ingredients I keep for my experiments. Beet juice, elderberry, madder root. It looks like it could be any one of them—or all of them mixed together."

"Vegetable dyes?" Rye asked.

Folly nodded. "Whoever filled those hogsheads knew exactly what they were doing. Blend the extracts together, set them with salt or vinegar and let them age for years, if not decades. They created a remarkably powerful dye."

"And enough of it to stain an entire river," Rye said,

staring at the sight below them.

"The current will take it into the ocean," Quinn said. "I bet it will form a slick up and down the coast for miles."

"You can be sure they'll be gossiping about this in taverns from Trowbridge to Throcking . . . and beyond," Folly added, and with her words Rye finally understood the full implications of the message.

"*That's* the magic of the Call," Rye marveled. It was simple, but deceptively clever. The message might stretch as far as the great river's reach, but word of mouth would take it even farther. The Call would be spread unknowingly by men and women near and far, and yet its true meaning would only be heard by those for whom it was intended. The Luck Uglies.

"We got it right after all," Rye said in relief.

"What do we do now?" Quinn asked.

"Now's the hardest part," Rye said, and Folly and Quinn looked to her hesitantly. She sighed and crossed her arms.

"We wait."

Over the next several days, the huff over the river died down as the village grew accustomed to, if no less discomfited by, its new landscape. While the water was not as deep bloodred as that first morning, it was still a rich sanguine and stained the boots, beaks, and claws of any man, bird, or beast who came into contact with it. Rye resisted her urge to return to her family at the bog hopper's shack, and instead stayed with Folly at the inn as Harmless had instructed. Quinn remained a regular presence at the Dead Fish between his trips to and from the Quartermasts' cottage and the blacksmith's shop. He also brought with him news of the bogs. There had been another Bog Noblin raid in Nether Neck. A house destroyed on Apothecary Row. A long, white-knuckled evening on Mud Puddle Lane as Rye's and Quinn's neighbors sat by their windows, eyeing two large Bog Noblins who had taken up positions at the far end of the dirt road. The beasts didn't attack, they just stalked the street quietly as if watching and waiting, until finally disappearing back into the woods with the arrival of dawn.

Rye hadn't heard from Truitt or the link children, and wasn't eager to venture back into the Spoke alone. But just because she'd promised Harmless she'd stay in Drowning didn't mean she was staying put. Each day she accompanied Quinn to Market Street. While he helped his father at the forge, Rye set her fingers to the cracks and crevices of an alley wall. The rooftops had once made her uncomfortable, but she had since spent many hours navigating their unlikely pathways with Harmless. Sometimes the roofs could offer a welcome relief from Drowning's claustrophobic streets and alleys. No matter how dense and crowded her village could sometimes seem, from its highest reaches it was clear that Drowning was little more than an outpost against the backdrop of the river and sprawling bogs, the rolling western woods, and the looming endless forest Beyond the Shale.

But the unique vantage point provided Rye with little clarity or reassurance. Slinister was surely one of the first to hear of the Call, and yet Longchance Keep remained still. No new arrivals appeared in the fields or meadows—never mind an entire brotherhood of Luck Uglies. And most importantly, she had seen no sign of Harmless. Rye began to wonder if the Call for the Reckoning had gone ignored, or worse. Perhaps she had indeed summoned it incorrectly after all.

On the fifth day following the Call, Rye found a high eave in the shadows of the village's tallest bell tower and its rusting whale weather vane. She nestled between two stone gargoyles, slinging her pack around a sharp-toothed guardian's neck so that it hung like a scarf. Harmless had taught her that rooftops could be unpredictable. Shingles weakened and beams rotted—those hidden pitfalls were more dangerous than falling off the edge itself. But any section of roof that could still hold the stone sculptures was likely to be able to support her weight as well.

She'd managed to reassemble her spyglass. With little optimism, she extended it to get a better look over the village walls.

But this time what lay before her caused Rye to spring to her feet.

Small ships ringed the coastline at the mouth of the river, their black leather sails fluttering like insects in the briny wind. In the distant shadows of Longchance Keep, dark shapes inched across Grim Green until finally gathering in loose clusters. Rye recognized them for what they were—horse-drawn carts and carriages. As the day wore on, pinpoints of fire sparked up around the Green and smoke drifted up from the new encampments.

"Rye, there you are," Quinn said, as he pulled himself over the gable of a roof and carefully stepped down toward her. "It's getting late. We should head back to the inn."

Rye lowered the spyglass. She was excited, but anxious at the same time.

"What is it?" he asked.

"Look for yourself," she said, handing him the spyglass. "The Luck Uglies are gathering outside of Drowning."

❦ ❦ ❦

Rumor of the mysterious new arrivals on Grim Green had reached the Dead Fish Inn by the time Rye and Quinn returned, and Faye Flood quickly whipped her sons into action in anticipation of some much-needed business. She slapped aprons on Fifer and Fallow, Folly's brothers closest to her in age, both of whom were dozing with their boots up on a table.

"What about Folly?" Fifer grumbled.

"Worry about yourself," Faye scolded. "Folly's minding Fox. Last time *you* watched your brother, you forgot where you put him."

Fallow grumbled. Faye handed their baby brother to Folly, and she strapped him into a harness she'd rigged over her chest. Fox didn't seem to mind, his chubby arms and legs dangling like a puppet's.

Folly joined Rye and Quinn. Rye tickled Fox's toes.

"You two better stay out of sight before my mother puts you to work plucking chickens for tonight's stew."

The three friends were interrupted by the call of the twins to their father from the inn's doors. Fletcher joined Fitz and Flint in the frame of the great portals, and Rye, Folly, and Quinn eased their noses between them for a better look.

Outside, the stillness of the Shambles was interrupted by the clop of hooves as a horse mucked its way down Little Water Street. It was a somber black animal with a body built for work over speed, and behind it rattled a squat, covered carriage with dark veils drawn over its windows. Atop the driver's box sat a stoic man in a wide-brimmed black hat with a kerchief over his face.

"Grave Sweeper," Fitz said.

"Strange to see one here," Flint added.

"You haven't gotten rough with any of the neighbors, have you?" Fletcher asked.

"Of course not. It's been months," Fitz said.

"Or at least weeks," Flint clarified.

"Hmmm," they all grunted together.

The Grave Sweeper's carriage rumbled to a stop, and something hopped down from the driver's box. Rye, Folly, and Quinn stared at the ground and averted their eyes. Even the twins looked away. Every villager in Drowning knew that to meet the gaze of a Grave Sweeper meant the foulest of luck—that he would soon be coming for you.

But it wasn't the Grave Sweeper himself who approached the inn. Instead, a hairy little creature in a tiny matching hat, kerchief, and long leather duster ambled toward the doors, its tail trailing behind. Before Fitz and Flint could move to stop it, it darted between their legs, into the inn.

Rye, Folly, and Quinn turned in surprise. It pushed

up from its knuckles and, hands on its hips, inspected the inn with keen black eyes under the wide brim of its hat. Finding what it was looking for—or perhaps not finding it—it scurried back to the doors, pulled the kerchief from over its face, and screeched, pointy white teeth flashing in its furry mouth.

The Grave Sweeper's companion was a monkey—a surly simian that Rye knew well. That meant someone else she knew couldn't be far behind. She pushed past the twins just as Bramble Cutty stepped down from the driver's box. She rushed out to meet him, Quinn and Folly close behind.

"Bramble!" Rye called, no longer fearful of the Grave Sweeper's gaze as she threw her arms around her uncle.

"Greetings, niece," he said, mussing her hair with his hand cheerfully. "You look well. You, too, Quinn and Foppy," he said, offering just enough of a sly smile to make Folly wonder whether he'd really forgotten her name again or was just having a go with her.

"I love your new scarf," he told her, tickling Fox's toe, where it dangled from the harness on Folly's chest. "You'll have to tell me where you came by it."

Bramble noticed Rye eyeing the Grave Sweeper's carriage.

"In case you were wondering," Bramble said, with a nod to his ride, "this isn't a permanent line of work for me. I, shall we say, 'persuaded' Trowbridge's real Grave Sweeper to let me assume his post for a bit. It's come in handy. You'd be surprised how many secrets the dead can reveal."

Rye squirmed at the thought of the carriage's cargo.

"It's also a perfect way to hide in plain sight," Bramble added. "Superstitions can be useful. Nobody—not even a Fork-Tongue Charmer—will look the Grave Sweeper in the eyes."

Rye knew that Bramble himself had been in hiding in recent months. Having deceived Slinister in support of Harmless, his well-being had been as precarious as Harmless's own.

"How have you been?" Rye asked. "So much has happened that I need to tell you—"

"In time, Riley," he said. "As happy as you are to see me, I have a little surprise you'll be interested in seeing first."

He approached the carriage door and opened it with a flourish. Rye recoiled. She had no interest in seeing *that.*

But the Grave Sweeper's carriage did not hold its usual cargo. Instead, Abby and Lottie O'Chanter climbed down onto Little Water Street, their smiles wide. Harmless followed, holding the side of the door with one hand as he eased himself carefully to the ground. The color had not yet returned to his face, but his gray eyes were warm as they met Rye's own. Even Mr. Nettle poked his woolly chin from inside, sniffing the air and blinking widely under the curled horns of his goat skullcap at the tall inn above him.

22 Truths of the High Chieftain

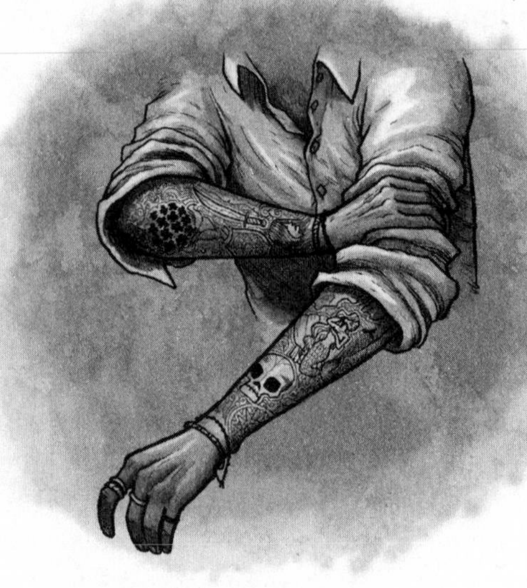

For the first time since Rye had returned to Drowning, the Dead Fish Inn didn't feel cold and empty. The presence of Rye's extended family—those related by blood and by friendship—warmed her more than the heat of the lamb shanks sizzling over the fire.

Plates were emptied and goblets refilled. After a long meal and carefree reunion, Bramble and Shortstraw set up a card game with Fletcher, the twins, and Folly's other oldest brothers. The younger Flood boys arm wrestled and jousted among themselves, sure to break a great number of dishes before their competition was done. Abby and Faye doted over little Fox, and were soon joined by Lottie, who seemed delighted to finally find someone smaller than herself around the inn. Mr. Nettle had donned his usual cheerful face, despite the itchy hives that plagued him every time he approached Drowning.

Rye sat with Harmless at the Mermaid's Nook, where, as was his habit, he kept his back to the wall, eyes watching all that transpired around them. Folly and Quinn fidgeted awkwardly, alone now with Harmless again for the first time. Rye knew that her friends recognized the changes in him. The old scars on his face loomed whiter against his cheekbones; the scruff of his beard was flecked as silver as a frosty meadow. She saw Quinn's eyes move to the sling that held Harmless's wounded arm, then dart away as if he'd spied something he shouldn't. Before Rye could say anything to help put them at ease, Harmless beat her to it.

"Folly, Quinn, it's so wonderful to see you both." He leaned forward, offering a broad smile. "Quinn, you've grown taller since we last spoke. You'll be as strapping as your father in no time. How's that hand treating you?"

"It doesn't hurt, but now I've got this." Quinn reached out, displaying the back of his hand where a discolored scar fanned across his skin—remnants of a jellyfish sting on the Isle of Pest.

Harmless whistled. "That's a beauty. Would you like to see my latest?" He pushed aside the loose fabric of his sling to reveal the skin of his damaged arm.

Rye shook her head adamantly in hopes of drawing Harmless's attention, but it was too late. Quinn had already caught sight of the angry red lattice of scar tissue cutting through Harmless's tattoos. Quinn's face lost its color and he looked like he might fall out of his chair.

"Yes, well, just a nick really," Harmless said, quickly covering it back up.

"And you, Folly," he said, turning his attention to her. He looked at her and paused, smiling at her hair that had now faded to light pink. "You look . . . different as well."

Folly swirled her hair around a finger and her cheeks flushed as rosy as her locks.

Rye gave Folly a sympathetic smile. "Folly and Quinn helped drain the hogsheads for the Call. Whatever was in there, it stained more than just the river," she said.

"In some realms," Harmless said, "hair the color of wild roses is worn by women of great wisdom."

"Really?" Folly asked, brightening. "Where are those places?"

"Oh, far away," Harmless said, waving his fingers

vaguely. "Very far from here." He grinned. "In any case, with your bravery and quick thinking, you have both once again done the High Chieftain a great service."

Folly and Quinn beamed. Harmless pressed himself against the table and gestured for them to come closer, mischief in his eyes. They leaned forward on their elbows.

"Unfortunately, my recent travels have left me without any reward to offer," he whispered. "But do you still have the gifts I gave you last time?"

"Do we?!" Quinn exclaimed.

"Shhh. You must be discreet," Harmless said, putting a finger to his lips and glancing around the inn.

"Do we?" Quinn repeated quietly. "Of course." He pulled the wooden stickman from the pocket and set it on the table.

"Ah yes, the twig boy . . . ," Harmless began.

"The Strategist's Sticks," Quinn said.

"Indeed," Harmless affirmed with a nod. "And if it isn't the . . . shrunken head," he added, as Folly pulled the silver chain from under her shirt to display the tiny skull strung on its end.

"The Alchemist's Bone," Folly said proudly.

"Yes," Harmless said with a smile. "I'm glad to see you've kept them safe. So tell me. What of their powers? Have you felt any effects yet?"

"The Alchemist's Bone is working," Quinn said enthusiastically. "Folly has the finest alchemy lab in all of Drowning right upstairs. She made mushrooms into a glowing paste that lit up the night sky of Pest. And she has a real knack for smoke and fire."

"Explosions are a bit of a specialty," Folly said with a shrug. "But the Strategist's Sticks are working even better. It was Quinn's plan to use the glowing mushrooms to disguise Pest's sheep as Shellycoats. And he's the one who finally deciphered the hidden message in *Tam's Tome*. Whenever we get stuck on a problem, Quinn and those sticks always seem to figure it out."

"I knew I put those gifts in the right hands," Harmless said, reaching across the table to clap them both on the wrists. "You've had them for barely a year, and look at what you've done already. Keep at your toils, and there's no telling what you can accomplish."

He sat back in his chair.

Folly perked up with new motivation. "I think I'll go gather some more ingredients for an experiment," she said. "I've heard of a potion that can melt metal locks. Want to help, Quinn?"

"Sure," he said.

"Rye?"

"I'll join in just a bit," Rye answered, and grinned as

her friends hurried off to scour the inn for hazardous substances.

The card players had broken into shouts and good-natured guffaws. Predictably, Bramble and Shortstraw won, but her uncle knew better than to set the stakes so high that he might wear out his welcome. Abby and Faye laughed and clapped their hands as Fox gummed Lottie's red hair. Miraculously, Lottie didn't protest, and pretended she was being devoured by a ravenous wolf.

As much as the good spirits of her friends and loved ones had lifted Rye's mood, Annis's ominous words now crept back even heavier as she watched them. What toll lay in store for them and Village Drowning?

"What burden sits on your shoulders, Riley?" Harmless asked quietly. His eyes studied her own. "I dare say you have the weariest face in all of Drowning." He offered a kind smile. "Next to mine."

Rye hesitated before answering.

"Folly and Quinn understate how much they've truly done with the gifts you gave them," she said. "They may not even realize it themselves. But without their skills, the Isle of Pest would have been conquered. The residents of Mud Puddle Lane would be left without food and medicine. This Call would never have been sounded. I doubt I'd even be sitting here right now without them—they've picked me up more times than I can count."

Rye reached down and stuffed both hands into an oversize boot. She removed the iron anklet Harmless had given her, placing it on the table.

"The Anklet of the Shadowbender," Harmless said quietly.

"I've squandered this," she said. "Folly and Quinn have worked so hard to unlock their gifts, and all I've done is stumble into one mess after another."

"Is that really what you believe?" Harmless asked.

"Isn't it obvious?" Rye said. It seemed that half her troubles were of her own making.

"Well," Harmless said, leaning forward again. "I see something else entirely. I saw a girl save an entire village because she wasn't afraid to break the rules to protect others. I saw a daughter reunite an entire island where a legendary village elder and her own mother could not. How? By doing the unthinkable: cutting the bonds that kept them apart, even at the risk of earning their wrath." His gray eyes held her gaze. "And before me I now see a young woman who has picked *me* up more than once, by being tenacious, and clever, and yes, more than a little impulsive from time to time. But the truth is, *I* wouldn't be sitting here right now without you. That you cannot deny."

Rye bit her lip. "But the anklet was supposed to allow me to disappear into shadows, to hurdle rooftops and travel as stealthily as a fox. Like you."

"Is that what it was meant to do?" Harmless asked, raising an eyebrow. "Do you remember my words when I gave it to you? I do, because I chose them carefully."

Rye recalled them. "You said the anklet would allow me to bend the laws of shadow and light," she recited.

"That's correct. And the reason why I chose them is because of what your grandfather once said to me. They were his last words, in fact. As Grimshaw lay there, and the High Chieftain's Crest passed from him to me in his final breath, he whispered this . . ."

Harmless's voice was a winter breeze.

"There are no such things as heroes. After all, for every man we call a hero, is he not cursed as our enemies' greatest villain? So don your mask, young master. Don't be afraid to bend the laws of shadow and light. And leave it to history to brand you as it deems fit."

Rye blinked, processing the strange words.

"It means a leader's choices are sometimes impossible ones," Harmless explained. "The right decision may not be best, and the best decision can be both right and wrong. So a real hero can only follow her heart."

Rye picked up the anklet and examined its runes between her fingers.

"Was this Grimshaw's? Did he give it to you?"

Harmless smiled. "Ah, well. Truth be told, I never saw that anklet until the day we plucked it from Leatherleaf's Luck Bag."

Rye's jaw dropped.

"Same with Quinn's stickman and Folly's skull," he added, with a sheepish shrug.

Rye had once suspected that Harmless might be exaggerating the charms' powers. But for him to admit it now, after all she'd seen them accomplish, seemed too hard to comprehend.

"But you said they were great heirlooms, powerful talismans. You said they were magic."

"I told you there were many different types of magic," Harmless clarified. "But neither you, nor Folly nor Quinn, derived your talents from these charms. That magic, your unique abilities, they're already within each of you. All you needed was something to believe in. And, sometimes, it's easier to believe in a charm or a totem than it is to believe in ourselves. So maybe, in that respect, there's some magic in them after all."

Rye was silent, taking in Harmless's words.

A shadow over her shoulder told her they were no

longer alone, and she looked up to find Bramble standing over them.

"A messenger was sent to Longchance Keep," he said quietly to Harmless. "He's just returned."

"What was Slinister's reply?" Harmless asked.

"He and the Fork-Tongue Charmers ride to Grim Green."

Harmless nodded. "Thank you, Bramble. If you ready the carriage, we'll leave shortly."

"Of course," he said, and placed a hand on Rye's shoulder. He gave her a wink of a pale blue eye before leaving.

"What's happening at Grim Green?" Rye asked.

"Slinister and I will meet face-to-face in the presence of our brothers," Harmless said, slowly rotating a platinum ring on the thumb of his injured hand as he spoke. "And if all goes well, we shall set the terms of the Reckoning."

"What sort of terms?" Rye asked, noticing that the ring was in fact a single thick nail—one that had been hammered and twisted to suit its new purpose.

Harmless gave her a reassuring smile. "Don't fret about them now, Riley. You'll hear them for yourself tonight."

Rye sat up in surprise. "Hear them? I'll be there?"

He nodded again. "You. Your mother. Lottie, too."

Rye couldn't believe what he was saying. "But we're not Luck Uglies."

"No, but you are the family of the High Chieftain." Harmless's jaw was tight. "And the results of the Reckoning shall affect us all."

A Murder of Uglies

Rye peered out the window of the Grave Sweeper's carriage as it bounced over uneven terrain. The O'Chanters rode in silence, Harmless's gray eyes flickering in thoughts somewhere far away, and even Lottie sat quietly, occasionally whispering soothing words to Mona Monster as the doll bounced on her knee. Rye picked her fingernails in her lap as she struggled to spot any sign of their destination in the darkness. Abby placed a reassuring hand over Rye's busy fingers. Abby wore her crimson cloak and tall leather boots, her black hair falling freely past her shoulders. If she shared Rye's concerns she didn't show it, and her mother's slight smile gave Rye some momentary comfort.

Shadows shifted outside and flickers of light flared along their path. Soon the coach rattled to a stop. Rye heard voices and felt the weight of the coach shift. She craned her neck, and thought she could make out the lanterns of a towering fortress atop a nearby crag. Longchance Keep. A path of torches slowly snaked its way down a rocky trail, and the O'Chanters sat silently inside the carriage for a long while.

Finally, the carriage's door opened and Bramble's eyes met hers from under his hood. He reached up to help her down. Harmless gave her a nod and she climbed out carefully, Abby and Lottie behind her.

They were in Grim Green, amid a temporary settlement built up around a roaring bonfire. A ragged black banner hung loose from a tall spike in the still air. Torches marked a wide perimeter, a crude fence of sharpened timbers erected around a cluster of tents and a makeshift paddock. Rye could smell the horses and the sizzling spits of dozens of small cook fires. All around them men had set aside their tasks and stood warily at attention. Rye looked for familiar faces, but the shadows of their cowls betrayed few secrets.

Bramble led Rye, Abby, and Lottie to a spot at the

edge of the assembly. Some of the gathered Luck Uglies nodded at Abby in recognition, and she placed her hands on Rye's and Lottie's shoulders and pulled them close.

Rye's eyes darted around the clearing, her heart quickening. She felt it lurch in her chest when she recognized one face, bright and defiant, at the far side of the circle. Slinister stared back at her, the bonfire reflecting off his crystal eyes. They were Annis's eyes, except where Annis's twinkled with wisdom, Slinister's flickered with menace. Behind him were the Fork-Tongue Charmers, their cheeks freshly streaked with white ash, lips blackened with soot. Rye spotted the Charmer named Lassiter at Slinister's side, as well as the shorter figure of Hyde nearby.

Thankfully, Slinister broke off his glare at the sight of Harmless. Slinister's jaw remained stoic, but Rye saw the slightest twitch of his lip over his knotted beard.

Harmless climbed down from the Grave Sweeper's carriage. His thick fur cloak was wrapped tightly around him, giving great breadth to his shoulders and obscuring the injured arm. His hood was the pelt of a wolf, its sharp teeth low over his forehead like a crown. He marched to the center of the clearing with all the menace of a great forest predator.

The Luck Uglies remained silent. Then, from the

crowd stepped a thick-chested warrior. He lowered his cowl, revealing an imposing face framed by long hair and a neatly trimmed beard the color of stout.

"High Chieftain," he said, with a bow of his head.

"Well met, Morrow," Harmless replied, clasping the man by the forearm. "It's been too long. I know you've traveled far and swiftly to be here."

"Of course," Morrow said. "We heard news of the Call for a Reckoning. It's a call none of us here have been asked to answer before, but we came without delay."

Harmless stepped away, lowering his wolf's head hood as he circled to look at the assembled Luck Uglies. "Yes, it's unfortunate that so many of us are reunited for the first time under such circumstances. But let it be known that it was I who summoned the Reckoning."

There was a physical stirring among the Luck Uglies, but no one spoke. Finally, the Luck Ugly named Morrow broke the silence.

"That news is surprising, as we were told that you fled into the forest Beyond the Shale," he said, casting a glare toward Slinister and the Fork-Tongue Charmers. He hesitated. "And that you'd missed a Call."

Harmless approached Morrow and met the taller man's eyes. His jaw was hard, but his glare harder. "All true," he said simply.

There was more rustling among the other men. They

cast glances to one another.

"Although . . . ," Harmless said, raising a finger and stepping away. He turned and faced the assembled crowd. "Those two simple statements, while correct, do not tell the whole story."

"The code is absolute," Slinister called out, his voice as brisk as the autumn air. The Luck Uglies turned their attention to him. "No more of the story matters."

"I'd like to hear what he has to say, Slinister," Morrow fired back. "After all, he is still the High Chieftain." He looked to Harmless. "We were told that you had been found in the forest, and laid to rest in the bogs."

Harmless shrugged. "Despite my means of transport this evening"—he gestured to the Grave Sweeper's carriage—"news of my demise was spread . . . prematurely."

A cold breeze cut across Grim Green, rustling the tattered folds of the black banner.

Harmless's icy glare caught Slinister's eyes. "But Slinister is correct in one respect. The rest of the story is of little matter now. Those of you who have been in and around Drowning already know what has transpired. And those who have traveled from far and wide need know only this. There is a division within the Luck Uglies. What started long ago as a rift between Slinister and myself has grown into an unbridgeable chasm in the brotherhood. As we gather here tonight, those who remain loyal to me and those who are loyal to Slinister would just as soon cut each other's throats as stand side by side."

The Fork-Tongue Charmers looked to one another, then across at the other Luck Uglies on the opposite side of the clearing.

"I could hold court here, and recite all of Slinister's wrongdoings, to try to convince you of his treachery." Harmless walked to Slinister, paused, and stared him hard in the eye. Slinister's gaze was unflinching, but his hand shifted slightly, as if ready to defend himself. "But something tells me half of you would remain unconvinced. And surely Slinister could detail a litany of my offenses, for I am not without my own shortcomings."

Harmless strode back to the center of the circle. "Or, I could exert my will," he growled, his voice rising. "My undeniable and absolute right as High Chieftain." His tone chilled Rye, and she saw that Harmless's eyes had turned furious, flaring as he now stomped around the ring of Luck Uglies, glowering at each of them. "And demand that you follow my lead as you have sworn to do."

He pushed aside his cloak and clawed open the buttons of his shirt so that the tattooed crest on his chest was visible to all he passed.

Rye saw some of the Luck Uglies avert their eyes to the ground. When Harmless spoke next the rage in his voice had shifted like the wind, and his tone was once again measured.

"But I suspect, were I to do that, I would still lose half of you. And we would be no better off than we are now."

Harmless stood silently for a long while.

"This brotherhood does not survive on half measures. As it now stands, we are nothing more than the loose band of outlaws and mercenaries the world has always called us. If I could step aside and bestow the High Chieftain's Crest upon an heir I would do so, if it might salvage this mess. But, alas, I have no sons"—he looked to Rye and Lottie—"only two extraordinary daughters." Rye saw that Harmless smoldered with pride, not disappointment. "So it seems that to preserve the brotherhood, Slinister and I must resolve our differences between ourselves."

Harmless drew a blade from the two scabbards at his back. He marched toward Slinister purposefully, and Rye tensed. Would they come to blows right now? The other Luck Uglies sensed it too and shifted uncertainly. Morrow looked as if he might step between them.

But as Harmless reached striking distance, Rye was surprised to see him throw his sword down flat on the ground at Slinister's feet. Harmless looked up, and held Slinister's jewel-like eyes.

"I call for a Reckoning," he said. "Slinister and I shall reconcile our differences tomorrow night, under the light of the full moon." Harmless pointed to the black banner. The wind had kicked up, and in its tattered folds Rye could now see the white silhouette of crossed swords and a four-leaf clover. "Whoever first raises the Ragged Clover atop the highest bell tower in Drowning shall earn the right to be called High Chieftain. And the rest shall agree to follow the victor's lead."

A murmur rumbled over the onlookers. Slinister looked surprised, then struggled to hide a smile.

"While you and I can set the terms of our own Reckoning," Slinister said, "such a prize would require the consent of the brotherhood. The full moon is nearly upon us, and some of our more far-flung brothers likely will not arrive in time to weigh in."

"Look around," Harmless replied. "By my count we have two thirds—a full Murder of Uglies. That's enough to approve what I propose."

Harmless reached under his cloak and removed the platinum nail-turned-ring from his weakened hand. He held it up between his thumb and forefinger, the ring glinting in the torchlight. "Shall we vote?"

Slinister smiled darkly. He unsheathed the blade

from his hip and laid it across Harmless's on the ground. "I accept your Reckoning," he said, and slid an identical ring from his own thumb. "And its terms."

Slinister pitched his ring onto the swords, where it bounced off the top blade with a clank of metal. Harmless nodded and did the same.

"Cast your rings," Harmless said, looking over his shoulder.

Nobody moved for a long while, then a solitary figure emerged from the pack. Bramble pushed his long black hair behind his ears, and his pale blue eyes bore into Slinister as he approached.

Slinister's face darkened at the sight of him. Bramble removed his own platinum ring and tossed it onto the swords, then stepped away and stood at Harmless's side. Another figure followed. His enormous girth stretched the limits of his belt, and the woolly beard on his chin and neck gave him the look of a lumbering bear. Rye had to shake her head to be sure the firelight wasn't deceiving her. It was the angry poet who had once chased her across Drowning's rooftops.

The poet tossed a platinum ring into the pile, then stepped next to Harmless and Bramble.

"Good to see you, Burbage," Harmless said.

"Good to be seen," the poet replied.

Slinister looked over his own shoulder and nodded.

Rye saw the Fork-Tongue Charmer named Lassiter approach and add his ring to the pile. Hyde stepped forward and did the same. Soon each of the Luck Uglies and Fork-Tongue Charmers emerged from the shadows and dropped their rings into the ever-growing platinum mound, until finally they had all taken positions at either Harmless's or Slinister's side, or hovered somewhere in between.

"Look at that," Harmless said after the last Luck Ugly had cast his ring. "It seems to be unanimous."

"I'd have it no other way," Slinister replied.

"May the best Luck Ugly win," Harmless said.

"Best Fork-Tongue Charmer," Slinister corrected.

Harmless stepped in close, and although speaking to Slinister, his words were loud enough for everyone to hear.

"You're still a Luck Ugly, Slinister, until the day you take your last breath." Harmless smiled, and the tips of his teeth flashed like a wolf's canines. "Even if that day has nearly come."

24

Men-at-Arms

The moon disappeared behind the clouds and the skies emptied in a torrent as soon as Rye and her family climbed back into the Grave Sweeper's carriage. The rain was furious and unrelenting, and when the carriage wheels became stuck in thick mud she feared they might never make it back to the Shambles. They finally arrived to find Little Water Street flowing with river water, and hurried inside the shelter of the Dead Fish Inn. They were joined by the Luck Ugly named Morrow and the group of men who had professed loyalty to

Harmless. Slinister and the Fork-Tongue Charmers had presumably returned to Longchance Keep, while those Luck Uglies who had not taken one side or the other remained hunkered down in their tents on Grim Green.

The mood around the inn was decidedly more somber as the new arrivals dried out by the fireplaces. Folly and Quinn had stayed up waiting for Rye's return as long as they could, but had finally retired upstairs with the younger Flood children. Folly didn't stir when Rye checked in on her, which was just as well—there would be time to explain everything in the morning. She retrieved her pack from Folly's room and descended back down to the inn's main floor. Abby placed a finger on her lips as she passed Rye on the stairs, Lottie asleep on her shoulder and ready to be tucked into bed.

Rye huddled on the hearth by the Mermaid's Nook, the heat of the fire warming her back and her fingers nervously tapping the pack in her lap. She watched the men around her. The inn buzzed with the hum of dozens of quiet conversations as Luck Uglies reacquainted themselves after years apart. The weight of the Reckoning seemed to temper their spirits if not their thirst, and Folly's parents did their best to keep their many cups filled.

Burbage—the angry poet, as Rye had always known him—sat with his elbows firmly planted on the carved-mermaid tabletop, a joint of meat thrust in a thick paw as he gnawed it with greedy teeth.

"Burbage, you're wasting away," Harmless said with a smile as he came to stand beside him. "You need to take better care of yourself."

Burbage rubbed grease from his beard and wiped his palm on a belly that didn't look to have missed many meals.

"Is it that obvious?" he bellowed. "Food's been scarce in Drowning. I'm bony as a wet cat and twice as cranky. Speaking of which . . ."

He pointed a sausage-like pinkie at Shortstraw, who rolled in the sawdust on the floor in an effort to dry his sopping fur.

"Keep your monkey an arm's length from me, Bramble. I've never tried one but I hear they taste like lamb."

Shortstraw frowned and bared his teeth.

"Take your chances," Bramble said. "This one's been giving me indigestion for years."

Rye pushed up from the hearth and approached the angry poet apprehensively. "I know you," Rye said. "I mean, in a sense. You chased me out of your bookshop last year."

Burbage raised an eyebrow over the joint of meat. "So I did," he replied with a grin that revealed gristle stuck between his teeth. "Of course, I had no idea who you were at the time." He dropped the well-picked bone onto his plate and tipped a velvet cap that looked as large as a pillowcase. "Name's Burbage, my lady. It's a pleasure to meet you."

"Rye O'Chanter," she said. "Likewise." Rye pursed her lips. "You're a . . . Luck Ugly?"

"You sound surprised."

"It's just—" Rye hesitated before continuing.

"Burbage was as spindly as a weed when I first met him," Harmless mentioned good-naturedly, from over Rye's shoulder.

"I was a late bloomer, that's all," Burbage said, puffing his chest and sucking in his gut. It hardly moved.

"But don't let his size fool you," Harmless added. "He's slipperier than an eel when he needs to be."

Rye recalled how nimbly Burbage had made his way across the rooftops. She remembered how tirelessly he had pursued them. She now had an opportunity to remedy a wrong that had troubled her. She reached into her pack.

"Here," Rye said. "This belongs to you. My friends and I never meant to take it. I'm sorry to say that the original's been ruined, but hopefully you'll find this one to be in better condition."

She handed him the copy of *Tam's Tome of Drowning Mouth Fibs, Volume II* that she'd retrieved from

Longchance Keep. He took it in his large hands.

"I won't be needing it anymore," Rye said.

"Well, that's most honorable of you, Miss O'Chanter." Burbage returned an appreciative nod and thumbed through the pages. "This *is* a fine specimen."

He closed the book with a thud.

"Gray," he said, "I believe this belongs to you." Burbage offered the book.

Rye blinked in confusion.

"Ah yes, thank you, Burbage," Harmless said, taking it. "You must be wondering about this," he said, glancing at Rye.

Rye nodded. "Well, *yes*. A few questions have crossed my mind."

"*Tam's Tome* is the work of Tamworth Wet-Blade," Harmless said. "Our distant relative—and the very first High Chieftain of the Luck Uglies."

"He's still alive?" Rye asked in disbelief.

"Certainly not," Harmless said. "Tamworth roamed the Western Woods when Drowning was little more than a frontier trading post. He didn't write *this* volume, but he penned the very first one. What started as his own personal journal was continued by those High Chieftains who followed him. *Tam's Tome* is more of a collaboration than a single work; each High Chieftain adds to it over time, forming a history of not just the

Luck Uglies, but the Shale itself. That's just one of its many secrets."

Harmless ran a finger over the cover. "Alas, I have been derelict in my own contribution as of late."

"Our High Chieftain has always been more a man of action than words," Morrow interjected with a smirk. "In the meantime, perhaps we should discuss the Reckoning, and how we will make sure the next volume isn't written in Slinister's hand."

"You're right, Morrow. I'm thankful to have your glum face around again to keep me focused." Harmless's words were more of a friendly tease than a taunt. He pulled up a chair and lowered himself into it wearily. Morrow sat down as well.

All around them, as if on cue, the other Luck Uglies' conversations grew quiet.

"What is the state of the village tonight?" Harmless asked.

"Silent," Burbage said, plucking a turkey leg from a platter. "For the first time in months. The Bog Noblins have stayed in the forest."

Harmless rubbed his chin. "My guess is that they've seen the gathering on Grim Green and are cautious. Hopefully their caution will extend another night. Once Slinister is addressed, we can turn our attention to them."

Burbage and Morrow exchanged quick glances, and Rye sensed that they didn't share Harmless's confidence in the outcome.

"Who will serve as your men-at-arms?" Morrow asked, setting down his mead.

The Luck Uglies at the other tables had all turned in their chairs to face them, hanging on Harmless's next words.

"I will," someone volunteered before he could answer. Bramble stepped forward and joined them at the table. "And I won't take no for an answer."

Harmless looked up and gave Bramble a tight smile. "Thank you, brother."

Bramble nodded.

"I will too," an unexpected voice said from the corner.

The men, and Rye, turned to Abby O'Chanter in surprise. She'd returned from putting Lottie to bed and stood listening in the shadows.

Harmless just shook his head at Abby in reply.

"I'm a better shot than any of you," she said. "Put me on a roof with my crossbow and I may just save all of your necks."

"Too dangerous," Bramble objected.

"No offense, Abigail," Burbage muttered, "but you're a woman. And you're not even a Luck Ugly."

Abby knotted her dark eyebrows at him.

"Under the rules of the Reckoning, the summoning party can select any two men-at-arms of his choosing," Harmless said. "Technically speaking, they need not be Luck Uglies—nor men for that matter."

Abby nodded in satisfaction.

"But," Harmless continued, "as valuable as your bow is, there's one thing more important to me than the High Chieftain's Crest." His eyes flicked to Rye and back again. His voice went quiet, and when he spoke it was as if there was nobody else in the room but Abby. "I have every intention of remaining part of the O'Chanter house for years to come. But Riley and Lottie have lived most of their lives without me. I am a luxury. You, Abigail, are the foundation on which their home is built. That's not something I'm willing to gamble."

Abby started to object, but Harmless put up his hand with finality.

"Then it shall be me," Morrow interjected.

"Thank you too, Morrow," Harmless replied. "But no."

Morrow narrowed his eyes, not in anger, but confusion.

"You're too even tempered, my friend," Harmless explained. "Too good of a Luck Ugly. Only one side can return from the Reckoning. If we lose—not that I intend to—the Luck Uglies will need someone like you in their ranks. Perhaps I can persuade Burbage to join me instead . . . ?"

"What are you trying to say?" Burbage howled, his open mouth full of turkey and outrage.

Harmless smiled. "Only that you are still as fine a climber as a two-tailed rat in a chimney. And you've lived here in Drowning right under the Earl's nose for the past ten years. If anyone knows its rooftops and alleyways, you do."

Burbage huffed. "Fine," he said with a wave of the greasy bone in his grip. "I accept your request . . . and your backhanded compliment."

"Then it's settled," Harmless said. "Bramble and Burbage shall be my men-at-arms. We will be joined by the luck of the O'Chanters. It has served me faithfully over the years, and will ride with me once more tomorrow night."

Harmless clapped his palm against the tabletop twice in affirmation. All around the inn, the Luck Uglies returned the gesture with a thundering echo.

Rye saw concern in Bramble's, Morrow's, and Burbage's faces, but they held their tongues. Her eyes went to her mother. Her face was grim. Rye suspected she would have more to say to Harmless, but would likely save her words for behind closed doors.

❧ ❧ ❧

Evening bled into morning, which flowed into afternoon, although time was gray and uncertain as the heavy rain continued throughout the day and cast the Shambles in a permanent state of gloom. At times the deluge was so fierce it rattled the timbers of the inn's roof and sent the candles of the bone chandelier flickering. Rye shared the previous evening's events with Folly and Quinn, who stayed put at the inn to wait out the storm. But for the most part, the Floods gave the O'Chanters and the Luck Uglies a wide berth, leaving them alone in the main room to prepare for the night ahead.

Harmless, Bramble, and Burbage had laid out their armor on tables. It looked light but effective: bracers, gauntlets, and chest plates made of leather and thick hide. They worked silently, each in their own thoughts as they adjusted straps and checked fittings. Harmless was slow and methodical by necessity, his one hand forced to do the work of two. Between his knees was a round, black lacquered shield the likes of which Rye had never seen before. Protruding from its face were thick, sharpened spikes, long and jagged like the tree branches in the forest Beyond the Shale. Harmless carefully oiled the ominous spikes with a stained rag.

He gave Rye a smile when he noticed her watching.

"A strong offense has always been my best defense, but my days of two-handed swordplay are behind me," he said, glancing down at his arm in its sling. "Sometimes we must adapt, and like a porcupine or a midnight sea urchin, a tough shell can help offset a weakness." He slid his weakened forearm through the shield's leather straps so that, with the help of the sling, it hung in front of his chest like a barrier. With his free arm, he tested the heft of a one-handed war axe. "At least I can still put this one to good use."

Rye looked at his gear set out on the table. There was a familiar hook-nosed mask, this one black as pitch, but its forehead and looming eyeholes were ringed with horns and spines similar to those on the shield. Next to it were several ropes of barbed chain, a flail-like ball of spikes on each end. He set the axe on the table and lifted one.

"Wraith Wings," he said, anticipating her question. "With practice they can be hurled with great accuracy, and keep your enemy at a distance. Particularly if you can wrap one around an opponent's neck."

Abby cleared her throat and gave Harmless a reproachful look. She set down a cloth bundle on the table, tightly folded in the shape of a triangle. It was black fabric of the weight normally used in banners. The Ragged Clover. Morrow was at her side.

"The rain has let up for the moment," Morrow said. "The Fork-Tongue Charmers have vacated Longchance Keep and moved to the Western Woods. The Luck Uglies on Grim Green have packed up and done the same. I'll be leaving with the others to join them, and make sure there is no mischief afoot. Once the Reckoning begins, no Luck Ugly or Fork-Tongue Charmer shall return to Drowning until the Ragged Clover flies atop the bell tower."

"Thank you, Morrow. No need for good-byes. I will you see you soon, my friend."

Morrow hesitated, then offered Abby and Rye a nod before turning and disappearing out the doors of the inn.

"Abigail, Riley, you both look exhausted," Harmless said. "I know neither of you have slept. Go, rest now."

Rye looked to Abby in alarm.

"I will come to say good-bye before I go," Harmless said reassuringly. "You have my word."

Rye rested upstairs in Abby's guestroom, where she drifted fitfully in and out of sleep for the rest of the afternoon. The passing thunderstorms outside must have seeped into her dreams, as she found herself plagued with images of rain and surging floods. At one point she stirred and found Lottie curled next to her, a mouth of crooked baby teeth open and drooling on Mona Monster. Her sister's company comforted her and she drifted off again. When she next awoke, it was to a presence in the room. A figure draped in black watched her from a chair in the corner. Harmless. She smiled and shut her eyes.

Rye felt a kiss on her cheek and a hand on her head. This time Harmless's palm was cool, but he left it there until it warmed to her touch. Rye breathed heavily. When she felt him take it away, she reopened her eyes sleepily. But the room was empty, and Harmless, if he had ever been there at all, was now gone.

Rye leaped up from bed and hurried out to the deserted hallway. Continuing down the stairs, she found the inn quiet once again. Bramble, Burbage, and the rest of the Luck Uglies had disappeared like phantoms, leaving just empty plates and goblets in their wake. Only Abby remained, shifting something over her shoulder.

"Mama, where's Harmless? Did he—" She stopped midsentence.

Abby had donned her crimson cloak and slung her crossbow over her shoulder.

"He went up to say good-bye an hour ago. They left soon after."

Rye couldn't believe she'd been in such a fog of sleep.

"What are *you* doing?" Rye asked, rubbing her eyes.

"I'm going for a walk in the village," she said.

Rye knew that wasn't her only intention.

"But you can't. That's against the rules of the Reckoning. You're not one of the men-at-arms. And no other Luck Uglies may enter Drowning."

"That's right," Abby said, kneeling down and putting a hand on Rye's cheek. "But I'm not a Luck Ugly. I'm just a simple villager on her way to check on our home on Mud Puddle Lane. You take care of your sister until I get back. And tell Mr. Nettle to stop scratching his hives—he'll just make them worse."

Rye was without words. Abby stood and put a gentle finger over Rye's lips before she could protest further. "I'll be fine. No one will even know I'm there. Not even your father."

She pressed her lips to Rye's head and was gone, slipping out the doors of the Dead Fish Inn.

Rye hurried upstairs to the balcony overlooking Little Water Street. She watched her mother stride purposefully down the empty mud road before disappearing into an alley to avoid the overflowing river. The late-afternoon sun peeked through storm clouds, burning the sky red. Rye's head swam. The Reckoning had arrived, and all that was left for her to do was sit idly and wait. She cast her eyes at Annis's barge floating silently on the tumultuous river and wished she could speak to her.

She jolted at the sound of her name.

"Rye!"

It was Folly's voice.

"Rye, where are you?" This time it was Quinn.

They both burst onto the balcony out of breath.

"Rye, you need to come downstairs!" Folly gasped.

"What is it?"

"Just come," Folly insisted. Rye hurried after her friends, down the stairs to the main floor of the inn.

She paused at the sight of the soaked figure in front of her, his brown leather coat dripping, the blue plume in his hat waterlogged and dangling over his eyes.

"Truitt?" she said. "You came through the wine cellar?"

"Rye, it's the Bog Noblins," he said. "They've attacked Drowning. They've overrun the village."

"Now?" she gasped. "How many?"

Truitt removed his hat and shook his head gravely. "All of them."

25 Battle for the Dead Fish Inn

"What do you mean by *all* of them?" Rye asked slowly.

"Every one of them," Truitt said emphatically. "The entire Dreadwater clan, gathered at the forest's edge. They're in the village. Breaking into buildings. Ripping the cobblestones from the roads. They seem bent on leveling Drowning . . . and everyone in it."

"The Dreadwater," Rye cursed. Her thoughts jumped to Harmless and Abby, to Bramble and Burbage, to Quinn's father at his forge. Not to mention the rest of the villagers trapped in their homes. "They must have seen the Luck Uglies retreat to the Western Woods," she said. "And they're done biding their time."

Folly's and Quinn's faces had turned ashen with the news.

"My father's still at the shop on Market Street," Quinn whispered to himself.

"Mud Puddle Lane was probably the first stop," Rye said, her thoughts turning to her neighbors. "And where are the link children?"

Truitt grimaced. "In the Cistern. I was on my way back to warn them but the rains have flooded much of the Spoke."

"At least they'll be safe there," Rye said hopefully.

Truitt just shook his head. "Not for long. If the water rises any higher, the Cistern will be filled. I need to help get the rest out of there."

"And go where?" Rye asked. "The village streets?"

"That's hardly any better," Quinn said. "Who is going to open their home with the town overrun by Bog Noblins? I don't think they'll have time to knock door-to-door."

"What about here?" Folly suggested. "We can lead them underground across the Spoke and up through the wine cellar. We won't need to set foot on the streets."

"Have you *been* to the wine cellar?" Truitt asked. He

waved for them to follow.

The friends were forced to stop halfway down the basement steps. Bottles floated in knee-deep water.

"Sometimes it gets damp in the spring," Folly said. "But I've never seen it like *this*."

"I barely made it through myself," Truitt said. "We're too close to the river. All of the tunnels under the Shambles are flooded. The only way back down is through the village itself."

They climbed the stairs back up to the inn.

"I stopped to warn you but I can't linger," Truitt said. "I'm on my way to Old Salt Cross—it sits on higher ground. The sewers under Apothecary Row should still be passable for now."

"I'll come with you," Quinn said. "I'm finding my father and bringing him here even if I have to drag the stubborn hammerhead on my back."

Again Rye considered Abby, Harmless, and Bramble. With their focus on the Reckoning—if there still *was* a Reckoning—they'd be walking right into a village under siege. It occurred to her that, all across Drowning, villagers must be sharing similar concerns. Loved ones, acquaintances, strangers—no villager would be left unscathed.

"Truitt," Rye said, putting a hand on his arm as he readied to leave. "Did you find Malydia?"

"Not yet, but the Fork-Tongue Charmers have just abandoned the Keep, and its gates are wide open," he said. "If they've left Malydia locked away there, I'll go find her as soon as the link children have reached higher ground."

Truitt moved to leave, but Rye held his arm tight.

"The Keep," Rye said, the option suddenly dawning on her. She looked to Folly and Quinn. "We can get the link children, Quinn's father, every villager we can find . . . to the Keep. Then close the gates. *That* will be the safest place in all of Drowning."

In their urgent chatter, the children hardly noticed the Flood family gathering around them. Faye took a quick head count; Floods, friends, even a stray Feraling.

"We've got one extra," Faye said, furrowing her brow. She looked Truitt up and down. "You're not one of mine, are you?"

The single thump on the inn's iron portals echoed like the boom of a stone fist. They all jolted at the unexpected sound.

"Someone's heavy-handed this evening," Fitz groused.

"We'll see who it is," Flint added.

The twins stomped to the door and slid open a narrow slit of a spyhole. Fitz lowered his head and peered out with one eye. He whistled in surprise.

"Now there's something you don't see every day," he gasped.

"Who is it?" Flint asked.

The iron portals clattered and shook, sending the twins lurching away and tumbling to the ground.

Fletcher rushed forward in alarm.

"Bog Noblins!" Fitz growled as he and Flint clambered to their feet. They quickly lowered the doors' heavy bar into place as the Bog Noblin pounded it again with the force of a battering ram.

"Faye, get everyone to the upper floors," Fletcher called, rushing to secure a window. "The doors should hold, but the boys and I will stay here just in case."

Faye gathered up Fox, the baby's eyes growing wider with each frightening shake of the inn. Mr. Nettle snatched Lottie by the hand and pulled her to the stairs. Rye followed them with Quinn and Truitt. Folly had held back, hands on her hips.

"This is my home too," she was saying to her father, although he ignored her protests. "I'm staying here to defend it."

Just then the inn thundered from another blow that shook its foundation. Overhead there was a snap of chains, and without thinking, Rye ran and pushed herself against Folly with such force that they were both sent tumbling to the floor. The sea monster chandelier just missed them, landing with an explosion of a thousand bones, large and small. Rye helped Folly to her feet as her brothers darted about, stomping out the scattered candles before they could set the inn ablaze.

"Okay," Folly said, her face pale. "I'll go upstairs."

They climbed to the third floor, and Rye, Folly, Truitt, and Quinn crammed onto the small balcony overlooking Little Water Street. Rye had seen the Shambles at its most frightening—silent and creeping with shadows on a Black Moon; riot-ravaged during a standoff between the Shamblers, soldiers, and the Luck Uglies; and, most recently, forebodingly shuttered and deserted under threat of the River Wyvern. But she had never seen anything like this. Below them, two hulking Bog Noblins stalked outside the inn's iron portals. Their gray skin clung to their powerful frames, and Rye could see the rust-orange ropes of hair dangling from the tops of their heads. One of them put a shoulder into the doors, rattling the windows of the inn.

"Do you think the doors will hold?" Quinn asked nervously.

"They always have," Folly said, although her voice wasn't entirely reassuring.

Rye's heart sank. At least they *had* doors. Harmless and Abby were on the streets. If Bog Noblins had already made their way to the Shambles, there was no telling what sort of condition the village was in.

From inside, they could hear Fox's frightened tears. A smaller body pushed between them toward the terrace railing. It was Lottie, her face scrunched in anger.

"Lottie, you shouldn't be out here," Rye said.

"Mean Gob Boglin made Baby Fox cry," Lottie huffed, and pressed her face through the rails so she might see them. Lottie narrowed her eyes. She coughed up something in her throat and pursed her lips. A thick wad of phlegm dangled from her mouth in a long thread.

"Stop that, Lottie!" Rye demanded. "You'll just make them more angry."

She shooed Lottie back inside, but her little sister's taunt had given her an idea.

"Folly, what about those potions you have? You know, the really dangerous ones?"

"Yes . . . ," Folly said hesitantly.

"Maybe you should get them . . . just in case?"

Folly bit her lip, then disappeared inside.

One of the Bog Noblins glared up at them, its dripping eyes flicking with malice. A butcher's meat hook dangled from one long earlobe and a long metal bolt was pierced through its lip. The creature sprang on its feet, slapping a clawed hand against the wall of the inn. Rye and Quinn leaped back from the edge. Fortunately, although much taller than a man, the Bog Noblin's leap fell well short. It let out a fearsome roar in frustration, and pounded the doors with its clenched fists. It left two dents in the doors' iron face.

"Perhaps we'd be wise not to taunt them either," Truitt suggested.

Rye had to agree, and was about to go inside when Quinn pointed and interrupted her.

"Rye, what's that on the bridge?" he asked.

Rye looked to where Quinn had directed. In the dim shadows of dusk, she saw lights at the far end of the great arched bridge. Torches. Held by what appeared to be a large number of men on horseback.

"Luck Uglies?" Quinn asked hopefully.

"I don't know," Rye said, confused. "They're supposed to be in the Western Woods."

Perhaps the Luck Uglies had called off the Reckoning, and would be able to look past their differences for one more day. But the riders were led by banner men, and Luck Uglies had never been ones to broadcast their arrival.

Folly returned, carefully removing two metal flasks from a small pouch at her hip. She handed one to Rye, and kept the other in her own hand.

"So if we mix these, they'll create an explosion?"

"Oh, yes," Folly said.

"Well, come on, let's do it before the Bog Noblins

get inside." She raised her flask over the rails.

"Wait!" Folly called, turning pale and grabbing her arm. "There's enough in here to blast the entire street into the river."

"Really?" Rye said, looking at the modest-size flasks.

"Yes, really. Just a few drops of each should—"

But Folly gasped before she could finish. The Bog Noblins had taken notice of them again, and the one with the hook in its ear charged, stepping on its companion's knotty back and hurling itself upward. Extending its arms, this time a clawed hand gripped the edge of the terrace. The children screeched and lurched away as the Bog Noblin hung there, its sharpened yellow toenails digging into the walls of the inn as it struggled to pull itself up.

Before they could retreat inside, the balcony shifted under their feet and tore away from the building. Rye found herself pitched through the air, and was able to throw her arms around a nearby storm gutter that ran vertically along the length of the inn. She hung there for a moment, still clutching the flask, and watched in horror as the remains of the balcony dangled, then fell, with Folly, Quinn, and Truitt still on it. The wreckage collapsed over the Bog Noblin, tossing Rye's three friends into the wet muck of Little Water Street. Fortunately, the Bog Noblin's head and the mud cushioned most of their fall.

The gutter jolted and creaked, and now Rye found herself tumbling as her weight pulled it from the building. She hastily stashed the flask in her coat pocket as she rode the gutter downward—there was no telling what would happen if the glass broke. She hit the ground hard, thankful that she'd had a lifetime of practice at falling—and that the overflowing river had rendered the street a muddy cushion.

As the four friends and the Bog Noblins struggled back to their feet, the doors of the inn heaved open, and Fletcher, the twins, and a small army of Floods rushed out to engage the monsters. They were quickly met by the Bog Noblins at the base of the steps, and the twins yelled for the children to run the opposite way as they swung a pair of two-handed claymores in their four burly fists, each of the mighty blades longer than Rye was tall. Rye and her friends didn't hesitate, and rushed down Little Water Street away from the inn.

The four children stumbled and staggered, their bones aching from the fall. They paused and looked back at the Floods as they struggled to hold their ground against the monstrous beasts. Rye cast her eyes to the water, where the lanterns of Annis's barge glowed on the middle of the river. She recalled what the old Luck

Ugly named Knockmany had once told her: Bog Noblins weren't strong swimmers. They wallowed in mud and shallow muck but were useless in open water. Perhaps Annis was in the safest place of all. Rye considered whether they should swim for it, but Folly's screech put an end to the thought.

"One's coming!" she cried.

The Bog Noblin with the butcher's hook through its ear had broken away from the skirmish with the Floods, and now lumbered down Little Water Street, gaining ground rapidly.

Rye looked to Folly and Quinn. The three friends had done this many times before. "You know what to do," she said.

"No, what?" Truitt asked.

"Scatter!" Quinn yelled, and grabbed Truitt by the arm, dragging him away.

Quinn and Truitt darted into an alley. Folly veered toward the river, disappearing down a dock. Rye made eye contact with the fast-approaching Bog Noblin and touched the choker around her neck.

"Pigshanks," she said. It was too much to hope that the O'Chanters' runes would suddenly spring back to life and frighten the Bog Noblin away.

She turned and ran directly down Little Water Street, assuming the Bog Noblin would follow. But instead it turned and made for the dock, its claws scraping wood as it headed in Folly's direction.

Rye stopped. A chill came over her as Annis's words rang loud in her ears. *The toll* . . .

She shook her head, chasing away the thought.

"No," she said aloud. Then, even louder, "No! You can't have Folly!"

Rye retraced her steps and charged down the darkened dock. Folly had reached the end and huddled at the edge of the water. The Bog Noblin was halfway there, between them now, and Rye could count the stumps of its spine along the gray flesh of its back. Rye ran her fingers over her cudgel, but she knew even the Shale's hardest ash wouldn't faze the Bog Noblin's thick skull. She glanced around the dock but found only some coils of rope and an old rusting anchor.

Folly caught sight of Rye from the far end of the dock. She shook her head, and gestured for Rye to run.

The Bog Noblin moved closer to Folly.

Rye reached into her boot and drew Fair Warning from its sheath.

"Rye, no!" Folly called out.

Fair Warning reflected in the light of the full moon rising over the mouth of the river. Rye stepped closer to the Bog Noblin, the blade shaking in her hand. She raised it, then crouched.

And tapped it against the old anchor.

Folly's eyes went wide in disbelief. The Bog Noblin looked over its shoulder at the sound of plinking metal.

"Rye," Folly pleaded. "Run! Please!"

Rye kept tapping the anchor. The Bog Noblin turned, its long mouth snarling as it now approached Rye.

"Folly," Rye called ahead, as steadily as she could. "You need to get off the dock."

"What?"

"Get off the dock!" Rye yelled, tapping the anchor more furiously. Folly rolled over the edge and disappeared beneath it.

The Bog Noblin was nearly on Rye now. Close enough she could smell the sour stench of the bogs steaming from its flesh. Rye hit the anchor one more time as loud as she could, holding her breath, pinching her eyes tight, and hoping that the sound would carry.

As the Bog Noblin reached for her, the surface of the water broke with a resounding splash and a heavy weight landed on the wooden pier, cracking the timbers as they buckled from the force.

The River Wyvern snapped its jaws tight around the Bog Noblin's hips. The red-bearded beast emitted a terrible wail, flailing its arms and legs as the giant reptile chomped down again and again with razor-like teeth.

Rye scuttled away through the wreckage of the dock, watching as the Wyvern's slippery black body padded back into the river, dragging the Bog Noblin with it into the depths, until a final thrash of its tail propelled them both underwater and out of sight.

Rye stumbled back to Little Water Street, where she fell down next to Folly in the mud. Folly just blinked her wide eyes under her damp pink hair.

"What was that all about?" Folly said.

"I thought I'd try feeding the River Wyvern," Rye said, her voice raw from nerves. She looked at Fair Warning's blade appreciatively before slipping it back in her boot. "I'm just glad he was still hungry."

They both sat quietly, catching their breath. But a rumble interrupted them as a great thunder of footfalls stomped down the street. They threw their hands over their heads, fearing they would be trampled by another onslaught of Bog Noblins. But instead, a cavalry of heavy war horses galloped past, kicking mud in their wake. The thickly armored horsemen worked their way down the embankments from the village, torches in their hands, gold banners held aloft.

Bewildered, Rye and Folly watched them race toward the Dead Fish Inn and take up the fight against the remaining Bog Noblin.

A rider at the rear of the cavalry stopped, his plated

armor gilded and his chest draped in gold-and-crimson tartan.

"Miss Riley! Lady Flood!" A muffled voice called out from under the rider's helmet.

Rye and Folly looked at each other openmouthed.

"Baron Nutfield?" Rye asked.

The rider lifted the visor of his helmet. Baron Nutfield's familiar nose was still ruddy, but his beard had been neatly trimmed and his face scrubbed.

"Apologies for the delay," he said. "We rode up the coast but the culverts are overflowing. The spill is so great the beach was impassable. We had to take the long way here."

Rye knew the twin culverts were enormous man-made tunnels that drained water from the Great Eel Pond under, rather than over, Village Drowning.

"Who are all these men?" she gasped.

"My soldiers, of course," Baron Nutfield declared. "They were all a bit stunned to see me after so many years but they're nothing if not a loyal bunch. It had been rather dull in my absence so they were hungry for an adventure. Consider them at your disposal. Where shall we send them?"

Rye and Folly looked at each other again, in stunned disbelief. Folly just shrugged.

"Uh, leave them here to secure the Shambles and

defend the Dead Fish Inn?" Rye said uncertainly. "Once that's in place, maybe you can send half into the village to rescue anyone they find and bring them back here?"

"Spoken like a true war maiden, Miss Riley," he said clenching a fist. He reached into his cloak and took a nip from a flask, wiping his lips with the back of his gloved hand. "Consider it done."

Baron Nutfield tugged the reins and the horse galloped after his troops.

Quinn and Truitt emerged from a nearby alley and hurried to meet them.

"Who was *that*?" Quinn asked.

"You wouldn't believe us if we told you," Folly said.

"I still need to get into the village without delay," Truitt said. "I'll take Mutineer's Alley." He turned toward the winding stone steps that led up to the village proper.

"I'm going with Truitt," Rye said. She planned on finding her mother, and directing every villager she came across to the safety of the inn or Longchance Keep.

"I'm coming," Quinn added.

"Me too," Folly said.

"Folly, no," Rye said, putting her hands on Folly's shoulders. "All of your family is here in the Shambles. With Baron Nutfield's help, the inn should be safe. Stay with them."

"You and Quinn are my family too," Folly said, clutching Rye's hands and pulling them free. Her voice was quiet, but stern. "I told you, we don't separate again."

Rye just nodded, and knew there was no battling her friend's resolve.

Truitt waved them forward. "Let's be on our way. Our path will only get worse the longer we wait."

They all climbed the steps to the top of Mutineer's Alley, peeking past its stone archway to Dread Captain's Way beyond. The road was empty, but the clatter and screams of conflict weren't far off.

"If the village is overrun, how will we get through?" Folly asked.

Rye looked up at the stone arch. Scowling, carved pumpkins leered down at them from their posts all along the road, their black robes billowing.

"Quinn, you said there are Wirry Scares all over the village?" Rye asked, an idea taking shape.

"At least the ones the squirrels haven't devoured yet. But they aren't going to help; the Bog Noblins couldn't care less," he added, throwing up his hands. "They ignore them like they don't exist."

"Perfect," Rye said. "That's just what we want them to do."

26

March of the Wirry Scares

Two towering Wirry Scares staggered awkwardly down the street, their snaggletoothed grins and sinister eyes glaring out from carved pumpkin heads. A stray cat inspected them curiously before darting into an alleyway.

Rye navigated from behind one pair of angular eyeholes. Her nose was filled with the smell of rotting produce and the world around her sounded dull and hollow, like the time she got her head stuck in the milking pail.

"Straight ahead, Truitt. Okay. Now step to the right."

Truitt strained beneath her. She sat atop his shoulders, both of them concealed by the billowing robes. She didn't know who had the worse job. Truitt did the carrying, but she was the one thrust neck-deep in a rotting pumpkin.

"Do you need a break?" she whispered.

"No," he groaned. "I'll be fine. But if you could stop squirming that would be helpful. You're heavier than you sound."

The first stretch of their journey was ominously uneventful, the streets deserted as the full moon rose higher overhead. But as they approached Old Salt Cross the structures around them began to glow. Not from window candles or lanterns—the homes and buildings were shuttered. It was Drowning itself that was burning.

Rye craned the pumpkin head and tried her best to glance up at the rooftops as they went. No Ragged Clover flew from the bell tower on the other side of the village. She saw no sign of the Luck Uglies or Fork-Tongue Charmers. Or her mother. She wondered again if it was possible that they'd abandoned the Reckoning altogether. More ominously, she worried whether the Bog Noblins had gotten to them first.

"Rye," Truitt said, straining. "The squirming? And . . . ouch . . . pinching?"

Rye realized she had been anxiously burrowing her fingers into Truitt's shoulders.

"Sorry." She loosened her grip and turned her attention back to the streets. There was little, if anything, she could do for her parents at the moment, but she could at least help some of the other villagers. "Keep to the right again up here."

But as they rounded a corner and headed toward Old Salt Cross, she gasped and lurched in shock, nearly sending Truitt tumbling.

"What is it, Rye?" Truitt whispered.

Rye had to swallow hard before speaking. "It's worse than I imagined."

What awaited them was mayhem. Rye had seen three Bog Noblins attack Drowning last year. Later, she saw enough of the creatures to fill an entire clearing and decimate Longchance's soldiers at the edge of the forest Beyond the Shale. But now the village streets were overrun by the hulking, riotous beasts. Frenzied and disorganized, they battered their way through windows and doors. Street lanterns toppled, leading to even more blazes. From the noise, commotion, and smoke rising from the distant streets around her, she knew that the assault wasn't limited to Old Salt Cross.

Several other Wirry Scares watched the scene unfold helplessly from their corner posts, entirely ignored by the Bog Noblins just as Rye had hoped. But one carefully stepped back toward Rye and Truitt. Its stick arms shrugged, as if to ask, *What now?*

They had no choice. Rye just waved the stick in her own hand, gesturing for Folly and Quinn to follow.

The living Wirry Scares continued on toward Apothecary Row, stopping regularly to be less conspicuous and to give Quinn and Truitt a break. When they paused to catch their breath at the corner where the four streets intersected, Rye noticed yet another stray cat studying them from the shadows. Its tawny fur was long and matted, but unlike most strays, this one was thick and powerful, its eyes more watchful than timid. Could it be something more than just a cat? The animal disappeared, and Rye didn't have time to give it another thought.

"The sewer grate is over there," Folly whispered from the jagged mouth of her pumpkin. It was on the opposite side of the road, which, like the other streets they'd crossed, was thick with rampaging Bog Noblins.

"Let's make a run for it now, before it gets any worse," Folly suggested.

"All right," Rye replied. "On the count of—wait. Look there."

Ahead, a man's body lay facedown in the puddles of the cobblestones. He appeared to be wearing thick leather armor, his head covered by a cowl. Rye's heart sank.

"Truitt, straight ahead. Quickly," she said, and they stumbled forward.

"Rye, wait for us!" Folly called after them.

Rye's panic grew as they drew closer to the fallen man. His build and armor were all too similar to Harmless's. In her eagerness to reach him she shifted awkwardly, and heard Truitt call out under her. She felt herself falling, and when she hit the ground just short of the prone body, the large pumpkin rolled off her and cracked in two.

Heavy footfalls splattered puddles as three Bog Noblins suddenly bore down on them. Rye wrapped her arms around her head, but never felt their claws. She peered through her fingers. They had each grabbed hold of the body, baring their teeth and snarling at one another like wolves laying claim to a fresh meal. As they fought among themselves Rye saw the ashen face loll to the side. It wasn't Harmless, but the Fork-Tongue Charmer called Lassiter. The fletching of an arrow protruded from his back.

A frantic, animalistic screech called out to Rye and Truitt just as the Wirry Scare manned by Folly and Quinn ambled up behind them. Rye turned toward the sound. Shortstraw's round eyes and white teeth gleamed from underneath the shelter of a toppled merchant's stall. Rye and Truitt clambered forward on hands and knees and rolled underneath.

Shortstraw hovered nervously by Bramble's side. Rye's uncle sat hunched in the shadows, his mask at his side, revealing a face tight with pain. His pale eyes jumped at the sight of them.

"Riley," he said between gritted teeth, "you have a way of turning up in the strangest places."

"Are you hurt?" she asked, and moved to touch him.

He raised a hand that had been clutched deep in his cloak to stop her. At his side was a broken sword. "I'll get by. And I appreciate your concern, but I think I've been poked and prodded enough for one night."

"Bog Noblins?" Rye asked.

He shook his head. "My old friend Lassiter. The Fork-Tongue Charmers ambushed us here."

Rye felt a pang in her gut as her hope for the Luck Uglies' assistance waned. "So the Reckoning goes on despite all of this?"

"Once the Reckoning starts, it cannot be interrupted until there's a winner. Although I must say, I don't think anyone had circumstances like these in mind." Bramble struggled to stifle an ominous, hacking cough. He wiped his mouth with the back of his hand. "I was in dire straits, but it seems a lucky charm has been hovering over our shoulders." He cast his eyes upward, where the toppled merchant's stall created a roof above them. "And unless there's another High Isle archer in Drowning, my guess is that your mother has found herself a nice perch somewhere. Tonight *her* stubborn streak was *our* good fortune."

"And the others?" Rye asked.

"That weaselly little Charmer turned tail and ran as soon as the first blades were drawn. He's probably halfway to Trowbridge by now—if a Bog Noblin hasn't snatched him up first."

Hyde, Rye thought. The boy might have been an expert at skulking and spying, but he didn't have the stomach to wear the cowl and mask.

"Your father and Burbage have taken to the rooftops," Bramble continued, pointing a finger over their heads. "Slinister, too, last I saw. The streets are becoming impassable. Which leads me to wonder how you—" Bramble paused, and shook his head. "I must be delirious. It seems a Wirry Scare has followed you."

Folly removed the pumpkin from her head as she and Quinn squeezed under the toppled stall.

"Flunky?" Bramble asked in disbelief. Rye was relieved he still had enough strength to tease.

"Wirry Scares might not frighten Bog Noblins, but they don't seem to interest them either," Folly explained.

"Even so, I'm not sure how long they'll stay disinterested if they catch wind of us under here," Quinn added.

"There's an entrance to the Spoke just across the street," Rye said to Bramble. "Can you run?"

"Running might be a tad ambitious, but I can stumble and flop." He strained to move into a crouch.

Rye turned to Folly and Quinn. "Can you put on your pumpkin and sneak over there to open the storm grate?"

Folly eased the pumpkin over her head. "Stumble and flop quickly," her muffled voice suggested to Bramble.

The Wirry Scare bobbled out from under the stall and staggered to the grate. Rye saw it crouch down and wave a clawed hand as a signal.

Rye and Truitt each wrapped a hand around Bramble's waist and helped him out from their hiding place. They struggled across the road to the grate, and pitched themselves into the sewer before any Bog Noblins could reach them.

Rye and her friends dragged themselves away from the mouth of the sewer, spill from the earlier rain draining down on them. Bramble followed, and found a damp wall to lean against. Shortstraw climbed to his shoulder and jabbered soft grunts of concern.

"Don't worry, my hairy friend," Bramble said, and scratched the monkey's chin. "I've still got life in me yet."

"This tunnel leads to the Cistern," Truitt said, pointing to one of several dark hollows that twisted into the distance. "Find yourselves some torches and I'll have us there quickly."

Quinn retrieved a torch from a casing, but a dull clack from the tunnel behind him made everyone else pause. Something heavy scraped across the earthen floor.

"That's the sound of the creeper," Truitt said in alarm.

Rye recognized it too. But this time she realized that she'd not only heard it here in the Spoke, but also in the forest Beyond the Shale.

Quinn turned his torch to the source of the noise, and recoiled in horror at the unexpected sight awaiting him. The jagged antlers and bony head of a Shriek Reaver stared back from the gloom, disoriented by the bright light.

"What *is* that?" Quinn asked, aghast.

"Really bad news," Rye whispered.

Quinn reacted quickly, casting his torch at the Shriek Reaver's knotted limbs. It lurched back momentarily, but Quinn's distraction proved short-lived.

"Run!" Truitt cried. "Follow me to the Cistern!"

Rye hesitated, grabbing Bramble by the arm to help him. She'd seen Shriek Reavers up close before, and there was no way her uncle could outpace it in his injured condition. But it was Shortstraw who moved next. As if he too shared Rye's concern, the monkey leaped from Bramble's shoulder and rushed at the Shriek Reaver, baring his small white teeth. The Shriek Reaver slashed at Shortstraw with its sharp, branch-like claws but missed, the quick monkey leaping past him. Shortstraw chattered at it, and the Shriek Reaver spun toward the sound, clacking its jaw and rattling its nub of a tongue.

Having caught its attention, Shortstraw scuttled off down a different tunnel, the Shriek Reaver whipping its body around and dragging itself after him at alarming speed.

"Hurry," Truitt called, and they all headed off after him, away from the Shriek Reaver and deeper into the Spoke.

Rye, her friends, and Bramble were silent for a long while as they navigated the subterranean catacombs, the only sound the splash of water at their feet and the drip of storm water above them. The leaks were so great that at times it felt like it was raining, and Rye understood why Truitt feared for the future of the Spoke.

Truitt didn't pause until they reached the stone steps that descended into the Cistern.

"What was that creature?" Folly asked. "It looked more horrible than the Bog Noblins."

"It's called a Shriek Reaver," Rye said. "They're some sort of guardians of Beyond the Shale."

"What's it doing down here?" Folly asked.

Rye had been wondering the same thing while they traveled. "Harmless told me that, last year, when we first opened the door to Beyond the Shale for the Luck Uglies, some less-welcome visitors had made their way through. I think that Shriek Reaver was one of them."

Bramble had been uncharacteristically silent throughout their journey through the Spoke. Rye turned to him.

"I'm sorry about Shortstraw," she said. He had never been a pleasant animal, but his last act was certainly a brave one.

Bramble just nodded. "He could be stubborn as a stump, but he was a good companion. And a better friend."

They all descended into the Cistern. It was still illuminated by hundreds of overhead lanterns, but the water had risen much farther up the stone steps and now submerged the first several levels of the link children's makeshift island. The narrow beams that formed a bridge now floated awkwardly on swirling water as the Cistern slowly filled.

"We've made it with little time to spare," Truitt said.

As they prepared to cross, a screech echoed behind them.

"Shortstraw!" Rye found herself calling, relieved to see the sopping wet monkey for perhaps the first time ever.

The monkey didn't pause to greet them and instead rushed across the beams, sending them bobbing on the water.

"No, Shortstraw," Rye repeated, shaking her head as her relief turned to alarm. There was a clatter of teeth and claws as the Shriek Reaver dragged itself down the stone steps.

This time no one needed to shout what to do. Truitt, Folly, and Quinn darted single file over the beams to the platforms at the center of the Cistern. Rye followed with Bramble, doing her best to support his back with her hands as they struggled to balance on the shifting bridge. The beams bounced violently underneath her, and Rye knew the Shriek Reaver had leaped on behind them. She didn't look back.

Bramble dove onto the more stable wooden island

first, and as his weight cleared the plank it lurched upward under Rye's feet. Rye felt herself stumbling, and her eyes fell on the water and the dark shapes cruising below the surface. She launched herself desperately, and landed stomach-first on the platform, where Truitt and Quinn dragged her from the edge.

Rye spun to check on the Shriek Reaver. It hurried over the bridge quickly but clumsily, its body not built to navigate the narrow beams. One clawed hand slipped and its long arm plunged into the water, sending it off balance. As it moved to right itself it fell over the edge, and splashed about as it clambered to drag itself back up.

Rye hoped the delay would give them time to retreat higher up the platforms, but the water began to stir and bubble like a frothing cauldron. The Shriek Reaver flailed its claws and warbled its stubby tongue. It wasn't drowning; it was trying to defend itself.

Countless white tails and fins thrashed in the water. Rye marveled as the frenzied school of eyeless fish snapped at the much larger creature. Eventually the Shriek Reaver retreated, dragging itself away in a tumultuous wake until it disappeared into the recesses of the Spoke.

"Snarklefish," Truitt said with a shake of his head. "They really will eat anything."

❀ ❀ ❀

The friends sat and composed themselves among the link children's pallets. The link children themselves had gathered around, the familiar faces of Hope, Darwin, and Poe pushing to the front. Bramble had sprawled out on some bedding to rest. Shortstraw perched on his chest and watched him like a doting nurse. Rye's eyes were on the water. She could see the Cistern continue to fill with every passing minute.

"Should we be on our way to the Keep?" Folly asked.

Rye was silent for a long while. "It's not enough," she said finally.

"What do you mean?" Folly said.

"You saw the village. The Bog Noblins have completely overrun it. Even if we warn the villagers, they'll never make it across Drowning safely. We can probably get to the Keep ourselves before the Spoke fills, but how long will we last there? And what will become of the rest of the villagers? Of our families?"

"Rye's right," Truitt said. "The situation is worse than any of us expected."

"Can we signal the Luck Uglies?" Quinn asked. Rye heard his voice rising, and knew that Angus's well-being must be weighing heavy on his mind.

Rye looked to Bramble. His eyes were shut, his breathing shallow.

"I don't think so, Quinn," she said. "They're all in the Western Woods, under strict orders to remain there until the Ragged Clover flies over Village Drowning. Who knows where Harmless is, or where the Reckoning stands? And if it continues, who's to say Harmless—or Slinister—will even be able to raise the Ragged Clover?"

Quinn wrung his hands. "So what's left to do?"

Rye's eyes drifted back to the rising water.

"Bog Noblins can't swim," she said, a desperate idea taking hold. "Harmless told me once that the twin culverts—the huge tunnels south of the village—drain the waters under, rather than over Drowning. If they were blocked, or destroyed, the village would flood. The Bog Noblins would have no choice but to flee. Or drown."

"Along with everyone else," Folly said dismissively.

"Not if we could warn them first," Rye said. "With enough voices, we could tell the villagers to climb to the top floors of their homes, or take to the roofs. They'll have a better chance of climbing away from a bunch of soggy, distracted Bog Noblins than fleeing across the village with them in pursuit."

Rye glanced around at the link children's gritty faces hesitantly. "It may be too much to ask of you."

"Don't underestimate us," Poe said.

Darwin scrunched his face, shrugged, and shook his

head at Rye in disappointment.

"Darwin says the same," Poe translated. "Just not as nicely."

"I meant that after all you've been through, I can understand why you might be reluctant to help the villagers," Rye explained.

"We're villagers, too," Poe said. "Even if the rest of Drowning forgets it sometimes."

"Nobody knows the streets like we do," Hope added, with a nod to her extended family of orphans and foundlings. "And we have plenty of lanterns."

"We would make a handsome army of Wirry Scares," Truitt said.

"Ooh," Hope said, looking up at her sister. "You're on the bottom. I get to wear the pumpkin."

There was a murmur of anxious, but confident, enthusiasm among the others.

"Even if we could warn the villagers, how can we destroy the culverts?" Quinn asked. "It seems an impossible task."

Rye reached into her pocket and carefully removed the flask Folly had given her. "Folly, do you still have yours?"

Folly retrieved the matching flask from her own pocket and examined it in her hand. They all stared at the containers.

"Rye," Quinn said, "you do realize what you're suggesting?"

Rye nodded gravely. "There's no other way. We need to drown the village."

27

A Toll Comes Due

The friends and link children all stood in silence, the full weight of Rye's words taking hold. There were a few whispers, but no objections.

"We should go," Folly said finally. "It will take some time to get to the culverts."

"You're right," Rye said. "But I need to go myself." She kept talking before Folly could interrupt her. "It can't be you. Or Quinn. If this doesn't work the way we hope, whoever destroys the culverts will be the most hated villain in Drowning. Your family runs the

Shambles, Folly. And Quinn, you need to warn your father—you're both important parts of Mud Puddle Lane and Market Street." Rye sighed. "My family, well, the Willow's Wares is long gone. We've already been declared outlaws. I've got the least to lose."

"Sometimes it takes a villain to save you from the monsters," Bramble muttered quietly.

The children turned to him. His eyes were half open. "Riley's grandfather Grimshaw said that once long ago," he added, then closed his eyes again.

"You can't go alone, Rye," Quinn objected. "You need help."

"You're right, Quinn," Rye said. "I'll need Truitt to guide me if he's willing." Truitt gave her a nod in reply. "In the meantime, you, Folly, and the link children take to the streets and warn the villagers. Bang on doors. Yell from the windows. Whatever it takes to get people to higher ground."

Folly stared Rye down with icy blue eyes.

"This is the last time, Folly," Rye reassured. "We won't split up again. But this only works if we all do our own part." She opened her palm and held it out.

Folly's face relented. She studied the flask between her own fingers, then moved to place it in Rye's hand. She hesitated.

"Mix the two liquids . . . that's all it will take," Folly

said, then carefully handed it over. "Just find a way to do it without standing nearby."

Rye passed Truitt the flask, keeping it an arm's length away from her body as she did so. She looked at her friends, old and new. Hope, Darwin, Poe, and all the others listened eagerly.

"After you've warned the village, be sure to get yourselves to safety. The Keep is on high ground. Meet Truitt and me there if possible; otherwise find a roof and stay put. Then we'll have done all we can."

Rye followed Truitt through the Spoke to the twin culverts. The trek was tedious and wet. At times they found themselves wading through waist-deep floodwater. In other stretches, they covered their heads with their coats to keep from being drenched by the leaking tunnels.

Throughout their journey, Rye considered how they might combine Folly's potions. Perhaps they could drop them from a distance, or place one then throw the other at it. But when they finally arrived at the spot where the Spoke dead-ended at the underground length of the culverts, she realized their dilemma. Spill from the Great Eel Pond rushed past them, flowing into each culvert and continuing toward the sea. Rye could see the tiny pinpoints of moonlight in the culverts' distant mouths.

But destroying one culvert wouldn't be enough—the water would just redirect into the other. They would need to destroy the entire drainage system here, closer to its source, to completely block them both. Her spirits fell.

"Truitt, there's no place to mix them. There's no ledge to drop one from. And we won't be able to place one and throw the other with any accuracy."

Rye studied the tunnel. The water was strong and swift as it roared into the culverts. But along the edges, smaller rivulets had carved shelves and grooves into the stone and earthen walls. Pools had formed in hollows where the water level had not yet filled so high as to spill into the main channel below. She placed her finger knuckle-deep in one hollow, and her eyes followed the tiny rivulet to its source. The underground storm water splashed and frothed relentlessly.

"Maybe the current itself will mix it for us," she said. "There's a small pool here. We can fill it with one flask while emptying the other farther back at the source. If we're lucky, we'll be far enough away from the reaction."

"Folly would be proud," Truitt said.

But Rye's hope diminished as she thought it through. One of them could fill the pool and flee down the culverts to safety. But the person who navigated deeper toward the Great Eel Pond and the water's source couldn't rush toward the explosion. And once the tunnel collapsed, both the culverts and the way back into the Spoke would be blocked. She bit her lip.

"Truitt, only one of us can leave through the culverts. The other will need to find another way."

"So you stay here and empty your flask in this pool," Truitt said. "I'll take my flask back toward the pond."

Rye hesitated before speaking. "But we don't know what's back there. It may be too difficult to find another tunnel."

"The dark doesn't frighten me, Rye," Truitt said, placing his hands on her shoulders as if he could sense her concern. "The Spoke is my home. I'll find my way out before it floods."

Truitt's mismatched eyes held Rye's own, and for a moment it was as if he could actually see into them.

"Go straight to the Keep and look for me at the mouth of the sewers. I'll wait for you there," he reassured, and offered a smile. "Now tell me exactly what I need to do."

Rye carefully took Truitt's hand in her own, then placed his fingers into the flowing water and gently guided them back.

"Follow this little stream as far as you can," she said quietly. "When you get there, whistle so I know you're ready. You can whistle, right?"

Truitt nodded. "Everyone can whistle. It's just like blowing a kiss good-bye."

Rye could feel her cheeks blush.

"Pour the flask I already gave you into the flowing water," she said. "Then run. Folly says there is enough here to destroy a village street. It should bring down the tunnel and dam the culverts. After that, the Great Eel Pond will spill right into Drowning."

She hesitated, then finally loosened her grip on his hand.

"Sounds easy enough." Truitt said, reaching into a pocket of his coat.

Rye's eyes fell to the ground, and her nervous fingers went to work on her already well-picked nails.

"Don't be so worried," Truitt said softly. "I'm not." He pressed two items into her hands. "I'd hate to lose these. Hold on to them for me? One you might find useful. The other is for Malydia."

Rye felt the hard ridges of the Everything Key, then ran her thumb along the smooth lines of the tiny silver-framed portrait of Truitt, Malydia, and their mother. She studied them between her fingers before looking up, but when she did, Truitt had already slipped away.

It wasn't long before she heard his high-pitched whistle over the churn of the current. Rye removed the flask Folly had given her and poured it into the pool. It shimmered like oil on the surface.

Rye picked a culvert and fought through a rush of water that nearly knocked her off her feet, following the pinpoint of moonlight that grew larger and larger ahead. She made it out of the culvert and stumbled onto the abandoned sands of the beach, where the water raged past her and spilled into the darkness of the ocean beyond.

There was a rumble from somewhere deep below, as if the earth itself had skipped too many meals. She felt a tremble under her feet, and she couldn't be certain if it was the ground or her raw nerves. Then the first billow of smoke emerged from the culverts behind her, quickly becoming a storm cloud of dust. Rye coughed and ran to escape the choking fog. She splashed through the deep runoff, watching as the cloud drifted up and cut a dark swath through the sky. Rye looked down to her feet. The flow slowed around her oversized boots until it became just a trickle, then dried up altogether.

Truitt, and Folly's potions, had been successful. Rye followed the beach toward the dim glow of Village Drowning.

The full moon disappeared as Rye slogged across Grim Green, and the clouds emptied just as she began her climb up the craggy hill that wore Longchance Keep like a jagged crown. The rain was punishing. Unforgiving. The type of rain that made her forget, momentarily, the weight of her worries as she struggled through sliding mud and focused only on getting dry.

Fortunately, Rye found the gates flung open, and she hurried across the abandoned grounds. She passed the stables and the well house, then descended down a set of slick stone steps at the base of the Keep. They led to a platform over the vast chasm that served as the castle's sewers. Overhead, openings in the facade drained swill down from the tower chambers into the sewer pits, while the platform could be used to toss carcasses and larger waste by hand. Rye knew that they emptied into the Spoke. And she knew that this was where Morningwig Longchance must have taken Truitt many years before.

Her chest tightened so fiercely she could no longer breathe. Not for what happened long ago, but for what she saw now. The sewers had spilled up and over the sides, black water overflowing. The underground tunnels were now surely filled. And she was alone.

Truitt had not made it out of the Spoke.

Rye dropped to her knees. Rain ran down her face and dripped from her nose for a long while before she moved again.

❦ ❦ ❦

It was only the thought of her family and friends that gave Rye the strength to push on. She rushed down the corridors of Longchance Keep, but found them deserted. As she approached the Great Hall, she heard the echo of a waterfall. She paused to peek through the doors. The Great Hall was abandoned, and a torrent of rain poured through the hole in the roof, water splattering and flowing in rivulets along the cracks of the stone floor.

Rye ran through the maze of hallways, searching for signs of life. In a familiar passageway, she came across the tapestry depicting the Descent tossed in a pile. The crack it had once concealed had since been battered and pummeled to rubble, and it was now large enough to step inside. A trail of coins littered the floor as if grabbed greedily by the handful. She didn't bother to enter the Treasure Hole—whatever riches the Fork-Tongue Charmers might have left behind were useless to her now.

Rye leaned against the wall in dismay. Clearly, none of the villagers or link children had made it back to the Keep. She wasn't about to wait there idly if there was still anything she could do to help in Drowning, but as she gathered her strength and readied to leave, her memory of Truitt and his words became an anchor. Truitt had intended to return here and free Malydia, and after all he'd done, Rye owed it to him to see those wishes through.

Malydia might not be in the towers or halls, but there was still one area of the Keep she hadn't yet searched.

The torch-lined labyrinth of cells was deserted except for the ghosts of those who'd once dwelled in the dungeons of Longchance Keep. Rye had little fear of the dead anymore; she'd long since learned that it was the living who were far more fearsome. But a sense of dread grew when her calls for Malydia went unanswered except by the echoes of Rye's own voice. She descended as deep as the catacombs would allow, until she finally reached an ominous black portal in the floor. Below it lay the deepest, darkest dungeon of Longchance Keep. Rye had been in there once before, and didn't welcome a return trip.

The portal's handle was secured with a thick but simple lock, and for a moment Rye worried that she might never be able to open it. Then her hand went to her chest, where the Everything Key hung from her neck. She removed it and inserted it into the lock, taking a deep breath as it turned with a click.

It took all of Rye's might to heave open the heavy portal at her feet, and when she did, the stench almost knocked her onto her back. She covered her face and leaned over the edge. The sound below was unmistakable and all too familiar. Water. Rye knew there was a secret entrance to the Spoke hidden in the deepest, darkest dungeon. With the Spoke now flooded, it must have filled the dungeon too.

"Malydia?" Rye whispered. Again, no response.

"Malydia," she called louder, and thrust her torch over the opening. It reflected off the deepening water below. "It's Rye. Are you down there?"

The ghoul that sprang from the depths was like nothing she had seen before. It was as white as a corpse and its two heads were covered in long, wet, black hair. Coal eyes blinked in pain and it thrashed its skeletal arms to shield itself from the torchlight.

Rye leaped away from the opening in shock. Fortunately the lowest cell was too deep for it to reach her.

"Girl," came its dry voice from the pit. "Return this instant."

"There's no one here," Rye said, unconvincingly.

"Quickly," the voice rasped. "The water's rising."

Rye carefully leaned over the edge, angling the torch so she could see what lay below. The ghoul twisted his neck and averted his sensitive eyes, but Rye could now see him better.

His clothes had rotted to rags, and his beard had

grown long and wild. Months in the deepest, darkest dungeon had rendered him almost unrecognizable. But Rye knew him well.

It was Morningwig Longchance.

And the imprisoned Earl had not grown a second head from his emaciated shoulders. Malydia's arms were wrapped around his neck, and she clung to his back so that she might not sink below rising water that now met his chest. Only the Earl's unusually tall stature had kept them from being completely submerged.

Rye blinked at the strange scene in disbelief.

"Don't just stand there," he barked. "Help us."

It seemed that Longchance's time in the forsaken pit had done little to improve his temperament.

"How?" Rye asked. "I have no rope. There's no ladder."

The Earl growled, jutting his chin upward to avoid swallowing the rising spill. "Just my luck—my rescuer is a helpless imbecile. Here, take Malydia."

Rye reached down, and with a last burst of energy, Longchance lifted Malydia up and clear from the water, extending his arms as high as he could so that Rye was able to snag a handful of her sopping clothes. Malydia's fingers clawed the edge of the opening. Her mismatched eyes seemed vacant as they met Rye's and she clambered up on her stomach. Malydia turned and they both leaned over the edge, dangling their hands as far into the pit as they could.

Longchance groaned and stretched, his gaunt hands clutching Rye's, then Malydia's, as he struggled to spit water from his mouth. Try as she might, Rye couldn't budge him, and she felt her body dragging into the hole.

"Longchance, wait! We can't lift you!"

The Earl's overgrown nails dug into Rye's wrists as he desperately struggled to pull himself up. Instead of trying to help, Rye found herself fighting to break free. Next to her, Malydia shrieked and kicked at the floor to keep from being dragged back down herself.

"Enough," Longchance said, and released them. His voice was resigned. Rye and Malydia fell back, breathing hard.

"Malydia, take this," he said slowly, sputtering water as he pressed his face above the surface. He reached up, and in his fingers extended a thick gold ring, topped with onyx and sapphire gemstones. The stones were carved in the shape of a clenched fist and coiled hagfish—the Crest of the House of Longchance.

Malydia hesitated, then reached down and took it between her own fingers.

"You are a good daughter, Malydia. With this ring

I bestow upon you all of my land and title. Henceforth you shall be Lady Malydia Longchance, Countess of Drowning." His eyes flicked to Rye. "And should anyone doubt your claim, Riley O'Chanter shall be your witness."

The Earl's lip curled. "Not my first choice, but at present, we are without any other option."

Malydia blinked at the hefty ring in her palm, then at her father.

He lay back, his arms floating akimbo like a weary lord flopping into bed for a long slumber. "I wish you luck," he said in a whisper. "Whether the title shall be a gift or a curse, only you can say."

The water filled the deepest, darkest dungeon, and Morningwig Longchance's face disappeared beneath the surface.

Rye sat with Malydia in the torchlight for a long while. Malydia still hadn't moved or spoken; she just stared at the ring in her palm. Rye didn't know how long Malydia had been locked away. She couldn't imagine what it must have been like to have been trapped down there with the Earl. But she did have a sense of what it was like to see your own father sink helplessly beneath the surface. As horrible as the Earl was, she was certain Malydia must be in turmoil. And now she had no choice but to share even worse news.

"Malydia," Rye said quietly. Malydia's mismatched eyes didn't move from the ring. "I need to tell you something."

Rye hesitated, the words nearly as difficult to say as they would be to hear. "It's Truitt. He's . . . not coming. The Spoke's been flooded, and Truitt was in it. He sacrificed himself for the village . . . for us."

Rye bit her lip and waited. Malydia looked up from the ring for the first time. The vacant glaze in her mismatched eyes turned sharp. Before Rye could explain further, Malydia lurched forward.

"You promised you would help him!" she hissed. "You let him drown?"

"No—" Rye said, but Malydia was upon her, clutching Rye's coat. The force of her weight drove Rye backward and onto the ground, precariously close to the open portal in the floor. The floodwaters in the deepest, darkest dungeon churned below.

"I knew you couldn't be trusted," Malydia growled, and her hands slid to Rye's throat.

"Stop," Rye gasped, and with all of her strength she pushed Malydia off. Rye flipped on top of the older girl, and Malydia's head dangled back over the lip of the pit.

Rye's hand went to her cudgel, her ears hot as embers. All of Malydia's vile words and past cruelty came back to her. This was the girl who had insulted her family, who had stolen her choker and imprisoned her in Longchance Keep. She'd long desired to give Malydia a well-deserved thumping, and now she could pitch her right back into the dungeon where she belonged.

Malydia's face trembled with fear. Rye gritted her teeth, then remembered something more. Malydia's effort to help her in the library, her bravery as the Night Courier, and Truitt's unwavering faith in his sister even when it seemed she didn't deserve it. Rye clenched her jaw and put her hand inside her coat instead.

When she removed it, she thrust the canvas portrait into Malydia's hands.

"This is your time now, Malydia," she said. "Village Drowning may not make it through the night. But if it does, it will need a leader with a clear head and a good heart. Remember Truitt. And who *you* really are."

Rye eased her weight off of Malydia and scrambled to the side, out of breath. Malydia pushed herself up so she was sitting. She trembled and clutched the tiny picture frame in her hands. She studied the portrait of herself and her brother as infants. And the face of her mother—perhaps for the very first time. Her eyes widened, and the harsh edges went soft. After another moment, they met Rye's own.

"I remember, Rye," she said, her voice now steady. "And I won't forget again."

28 The Reckoning

Rye expected that the flood would come by way of an enormous, crashing wave. Or perhaps in a powerful, bursting torrent, as if a hole had been punched in a dam. Instead, what she found when she made it to the village was something less awe inspiring, but even more chilling. A steady current of water crept through the streets and alleyways, like fingers of spilt wine in the cracks of a tavern's floorboards. But the fingers didn't stop. They grew thicker and deeper as if filled from a bottomless cask.

The water carried with it a stream of debris. Small items at first: sticks, branches, loose hay bales. Then larger items: feed troughs, carts, vendors' stalls toppled by the Bog Noblins. The floating islands of debris soon became mountains, and the climbing piles of wet refuse were joined by bodies—gray skinned and waterlogged, their rust-orange hair floating kelp-like across the surface. The Bog Noblins who had not been caught in the flood now struggled to flee, retreating to higher ground beyond the outskirts of the village.

Rye looked to the rooftops, where lanterns glowed atop residences. The villagers had indeed heard the warning, but the extensive flooding must have made it impossible for Folly, Quinn, and the link children to retreat to the Keep themselves. The remains of several Wirry Scares drifted past her on the current, but she was relieved to find the bobbing pumpkin heads unoccupied. She took her best guess as to where she might find her friends and made her way to Market Street as the rain finally began to ebb. When the winding cobblestones became impassable under high water, she took to the rooftops herself.

Rye had just pulled herself atop the butcher's shop when she spotted a drenched and bedraggled figure desperately pulling fellow villagers to safety. The woman plucked out a young boy clutching a floating oaken bucket. With desperation-fueled strength, she dragged out an elderly villager struggling to tread water. When the woman paused to push her sopping black hair from her face, Rye cried out and ran to meet her.

"Mama!" she called.

Abby caught Rye in her arms and held her tight.

"Riley," she whispered, pressing Rye's cold, wet cheek to her own. "Quinn and Folly told me about what's happened. They're with Angus now."

Rye released her mother. Abby's crossbow was gone, and her face was tight with unmasked worry.

"What about Harmless?" Rye asked urgently. "Is he here as well?"

Abby shook her head. "I don't know. I suspect he's not far, but I've lost track of him. See if you can find him. Tell him he must abandon the Reckoning. The flood is rising faster than we can keep up with; we need every available hand to help."

Rye glanced across the rooftops, where she could see other villagers, and the smaller figures of link children, doing their best to rescue those trapped by the rising water. She moved to go, but Abby put a hand on her shoulder.

"Riley, be careful," she said. "But hurry."

Rye nodded and tore off as her mother turned back to the villagers' plight. She leaped across gables and arches. She heard the clamor of frightened voices as families called to one another from windows below, coordinating their own escapes. Rye struggled to make out other familiar voices among them. Eventually the bell tower rose up over her, and, hardly realizing it, she found herself on a steeply pitched roof at its base. She stopped abruptly.

A man stood at the edge, hands on his hips, eyes on the tower and its rusting whale weather vane high above.

He turned, and Rye caught her breath. Slinister's familiar mask stared back at her, its gaping maw black and looming. But this mask wasn't scaled or leathery—its plated steel flashed with menace. It was a war helmet fit for a Reckoning.

Rye ran up the pitched shingles, hoping to put as much distance between herself and the Fork-Tongue Charmer as she could. At the peak, she found a heavyset Luck Ugly seated patiently, a thick broadsword across his knees.

"Burbage?" she called.

"Riley?" he said in surprise from behind his own mask.

"Slinister is right behind me. He's on his way."

Burbage's hook-nosed mask bobbed as he nodded. "Yes, it's about that time."

He rose to his feet and stretched.

"Where's Harmless?" she asked.

He cocked his head to the other side of the roof. "He's right down there. You should go and wait with him."

"Are you coming?"

"No. It's my turn to have a run at that slick-tongued shad," he said, and twirled the enormous sword in his hand. "There's nowhere left to go." He pointed the blade overhead, where the bell tower rose above them.

Rye swallowed hard.

"Go on," he said, shooing her. "Scoot."

Burbage marched down the roof to where she'd seen Slinister.

Rye rushed the other way to find Harmless. It wasn't difficult. He stood pensively at the edge of the neighboring roof below, the High Chieftain's mask in his hand and his gray eyes staring out at the watery village around them.

"It's Slinister," she said, out of breath. "He's coming."

"Yes, Riley," Harmless said. Any surprise he had to see her quickly disappeared. He asked for no explanation. "It seems the time of reckoning has come for us all."

"You have to abandon the Reckoning," she pleaded. "Mama is here on the roofs. She sent me to find you.

The village is drowning, and she needs your help."

Harmless didn't reply. He cast his eyes up at the bell tower, then to the crowded rooftops below them.

"Please," Rye implored. "Is no cost too great for the High Chieftain's Crest?"

Harmless's eyes met her own. He breathed heavily, as if laboring over a great burden. Then he placed a hand on her shoulder.

"Come," he said. "Take me to your mother, and we'll do whatever we can to help."

They took a step up the pitch of the roof, but Harmless's grip tightened as someone else appeared at its peak. Slinister. Burbage slowed him, but hadn't stopped him. The Fork-Tongue Charmer paused to catch his breath as lightning bounced from a distant cloud.

Harmless crouched, hooked his mask on his belt, and put his mouth close to Rye's ear. "Whatever you see, whatever I may say, stay here. Do not intervene."

"But your arm," Rye said, looking at the wounded limb that clutched his shield. "You've been weakened while Slinister remains strong. It's not fair."

"Trust me," Harmless said. His gray eyes glinted. "Just this one last time. And promise me you'll stay put."

Rye's stomach fell.

"Say it," Harmless said.

"I promise," Rye mouthed, in a barely audible whisper.

He pressed his lips to her head, then grazed her cheek with his palm. For the first time in a long while, his touch warmed her cold, damp skin. He gave Rye a reassuring smile as he turned and left her. She took cover behind one of the stone gargoyles.

Harmless ascended the pitched roof to its peak, just as Slinister caught sight of him and watched his approach warily. The former comrades and friends regarded each other in silence.

Slinister glanced up at the bell tower overhead, the electrical storm casting them in its shadow as it lit the sky.

"So this is where it ends," Slinister said, his voice muffled and deep behind the hollow of his steel helmet.

"The High Chieftain's Crest is yours," Harmless said. "Join me in assisting the villagers and I'll concede it to you. All I ask is that we signal the Luck Uglies together, so that they may return from the Western Woods and help us."

Rye couldn't believe her ears. Was Harmless really willing to hand over his Crest—and possibly more—for the sake of the village?

Slinister seemed similarly dazed. He glanced over

his shoulders, as if Harmless's words were a creeping spider waiting to bite. "Is this a ploy?" he asked. "Some sort of treachery to put me off guard?"

Harmless shook his head. "It's no ploy, Slinister. Just an opportunity for us both to right our past wrongs."

Slinister was still for a moment. "Your selflessness is admirable, Gray," he began. "But it is also your greatest weakness. I have long sought the High Chieftain's Crest, but it is not an honor I wish to barter for. Once I assume it, I won't be bound by promises to you or anyone else. I'm afraid you have struck your last bargain."

Slinister drew a long, serrated blade.

Wearily, Harmless affixed the High Chieftain's mask back over his face. His features disappeared behind the jagged scowl of the fearsome veil, and even his eyes were shadowed by its horns and severe ridges. Now, on the rooftops, Rye saw that the mask was the face of a gargoyle.

"I have neither the time nor the appetite to persuade you," Harmless said darkly. He reached to his belt, and raised the fearsome war axe in his hand. "So it seems there's nothing left but to finish what we have started."

"Is that supposed to rattle me, Gray?" Slinister asked, gesturing his blade toward Harmless's weapon. "Send me into a rage by wielding the same axe you used to cleave my skull last time? It didn't work then, nor will it now."

Harmless just crouched, making himself small behind his spiked shield, axe at the ready. Then, faster than Rye could blink, he struck.

But Slinister was ready and ducked his blow, Harmless's axe gouging a chimney with a shower of sparks.

Harmless lurched forward, trying to bash Slinister with his shield, but Slinister stepped away, wary of the sharpened spikes.

Slinister planted a heel into Harmless's calf. Rye heard Harmless groan and drop to his knee. Slinister's boot was fitted with a long spur, and when he pulled it free from Harmless's leg it was slick from the fresh puncture.

A quick lash of Slinister's sword hilt and Harmless was disarmed, his axe tumbling onto the rooftop. Rye caught her breath in her throat as Slinister raised his blade. He brought it down on Harmless, hacking at his shield like a woodcutter. After the first few strikes it was clear that the shield was his target, and he attacked it with such ferocity that he eventually cut away the sharpened spikes until they were little more than dull stumps. Slinister cast his sword aside and ripped the shield from Harmless, flinging it away, leaving Harmless's bare arm dangling in its sling.

Slinister lifted his boot and brought it down onto Harmless's crippled arm. Harmless buckled in pain, twisted, and fell on his stomach. Rye leaped up and was about rush from behind the gargoyle, but her father's eyes caught her own. They flickered in pain from behind the horned and twisted face of his mask. He gave her the subtlest shake of his head, and she forced herself to wait.

Slinister stood above him, grabbed him by the shoulders, and tossed him over so that he lay sprawled on his back.

"How foolish do you think I am?" Slinister growled. "I know you poisoned the spikes of your shield—ten years is a long time, but I've seen you do it before. What was it? Asp's Tongue? Death Bell?"

"I've always preferred midnight sea urchin," Harmless said through gritted teeth. "Far more effective."

Slinister dropped a heavy fist down on Harmless's face. Rye sucked in her breath at the sound of a crack. The mask. Or Harmless's bones.

But Slinister wasn't done. Another fist. And another. His fury was relentless, and he paused only briefly to shake out his own hands, red and bleeding from the force of his own blows. Rye pinched her eyes tight, the sound sickening her. She couldn't stand by and wait; it was too much. When she opened her eyes, Slinister had stepped away, bending to retrieve something from the roof. Harmless was deathly still, his feet trembling weakly. His one functioning arm flopped like a blind fish out of water, fingers twitching. The High Chieftain's mask lay in pieces around his head. She couldn't bear to look at his face.

Slinister found what he was looking for. Harmless's war axe. He clutched it in his bloodied knuckles, and marched back to his fallen victim. Slinister braced a hand on his own knee for support, and raised the axe, like a lumberman measuring a log for splitting.

"And so it ends," Slinister said.

Rye ran out from behind the gargoyle. "No!" she called.

Slinister's steel mask jolted in her direction. Rye didn't know what she expected to accomplish, but the axe trembled in his hand. He moved to raise it again, but it now seemed to be a great weight in his fist. His grip gave way, and the axe fell onto the rooftop. Slinister put a hand on his chest.

Harmless's fingertips dug at the roof. Slinister stepped back and thrust his hands to his helmet.

Rye hurried forward and threw herself on top of Harmless before Slinister could attack again. But Slinister was now desperately unclasping his helmet, clawing it free and throwing it aside. His face was ashen, his eyes blinking wide.

"Slinister," Harmless sputtered, through broken lips. "You were wrong."

Slinister looked at him, gasping for words between labored breaths.

Harmless's fingers had found what they were looking for. It was a broken shard of the High Chieftain's mask. He raised it as high as he was able.

"I didn't poison the shield," he whispered. "I poisoned the spines of the mask."

Slinister's eyes flared in horror. He pressed his fingers around his own throat as he coughed and heaved, staggering away from Rye and Harmless.

There was a crack of timbers and shingles. A weak portion of the waterlogged roof gave way, and Slinister Varlet fell through the open hole in a rain of wood, disappearing into the building below.

Rise of the Ragged Clover

Rye shivered as the wind picked up, a stray drizzle still sputtering through the air. Harmless had pressed himself up on his elbows and was able to struggle to his knees. Rye bit back her emotions when she saw his face. The High Chieftain's mask lay in pieces around him, but he lifted his cowl over his head so that its shadows might shield her from the sight.

"Are you in terrible pain?" Rye asked.

"It's not the worst beating I've taken," he said, with a tiny curl of his swollen lips.

Rye heard the call of voices far below them. She walked to the edge of the roof and looked down. Folly and Quinn! On a lower rooftop across the waterway that was once Market Street, she could see her friends struggling to pull fellow village children from the floodwater and onto their roof.

Folly's voice cried out as a young villager slipped from her arms and slid back into the water. Quinn dove in to save him.

A renewed sense of urgency gripped Rye's stomach.

"They still need help," Rye said. "The water's rising fast. I'll go myself." She made for the roof's edge.

"No," Harmless called, and pushed himself to his feet. He approached Rye and put a hand on her shoulder. His gray eyes studied her face from their swollen sockets. There was concern in them that he couldn't mask.

"You're cold and exhausted. You've already seen and done more tonight than you should have ever had to."

"I'm fine," Rye said, although she could feel her strength wane with every word. She stared down at the villagers struggling below them.

"*I'll* go help Folly and Quinn," Harmless said. She felt him throw a heavy, oversize cloak over her shoulders. "You stay here and rest a moment. Try to keep warm. I'll be back shortly to signal the Luck Uglies, then find somewhere dry and safe for you."

Pressing his arm to his side, Harmless stepped over the edge and began to descend the building.

Rye watched him go until he disappeared into the shadows of the village. In the dull predawn glow, she saw the shadows of villagers gathering on the roofs of their homes. Market Street had been rendered a canal, the first-floor shops submerged under ten feet of water. Windows were broken, facades cracked and battered by the Bog Noblins' assault. But of the Bog Noblins themselves, Rye saw little. The rancid black smoke of the burning buildings had turned white and billowy, the river water quenching the fires' rage.

Yet, from her perch, Rye could see neither Mud Puddle Lane nor the Shambles. She looked up to the bell tower. She'd never been that high, but it would provide the only vantage point to see how her friends and neighbors had fared. She clutched the cloak tight around her neck and began to climb. Over the gargoyles, past the gutters. She paused to catch her breath at the bell house itself, pulled the long cloak from where it dragged under her feet, then began the final ascent over the decorative curves and shingles of its rooftop. She grasped the stem of the rusting whale weather vane in her fist and pulled herself up. Close up, she realized that the whale was nearly as large as she was.

The wind was harsh this high, and Harmless's cloak caught a gust like a sail, nearly sending Rye right off the bell tower. She pulled it from her shoulders and wrapped it over the weather vane so it wouldn't fly away. Rye crouched and looked around her just as dawn broke over the village. Drowning had been transformed, its streets now a maze of twisting waterways. The view was sweeping, but it left her feeling isolated and lonely—detached from her friends and fellow villagers. Then, suddenly, she wasn't alone at all.

A thick hand appeared on the roof, followed by a broad-shouldered frame. She immediately recognized the familiar pattern inked into the shaved scalp and the elaborate braid. Rye gasped. She would have stepped back, but it would have meant plummeting into the village below them.

Slinister pulled himself onto the bell tower. He steadied himself on his hands and knees, a billowing banner the color of his green-black tattoos clutched in his fist. But when he looked up and saw Rye, his face was strained and ashen. Slinister seemed as stunned to find *her* as she was to see *him*.

"I should have known you had it in you, Rye O'Chanter," he said. He looked out at the smoldering village below them.

Rye shook her head in confusion. "Had what in me?"

"I've made my bet and lost," he said, his eyes still on Drowning. He opened his fist, and his somber green version of the Ragged Clover banner dropped from the tower, scattering in the breeze. "There's nothing left for me now. The poison was diluted, but still strong enough. It won't be much longer . . ."

It was no answer at all.

"Are you going to throw me off the bell tower?" Rye asked.

Slinister's eyes met her own. "I've committed many monstrous acts, but that won't be one of them."

"You buried my father in the bogs. You burned down your home with your adoptive parents still inside. There's nothing I'd put past you," Rye said angrily.

She clutched the weather vane firmly with one hand. Her other drifted toward her cudgel. With Slinister weakened by the sea urchin's toxins, maybe she stood a chance.

Slinister coughed a desperate, choking hack. "I never burned down the Varlets' homestead," he said. "I returned to our farm to find it smoldering. Someone started the fire in the stables—undoubtedly meant for me."

Rye felt her own chest tighten as Slinister swallowed back another heaving gasp. "It must have spread to the farmhouse," he rasped. "Did I flee Pest afterward? Of course, before someone could return to finish the job. But I didn't start that fire."

Rye shook her head in disbelief. Had Slinister truly been innocent of the most heinous crime he'd been accused of?

"I don't believe you," she said. "You're trying to deceive me again."

"What do I have to gain from that?" Slinister asked, the usual pride and fury in his voice replaced by a deep sadness. "The poison is in my blood. My fate sealed. I have no wish to harm you. My quarrel was with your father. Never with you." He coughed again, uncontrollably, covering his mouth with the back of his hand. When he was finally able to choke it back, he forced out the last words Rye would hear him speak.

"You'll make a fine High Chieftain one day."

Rye was stunned. She looked at Slinister's ashen face, his sullen eyes, and for a moment, all she felt was pity for Slynn Varlet, the boy who became the monster everyone told him he would be.

But then the look in Slinister's eyes changed, hardening like jewels and flaring at her, and he drew Harmless's own war axe from his belt.

Rye's ears burned. The Charmer had used his guile once again. She quickly fumbled for her cudgel, but couldn't free it.

A dull clatter echoed behind her. She turned quickly, and her jaw dropped in horror. The Shriek Reaver, wet and dripping, had dragged itself up from the floodwater, its serpentine body of roots and bone coiling as it settled itself atop the bell tower. Its clawed tendrils dug into the shingles, and it cocked its head as it seemed to gather its bearings. Steam rose from its stag-like skull and antlers. It turned its hollow eye sockets toward Rye and froze, as if surprised by its discovery.

Then, without hesitation, it sprang.

Rye felt a firm hand grasp her arm and shove her aside. She fell atop the crown of the tower, digging her fingers into the shingles as she slid helplessly downward. She planted her boots and slowed her descent to a precarious stop just before sliding over the edge. She looked up as she clung desperately to the roof.

Slinister had taken her place and now bore the brunt of the Shriek Reaver's attack. He clutched it by its throat with one hand, the creature's oversize teeth clamping inches from his face. It brought its claws down, piercing deep into Slinister's arms. He grimaced but did not let go, hacking at its body with the axe. The Shriek Reaver's trunk swam in the air as it tried to avoid his blows. It wrapped the switch of its tail around his feet, and Slinister stumbled but did not fall.

The Shriek Reaver clucked its shriveled tongue

and plunged its second set of claws through Slinister's shoulder, trying to break his death grip on its throat. Slinister cried out and dropped the axe, took hold of the monster's arm with his free hand and, with massive strength, tore it free from not only his shoulder, but off the Shriek Reaver itself.

The beast's teeth clacked and a sucking rasp escaped its lipless mouth. Its body coiled through Slinister's legs, wrapped his chest, and whipped itself around his neck. Constricted, the veins in Slinister's temples bulged.

Rye saw the fierce glint in Slinister's eyes fade as they rolled back into his head, but before succumbing, he took a deliberate step backward—off the edge of the roof. Together, the Fork-Tongue Charmer and the Shriek Reaver plummeted off the bell tower, crashing hard against a gable before hitting the water and sinking far below.

Rye dragged herself up the face of the bell tower's steep roof and leaned against the rusted weather vane. The flood had cleansed the remaining stain from River Drowning, and now the water reflected golden in the morning light. The fires had been extinguished and now only the sky burned red. Storm clouds raced away for the horizon, the morning light painting them crimson.

Rye looked down at what she had done. Below her,

the shop fronts and homes lay submerged beneath the rising water as far as she could see. The roofs and gables were filled with villagers, taking refuge from the flood. How could she ever face them? Would they ever forgive her once they discovered what she had done?

Rye drew Fair Warning from her boot and used it to carve something into the crown of the bell tower—something in case she wasn't welcome in her own village again. When she was finished, she put her head in her hands, overcome with sadness.

But all over Drowning, the villagers' heads craned skyward. They watched not the sun, but the bell tower. The wind had whipped Rye's cloak in knots around the weather vane, its folds billowing like a black flag. On the cloak was an emblem. Crossed swords and a four-leaf clover. And, of course, it wasn't a cloak at all.

The Ragged Clover flew over Village Drowning.

30
An Heir of Unknown Intentions

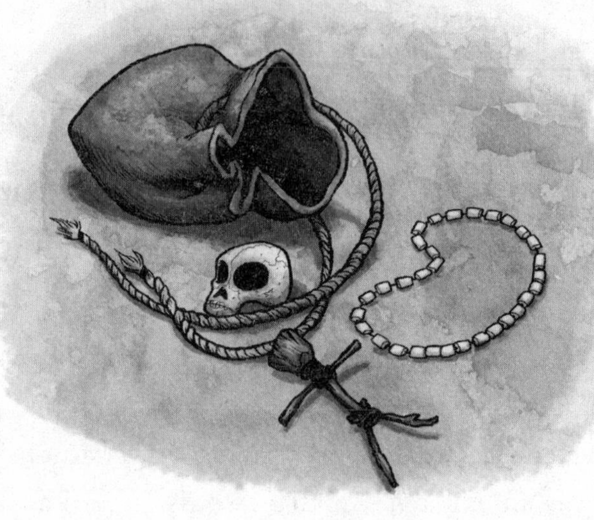

Rye, Folly, and Quinn joined Hope, Darwin, and Poe on the platform overlooking the sewers of Longchance Keep. All the link children had made their way safely to the old castle, Malydia having opened up its rooms to them. Rye insisted on checking on their well-being before returning to where her own family had gathered in the Shambles, and Folly and Quinn, ever loyal, insisted on accompanying her. They found the link children to be wet, battered, yet still standing—much like Drowning itself.

But the link children had taken the news of Truitt's loss hard. Hope was one of the youngest and most distraught, and all the joy had vacated the little girl's once bright eyes. Rye rarely suffered from a shortage of words, but now found that words of comfort could be the most elusive ones of all. Rye looked to Folly and Quinn, then came to a decision. She stepped forward.

"Hope, I have something for you. It's an old and powerful talisman. It's served me well, but I don't need it anymore." Rye reached into her boot, unclasped the iron anklet, and extended it in her palm. Folly and Quinn exchanged wide-eyed glances.

Rye cleared her throat. "This is the Anklet of Ugly Luck. When times seem darkest, and fate has dealt you an unfortunate blow, it will help guide you to the silver lining. Just remember to keep looking, for Ugly Luck's twists sometimes take time to reveal themselves."

Hope took the anklet carefully. There was the faintest glimmer in her eyes as she examined the tiny runes in amazement. Rye offered her a warm smile and stepped back.

Folly and Quinn glanced at each other once more, and Rye was surprised to see Folly step forward.

"This is for you, Poe," Folly said, taking Rye's place. She removed the Alchemist's Bone and the chain from around her neck. "It's the Bones of the Beloved." Folly paused and thought for a moment, then grinned. "It carries the strength of those you've lost, and will help you stand strong even when you feel weak."

"And I have this for you, Darwin," Quinn said eagerly, taking the Strategist's Sticks from his pocket. "It's called the Totem of Bravery."

Rye was too filled with emotion to hear the rest of her friend's words. She had never been more proud of Folly and Quinn than she was at that moment.

After they had finished, the link children filed back inside the Keep. Rye encouraged Folly and Quinn to go on ahead to the Dead Fish Inn—she'd be close behind. She sat alone at the edge of the platform, looking into the sewers below. They still swirled with water, and Rye knew she had seen the Spoke for the last time. Silently, she offered Truitt a proper good-bye, and shared with him all that he had meant to her.

Reluctantly, Rye stood to leave, but something caught her eye. It rested below her, on a stone just above the water's surface. She got on her hands and knees and was just able to reach it with her fingertips.

A wet and ragged blue feather. Just like the one from the Night Courier's cap.

Rye looked around her, but she was all alone.

Of course, there was no way to know whether the flood had washed it here or a certain heir of unknown intentions had purposefully left it behind. But Rye chose to believe the latter as she left the sewers of Longchance Keep with the feather—and the fond memories of a dear friend.

Rye rowed a small boat across the transformed landscape, Drowning's rooftops and chimneys breaking the surface like tombstones in a watery graveyard. The face of a stone gargoyle on an eave stared at her as she passed, its expression puzzled and a bit sad, as if it too was unsure of what to make of all of this.

Mutineer's Alley was a gentle waterfall, floodwaters rolling down its steps from the village to the river, which had swollen and swallowed most of the Shambles. The great arched bridge now looked more like an enormous stone walkway, the river's current filling its arches almost all the way to their peaks. Only one other structure remained visible. The roof and upper floors of the Dead Fish Inn had survived the worst that the River Drowning could throw at it.

Someone had moved the inn's black fishbone banner to a chimney, where it flapped defiantly, ever resilient.

Rye expected to find solemn faces inside. Instead she heard laughter. And splashing. Folly's brothers had stripped down to their britches, and took turns jumping from the railing of the top-floor hallway into the water-filled main room below.

"Boys, stop that!" Faye called in exasperation. "You'll catch the Shivers! And who knows how filthy that water is?"

The Flood boys seemed unfazed by the warning, and Fallow leaped off the railing belly-first.

Rye looked at the many familiar faces around the Dead Fish Inn. They were tired. Haggard. Resolved to the long task ahead. But they were all there, and they were smiling.

Harmless sat quietly with Abby, who pressed a poultice to his swollen face. Folly tried to corral Lottie and Fox before they replicated the Flood boys' acrobatics, while Mr. Nettle and Shortstraw took turns scratching each other's backs with their toes. Quinn was joined by his father, Angus—whom Rye had never before seen at the Dead Fish Inn. They'd discovered that the blacksmith's largest shields made excellent floats for transporting supplies. Baron Nutfield and his men surrounded several salvaged casks, and she was relieved to see them joined by Burbage. His encounter with Slinister had left him battered but unbroken, and he and Bramble nursed their injuries over well-filled mugs.

The mystery of their good cheer baffled her at first, but then she realized the secret. There would be many days to mourn what they had lost, but now was the time to appreciate all they still had.

Rye hurried to Harmless and Abby, and did just that.

When she later found herself sitting on a balcony overlooking the river, Harmless stepped out and joined her. He dropped into the empty chair at her side and put a boot up on the railing. Rye's eyes traced the course of a crimson-sailed junk as it eased its way toward the harbor.

"Annis is on her way home," Rye observed solemnly. She suspected that, one way or another, the old woman already knew what had befallen Slinister. "And I didn't get to say good-bye."

"Don't fret over it too much," Harmless said. "It never hurts to have a friend in the Lower Isles. And I'd guess the old bird may still have more days in her than you and I combined."

Rye squinted at the horizon and the thought of those distant islands. "I think I'd like to visit Pest again someday soon. Last time, I left Waldron and the Belongers without saying good-bye."

"I have no doubt they'll be delighted to see you."

As the crimson sail grew smaller, it passed three larger ships that had sailed in from the harbor and braved the swollen river, mooring just off of Slatternly Flats. Rye leaned forward in disbelief. The three were identical. She brightened at the sight of the soaring gulls on their emerald banners. *Slumgullions.* The crews unloaded supplies from their longboats and plucked stranded villagers for safe passage to higher ground.

"It's Captain Dent!" she cried cheerfully. "And even more *Slumgullions.*"

"The Captain always lends a hand to those in need," Harmless said.

Rye gave him a suspicious glance.

"Of course, once the village gets back on its feet, it will need plenty of ships . . . and a Captain-for-hire with the knowhow to move goods in and out quickly," he added, giving her a knowing shrug. "I'm sure he'll be eager to pitch in there as well."

"Will the Luck Uglies be on their way?" Rye asked.

"They've seen the Ragged Clover," Harmless said. "I expect they'll be arriving soon as well."

"What then?" Rye asked.

"Then we'll have some work to do. Rebuilding a brotherhood."

"And a village?" Rye said hopefully.

Harmless shrugged. "Alas, I don't know that is where the Luck Uglies' greatest strengths lie. As much as I have long sought to bring the Luck Uglies out of the shadows, perhaps they can best serve Drowning from the darkness. After all, sometimes it takes a villain . . ." His words trailed off, and he noticed Rye's look of concern.

"Of course, you will be entitled to have your say," he added.

Rye turned from the river to look at him. "What do you mean?"

Harmless smiled. "You are my heir. And, someday, as is your right, you may become the High Chieftess of the Luck Uglies."

Rye thought she must have misheard him.

"But I'm a girl. The title only passes to sons."

"Ah, yes. Historically that may be true. But remember the terms of the Reckoning. It was agreed that whoever raised the Ragged Clover over Drowning would have the right to become High Chieftain."

Rye recalled the words carefully.

"It was, in fact, *you* who raised the Ragged Clover," Harmless said.

Rye paused. Was that why he had left her alone on the rooftop to assist Folly and Quinn? Was that why he'd wrapped the Ragged Clover around her shoulders?

"But the Luck Uglies never would have agreed to those terms if they knew what that meant," Rye muttered.

"Don't underestimate yourself, Riley. Your heroics are extraordinary. Anyone can see that."

Rye looked down at her boots.

Harmless paused, then gently placed his finger

under her chin and lifted it. "Of course, while it is your right to become High Chieftess, it is not your obligation," he said. His eyes searched her own. "As I've told you before, there are plenty of other boots to fill."

Rye hesitated. "It's all just a bit . . . overwhelming at the moment. I look around the village and struggle with what I've done."

"You followed your heart and made a difficult choice," he said slowly. "As bad as it looks now, Drowning may very well be better for it. The moats of water surrounding the village will keep out Bog Noblins better than any swords or walls. And an unusual number of stray cats have turned up in recent days. At least, I *think* they are cats." He gave Rye a wink. "Besides, your friend Leatherleaf is still out there. Who's to say there aren't others like him? With time, and effort, maybe a day will come when we won't need to keep the Bog Noblins out at all."

Harmless cast his eyes out toward the river, as if watching the distant horizon. Rye followed his gaze, but if there was something out there, it was beyond her vision. He seemed content to sit in silence for a long while.

Rye's shoulders were heavy, as if bearing a great weight. When she finally spoke, her words came slow and painfully, and she turned her whole body in her chair to face Harmless.

"I don't think I can do it," she said quietly. "I can never be a High Chieftain."

"You can do anything you set your mind to, Riley," Harmless said, his eyes still on the river. "You've proven it to me. You've proven it to the Luck Uglies. You just need to believe it yourself."

"No," Rye said, and of all the challenges she'd faced since first meeting Harmless, her next words were the hardest. "I don't *want* to be High Chieftain. I don't want to use fear as a weapon and struggle for power. I don't want to be the one to lead the Luck Uglies out of the dark if it means I must first step into the shadows myself."

Harmless took his foot off the railing. His eyelids flickered then fell. His shoulders slumped.

"You're certain?" he asked quietly, without meeting her eyes.

"I'm sorry," Rye said quickly. She felt guilty and ashamed. It was as if her words had left her father deflated. "I never wanted to disappoint you. It's just—"

His heavy gasp interrupted her. "I'm so relieved," he said in a whisper, the thought escaping him like an imprisoned ghost suddenly released from its bonds.

"Relieved?" Rye asked.

Harmless looked up from his boots, his gray eyes meeting her own. "And proud," he added. "Of all the choices you've made, this one is the bravest."

"I don't understand. You don't want me to be High Chieftain?"

Harmless leaned forward. "All I've ever wanted is for you to follow your own path—the one *your* heart desires. Do I think you are worthy of the High Chieftain's Crest? Surely. But I also know you are capable of so much more. All I have sought is to unlock every doorway I could for you, then let you step through the one you see fit."

Rye blinked her wide eyes slowly. "But what if I don't know which one to step through?" she asked.

Harmless just smiled before answering.

"Sometimes, discovering the wrong ones is as valuable as finding the right."

31 How It Ends

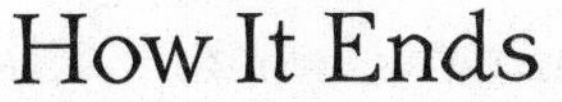

The O'Chanters finally returned to their long-neglected cottage on Mud Puddle Lane. Thanks to the peculiar whims of geography, the run-down neighborhood was now the highest patch of ground in all of Village Drowning, its cottages the only ones left unscathed by the flood. From their yard, they could see where the water stretched all the way to the harbor. The Ragged Clover no longer flew over Drowning, and Rye happened to be outside the day the banner had sailed off the bell tower in a sudden gale, like a phantom gathering its cloak. It never did come to rest, and Rye had watched the Ragged Clover dance over the exposed rooftops until it disappeared amid a flock of rooks resting on a gable that once marked the northernmost end of Market Street.

Soon after, Rye was delighted to discover that her messenger pigeons had also returned home to roost. Her favorite, Molasses, had even brought her a message tied to his foot. She reread it now as she sat inside at the dining table by the fireplace.

> FOX HAS HIS FIRST TOOTH. HE USED IT TO BITE FALLOW. I THINK HE'S GOING TO BE THE BEST BROTHER YET. WE'RE EXPANDING THE INN BIGGER AND BETTER THAN EVER. GET QUINN AND VISIT SOON!
> —FOLLY

Rye folded the slip of paper and stuffed it into a pocket. Abby busied herself refilling two goblets of cranberry wine while Harmless rested across from Rye, his palm atop a thick book on the table. Rye's eyes flicked to the copy of *Tam's Tome.*

"Can we read more tonight?" she asked.

"Your mother still doesn't think it's appropriate bedtime reading," Harmless said, casting a glance toward Abby.

Abby narrowed an eye in reply, but as soon as she turned her back, Harmless gave Rye an enthusiastic nod of reassurance.

"Will you write the next volume of *Tam's Tome*?" Rye asked.

Harmless sighed. "I suppose I should get around to that. I've been putting it off for quite some time."

"You can't tell a story and leave out the ending."

"True," Harmless said. "But sometimes, when you get to the end, you realize that the journey was the best part."

There was a squeak of hinges and the pad of familiar paws across the floor.

Rye felt a thud on her lap. Two green eyes blinked out from a furry black mane.

Shady kneaded Rye's thighs gently, circled twice, and plopped himself in a warm ball on her legs. Harmless had cut a small hinged flap into the cottage door so that Shady could come and go as he pleased, and the Gloaming Beast had taken to checking on them before his nightly prowls.

"I see someone's back to say hello," Abby said cheerfully, setting a goblet in front of Harmless. She greeted Shady with a scratch of his head, careful to keep her wine out of reach of his thirsty pink tongue.

Abby eased into a chair, trail-weary after spending

the day escorting Mr. Nettle back to the Hollow. The Feraling had decided he might try his hand as an innkeeper and promised to visit often—come hives or high water.

Abby raised her goblet. Testing out his left arm, Harmless lifted his own goblet with a grimace and clinked it against Abby's.

"Come spring, I'll head down to Trowbridge to visit my old friend Blae the Bleeder. If anyone can patch this up, he can." Harmless set down the wine and rubbed his ailing shoulder. "Of course, you're welcome to come, Riley. We could make it a little adventure. There's far more to the Shale than this watery little corner."

"I'd like that," Rye said.

Harmless cast his eyes at the crackling embers in the fireplace.

"In the meantime, we will all settle in for a long winter. I, for one, plan to get fat on your mother's brown-sugar-and-raisin porridge." Harmless placed his hand on his gut and gave Abby a wink. "With a little luck, I may even be able to convince Good Harper to return to Drowning for Silvermas."

Rye looked out the open windows. It was a beautiful late-autumn day, the kind that made winter seem deceptively distant. The neighborhood was quiet. Most of the Puddlers had taken up boats and rowed into the village itself, assisting the now-less-fortunate villagers in Nether Neck and Old Salt Cross who had been hardest hit by the flood. Quinn was with Angus, salvaging what they could from the blacksmith's shop on Market Street. They planned on reopening Quartermast's right here on Mud Puddle Lane. Lottie had the street to herself at the moment, and Rye could just make out her sister stalking insects in the weeds where the end of the lane dipped and disappeared into the dark water.

"Quinn tells me that Malydia has actually rolled up her sleeves," Rye mentioned, her eyes still on the rooftops in the distance. "She's been working shoulder-to-shoulder with the rest of the villagers."

"Hmm," Harmless said. "That must have been an unexpected sight."

"Do you think the enlightened Lady Longchance will do a better job than her father?" Abby wondered out loud.

"I think so," Harmless replied after a moment.

"And if she doesn't?" Abby asked. "Malydia's very young, and will rule Drowning long after we're gone. If things take a turn for the worse, who will be left to answer the Call?"

Rye glanced at Harmless, awaiting his response. But Abby's question hung in silence.

"I think the answers to those problems will find us

another day," Harmless said finally, and raised his goblet again. "For now, let's just welcome what tomorrow brings us."

Their toast was interrupted by a loud voice outside. It was Lottie—calling for someone.

"What has your sister gotten herself into now?" Abby said, craning her neck to see out the window.

"I'll check on her," Rye said, depositing Shady onto her mother's lap.

Rye stepped outside the cottage. Lottie wasn't at the door but stood at the far edge of Mud Puddle Lane, watching the brackish water lap at her feet. She no longer yelled, but seemed to be speaking softly.

"Lottie?" Rye called, but received no reply.

The water rippled in front of Lottie. Rye squinted to get a better look.

Blue-black scales broke the surface.

"Lottie!" Rye screamed this time, but her sister didn't move.

The River Wyvern dragged itself ashore silently. Its eyes darted and tongue flickered at the sight of the little red-headed morsel before it.

"Lottie!" she cried again, rushing from their yard. Rye tore down the street, panicked at the scene awaiting her.

Lottie was staring up at the reptilian eyes. The

Wyvern examined her hungrily, its maw gaping. Lottie blinked and slowly reached into her pocket.

The River Wyvern tilted its scaled head. The sharp, ridged sail fin atop its back flared and pointed to the sky.

Lottie extended a hand and Rye's heart raced.

The River Wyvern recoiled slightly at first but didn't attack. Lottie whispered something, opened her palm, and a handful of crawly insects scuttled over her fingers. Rye's jaw dropped and she jolted to a stop.

The reptile cracked its mouth, extended the tip of its thick pink tongue, and shut its eyes.

"Lottie?" Rye tried one last time, confusion creeping into her voice.

The River Wyvern's eyes snapped open, and it narrowed them at Rye warily. Lottie looked back with an irritated glare.

"Is that—" Rye began, in disbelief. "Have you been—"

"Shhh, Rye," Lottie scolded. "Don't be a beeswacker."

The River Wyvern blinked at Lottie, then slowly sank beneath the water, disappearing with a silent flick of its long tail.

Before Rye could speak, Lottie marched back and pointed a finger.

"You no tell anyone about Newtie," she commanded.

"He came home, and he's *mine*."

Rye just nodded, speechless.

Lottie huffed with finality, then stomped back toward the cottage, where Harmless and Abby had appeared in the doorway. She glowered back over her shoulder at Rye one last time, and thrust her finger to her lips, as if to say *Shush*.

Rye took another look at the water, but its glassy surface betrayed no secrets. The slightest smile cracked the corner of her lips.

Perhaps there'd been a High Chieftess among them all along.

After all, even the fiercest dragons had to start out as the tiniest of newts.

Rye did her best to wipe her smirk away, and hurried to rejoin her family.

EPILOGUE

R Is for Rye

It's become a rite of passage for the brave and foolhardy children of Village Drowning to row out to the tallest bell tower on the night of a full moon. They climb to the top, their path lit only by the flicker of moonlight on the winding canals. Once there, they carve their own initials under the old symbol left in the wood.

A capital letter *R* with a circle around it.

R as in Rye.

The girl who drowned a village in order to save it.

Of course, this is not to say that Rye didn't accomplish

other extraordinary feats over her many years. It's just that, thankfully, most were not the type to attract the attention of Tam or his quill, and such stories are probably best left for a quieter kind of tome.

As for stumbles, there would still be plenty. But Rye had lots of practice falling down.

And she always got back up.

The End

Banter like a Local: A Tourist's Field Guide to Shale Lingo and Lore

Beeswacker: An eavesdropper, as in someone who can't mind her own beeswax. Originally coined by Lottie O'Chanter. Be careful where you stick your nose in Village Drowning, where both unpleasant odors and fiercely guarded secrets remain plentiful.

Bog Hoppers: It's been said that nothing good ever came from a bog, but these migrant workers once harvested the wild marshberries favored for fermenting and baking. With the return of the Bog Noblins, hoppers found themselves to be part of the marsh's food chain, and the profession dried up faster than a Dead Fish Inn cask during a Black Moon Party.

Brindleback: These large, squirrel-like rodents aren't indigenous to the forest Beyond the Shale. Rather, a cage full of the furry nuisances escaped from an ill-fated gypsy circus generations ago and they've since made themselves at home in the forest's trees. Brindlebacks have been known to pilfer rations, eat the lining of trousers, and soil fresh water supplies. However, the critters possess one redeeming quality: during a particularly long winter, this traveler found that, in a pinch, they do indeed taste like chicken.

The Descent: Where did you hear about that? I know nothing of it. And you shouldn't either, beeswacker, unless you're looking to find yourself ears-deep in a bog.

Feraling: These reclusive human denizens of the forest are expert trackers, gatherers, and survivalists. Their numbers are quite sparse as an unfortunate myth circulated that stew rendered from a Feraling's bones brought the drinker good luck. More often than not, it brought parasites. Feralings tend to be naïve and aren't terribly fearful, which made the whole bone-boiling business particularly inconvenient for them. But don't call them goat boys. That's just offensive, and is likely to get you kicked.

The Reckoning: La-la-la . . . I can't hear you . . . These strange terms you keep muttering about are liable to get us both snatched in the middle of the night. Next question.

The Rill: Numerous wild creatures slither, creep, crawl, and thrash through the forest Beyond the Shale. Yet, the deep woods remain inhospitable to beasts of the two-legged variety. Folklore tells us that the ancient stream known as the Rill and its rivulets are impassable to non-humans. Those men and women who successfully braved the forest learned to build their encampments within these strange boundaries. Whether the Rill's power is real or imagined, it's always best to sleep within its confines, lest a toothy forest denizen make you its next meal.

River Wyvern: In truth, the enormous reptile rumored to have taken up residence in the River Drowning is more cold-water lizard than mythical Wyvern. After all, while it has proven itself to be a voracious eater, nobody claims to have seen it fly or breathe fire. But the town criers have never been ones to let facts get in the way of a catchy name or sensational headline.

Shriek Reaver: Some cultures tell stories of spriggans—malicious fairies who defend barrows and woodlands from humankind. Beyond the Shale's ancient and mythical Shriek Reavers are said to rise when humankind creates an imbalance in the forest, and these single-minded guardians won't rest until the scales are tipped back in the forest's favor.

Snarklefish: These blind cave fish are known to inhabit the sewers of Village Drowning and other subterranean waterways. While the largest don't grow much bigger than a trout, their small size belies an enormous—and indiscriminate—appetite. Many an unwary angler has lost a finger to a snarklefish bite, and if you're foolish enough to scrub your dirty bits in a snarkle pool you just might find yourself picked clean to the bone.

***Tam's Tome of Drowning Mouth Fibs*:** A multivolume history text with editions curiously numbered in descending order. Copies of the oldest volumes are exceedingly rare, as the controversial tome has been banned, burned, and relegated to the rubbish bin at various times since its first publication. To date, no one has come across a copy of the long-awaited finale, *Volume I*, and it is widely suspected that the reclusive, ageless author has either lost interest or finally grown jaded with the publishing industry.

Treasure Hole: While you might hide your valuables under the rug or in a sock, there's not enough hosiery in all the Shale to stash a self-respecting noble's trove of accumulated goodies. Instead, it's customary among the upper class to build elaborately hidden treasure holes in their castles and keeps. The bigger the treasure hole, the more tightly guarded its secrets. And someone who stumbles across an unguarded treasure hole may find themselves, quite literally, with the keys to the kingdom.

Who-Could-Stay-Quiet-the-Longest Game: A game played by children of Village Drowning, often at the urging of their parents. Rye O'Chanter has many talents, but her proficiency at this game isn't one of them. To date, her sister, Lottie, is the only player known to be worse.

Acknowledgments

It takes a village. . . .

Writing may be a solitary endeavor, but it takes a small army to bring a series like the Luck Uglies to life. So many talented people have helped me along the way that I can hardly do them all justice. But here are just a few who deserve enormous thanks:

Michelle Andelman, who plucked this unknown author's manuscript from her slush pile, and Markus Hoffmann, Lauren Pearson, and all the other fine agents at Regal Hoffmann, past and present.

Harriet Wilson, my wonderful editor who saw fit to introduce the Luck Uglies to the world, and whose vision for the series has always been so closely aligned with my own.

Phoebe Yeh, whose footprints will always be part of Village Drowning's cobblestones.

Christopher Hernandez, Tara Weikum, Gina Rizzo, Amy Ryan, Sarah Dotts Barley, and everyone at

HarperCollins who rolled up their sleeves and played in the bogs.

Illustrator Pétur Antonsson, who paid attention to every detail and made each book a beautiful sight to behold.

And above all, Wendy, Caterina, and Charlotte. You are my muses, tireless cheerleaders, and best friends. None of this would have happened without you.